Woodsedge

Woodsedge

Barbara Knight

Walker and Company
New York

First published in the United States of America in 1987 by the Walker Publishing Company, Inc.

Published simultaneously in Canada by John Wiley & Sons Canada, Limited, Rexdale, Ontario.

Library of Congress Cataloging-in-Publication Data

Knight, Barbara.
  Woodsedge.
  I. Title.
PS3561.N437W6   1987   813'.54   87-6076
ISBN 0-8027-0956-7

Printed in the United States of America

10 9 8 7 6 5 4 3 2 1

Dedication
To two Knights of Kentucky
John Richard, my husband
and
Margaret Rose Sanford, his sister

Woodsedge

Chapter One

"MAY I COME IN?"

In the bright sunlight on the porch at Woodsedge, Bailey Comstock, reporter for *The Shearerville Sentinel,* glittered almost as brilliantly as she had at the Club on Monday. She was probably the last person on earth I wanted to see, but I stood aside and she stepped into the hall, her eyes darting eagerly from side to side. I quickly closed the door of James's study, and when she moved toward the parlor, I indicated the long hall sofa and made my voice firm. "Please sit here, Miss Comstock. I would offer to take your coat but I can only give you a minute."

Her hands in elegant skintight gloves paused in the act of unbuttoning her coat. For a long moment she stared cooly at me, and then she shrugged. "Oh, all right. I suppose you are terribly upset and I apologize for disturbing you, but I really must know whether it's true that James Brandon was shot."

The word hung in the sudden stillness in the front hall at Woodsedge, where James Brandon had stood, his jaw jutting and his eyes blazing, such a short while ago. I pulled the muscles in my face straight and tightened them against a surge of emotion. "The hospital can tell you better than I can, Miss Comstock, or the county sheriff, ah, Deputy Strawbridge. I really don't know exactly what happened."

Certainly true! Literally true!

"But you were there, weren't you?"

"Yes, but I didn't see." I bit back an impulse to add an apology and explanation, and waited for her to go on.

"Where were you?" she asked, eyes cool and challenging.

It was a good question. To say I didn't know where I was when James was shot would be absurd. I started to open my mouth like a well-rehearsed schoolgirl to tell her where I was, where James was, and who fired that shot—*those* shots!—when I remembered my promise to Pete Strawbridge. "I can't answer that question, Miss Comstock. It's a police matter, you see, and I . . . can't make any statement to you at all."

She looked at me as though I were a sick or stupid ten-year-old. Then deliberately, all her gestures controlled, she took out a little notebook much the same as the one Sheriff Dennis had used. She flipped a page or two, clicked the knob at the top of her pen, and poised it over the pad. Her smile was cynical. "You *are* Joan Brandon, aren't you? Visiting for the holidays? From New Hampshire?"

"All of that."

"And James Brandon *is* your cousin? Your *first* cousin?"

"You know that."

"I understand you still have a lot of relatives here." It wasn't a question so I didn't answer. "So nice. I think I met your brother once, ah, Perkins Brandon? Isn't he in the Navy?"

"Perk. Yes."

"I understand you used to visit here regularly when you were a child. Woodsedge was your father's parents' farm, wasn't it?"

"Yes."

"And it belongs to you and your cousin now, right?"

"I'm sure it's a matter of public record, Miss Comstock."

"Your cousin James Brandon?"

"The same cousin who is now in the hospital, and I will not say anything about that—at all, Miss Comstock." I stood up from my chair across the hall from her.

"There is one more matter of public record, Miss Brandon," she said as she got to her feet and stood in front of me, her eyes sparkling. "The police record in Shearerville logged a call from you on December twenty-third reporting that you found a dead body in the woods while you were walking your dog. The police referred you to the county sheriff's office. Sheriff Dennis came out here and went up to the woods with you and your cousin. What happened next, Miss Brandon? Why was nothing more recorded about what happened next?"

"Obviously, Miss Comstock, if that were public knowledge you would know it. I suggest—"

Miss Comstock rolled her eyes in the insulting signal of patient resignation and clicked her pen sharply. "What *did* Sheriff Dennis find up in the woods, Miss Brandon?"

"You will have to ask Sheriff Dennis, won't you? *If* you can find him, that is. Or, better still, ask Deputy Strawbridge. Now I must—"

"Perhaps I should ask Rob Dunstan?"

"If you like."

"Or Henrietta Dunstan, shall I ask her?"

"Be my guest!" I gave her what I hoped was an enigmatic smile. She seemed a little disconcerted. I was moving toward the door, hoping she would follow, when the phone rang.

My heart thudded as I took an automatic step to answer it. News of James at last? Alive still, or . . . ? Or perhaps Rob? I wanted more than anything in the world to answer that phone, but I knew Bailey Comstock was perfectly capable of following me into James's study or of slipping off to explore the house. I raised my chin a little higher and bit off my words as I opened the door. "I'm sorry, but you really must . . ."

With a shrug of resignation she finally put her pen in her purse and her notebook in her pocket, carefully buttoned her coat, and then walked slowly, with great dignity, out of the house. I closed the door quickly and ran to the study, but the phone was silent again. There was nothing I could do but wait.

I pulled the stained, red damask curtain aside and watched her drive away, and then dropped the curtain back over the window and crossed the hall to turn on the gas log in the parlor so it would be warm and welcoming for Dad. I stood for a moment looking out over the desolate rose garden to the lane beyond the hedge, and a warm surge of excitement and—in spite of everything—joy started my pulse racing again.

Rob . . . Rob . . . !

I looked at the clock on the mantel. At least another hour. . . .

Amazing that in only two weeks so much had happened, so many things would never be the same again! Hard to believe it had been only two weeks, two days, and slightly more than two hours since I took exit eight off the interstate to the junction with the old Nashville Pike. Right 16 miles, Shearerville. Left 14 miles, Fort Harrington. I was sure it couldn't have changed that much in twelve years. I turned right to search for Carter's Lane and the road to Woodsedge.

"Either way you'll get lost," James had said. "And if you miss Carter's Lane you'd better go on into Shearerville to find the county road. It'll be miles. . . ."

Hector sat like a snooty dowager in the seat beside me, and I ran my fingers under his collar, deep into his thick coat. "Just a little while, pup. Just a little while." I curled my shoulders forward and back to ease the mounting tension and lit another cigarette. I didn't deny to myself that I was uneasy about seeing James, but no amount of curiosity or longing to see Woodsedge again would have dragged me down here, alone this way, without Perk, if I were really afraid of my cousin.

Alone this way, without Perk. . . .

I pulled my mind back to the road. Rolling fields slipped away on either side, farms seemed prosperous, fences tight and barns straight, shining tin roofs . . . then trailer parks and billboards and lights from the new mall. Traffic was getting heavy. By pure luck I found Carter's Lane tucked coyly between two red brick houses, and a minute later I was out in the country, driving too fast down the winding road. I slowed and checked my gas gauge. If Carter's store, at the junction of Blair Road, was still open, I would stop— just for old time's sake.

It was not only open, but new and shiny, bustling with vending machines and flashing signs. I pulled up at the self-serve pump and managed to spill only a little gas as I looked around at the various pickups with the names of the farms they belonged to blazoned on their doors. I was wondering why "Hilliard-Dunstan" on a battered Chevy seemed familiar, when the driver, a tall man with a quick stride, obviously in a hurry, came out of the store, stopped in his tracks and did a classic double take when he saw me standing there. I thought for an instant he intended to speak to me, but he only nodded briefly, stepped into his truck, and drove off down Blair Road.

I felt I should have recognized him. . . .

And then, realizing I had subconsciously expected to find someone I knew here so close to Woodsedge, I shrugged the feeling aside, paid for my gas, and drove on for a mile or two and turned westward onto the county road, where all the landmarks were familiar. I savored each of them, the big farmhouses set among now leafless trees, barns with their roofs bright with sky-shine, Shiloh Church, the Grange Hall, a cluster of silver grain elevators, mail boxes that still bore the old family names. . . .

And there at last was our lane, Brandon Lane! Left onto gravel, and Hector stood up, wagging his whole body eagerly as the sound from the tires changed. I rolled the window down and pulled the air into my lungs, but there was no summer scent of honeysuckle or corn ripening. The

5

sharp tang, which I knew must be tobacco curing, was new, all new for me, as well as for Hector. "Rabbits out there," I said, and he sniffed excitedly, even though he had never encountered a rabbit in all his young life.

Half a mile ahead the house was glowing, the yard lights full on and silvery green. The old walnut trees Two-Greats Grandfather had planted stood stark and ragged against the afterglow. Fields on either side of the lane rolled away into darkness. The gravel was pearl grey in my headlights as we passed the garden steps, the mailbox, and the yew hedge— so high! The driveway was new. It divided to send an arm to the porch, and there, in front of the open door, stood Alison, waiting like a medieval chatelaine at the door of her castle to welcome me.

"Thank you, God!" I shut down my engine and opened the door for Hector. "Go, pup!" He ran off into the gloom, and for an instant I felt very alone, very unsure. I picked up the sack of his food and went up onto the porch to greet my cousin's wife.

"James just called," Alison said, after the first awkward hugs. "Let's leave your things for him to bring in. He'll be along in a little while." She held me in front of her with strong hands on my shoulders, and I felt shabby and tired as I stood there in my jeans and fisherman's knit, clutching the bag of kibble like some urchin begging shelter. "You look wonderful! A little thinner, maybe, and I expect you're tired after your long trip."

"I am, a little," I admitted. *And you're taller than I remembered. Heavier? More mature? Contacts, not glasses. . . .*

"Will your doggie be all right out there? He won't run off?"

"Oh, yes. I mean, no. It's his suppertime." I held up the sack of dog food as though offering it to her.

She ignored the sack. "Isn't he pretty big? I thought spaniels were little lap dogs."

"You're thinking of cockers, I guess. He's about right for

a springer. Ah, where . . . I mean, I asked James if I could . . . I had hoped he could sleep in my room."

"James fixed a nice place for him in the brooder house," she said firmly. I was not surprised. No Kentucky Brandon ever allowed dogs in the house. "Fresh hay and a new latch on the door."

I remembered the shed built for Grandmother's baby chicks. I couldn't complain. "Oh, fine! That will be great." My voice trailed away as we entered the hall. I looked around me almost with awe. All so different! Richly carpeted and wallpapered, undeniably splendid and not at all as I remembered it. A pink-and-silver Christmas tree stood where the ancient whatnot had been, alight with glitter instead of the shadowy treasures I had never been allowed to touch. "You've done so much! I wouldn't know the place! It's . . . just beautiful!"

"You're in your old room. You won't find much changed back there." Was there a chill in her voice? "Would you like to freshen up? You'll have your own bath. That's as far as we've gone with our renovations."

"Yes, thank you."

We went through double doors, creamy white paint instread of thick black varnish, into the back hall, shorter and narrower than I remembered, where bedroom doors, also creamy, opened on either side, to the final door where the back porch began and the dining room opened on the right. The door to "my" room, on the left, was open, the lights on, and Alison stood aside to let me enter.

"Oh, lovely! It hasn't changed a bit! Not even curtains. I'm so glad!" I stopped when I realized I was implying resentment at the changes in the front of the house. "I mean, the rest is beautiful. You've done absolute wonders and it's just gorgeous—"

"But this is the way it was." She laughed lightly, and I was pretty sure I had imagined the chill. "I know how you must feel, coming back to an old place after twelve years. I'm glad it isn't all changed. Here, let me show you the bath. We just made a door into the back half of the old one, through the bookcase." She showed me an elegant little room straight out of a slick decorating magazine.

"The front half opens into your grandfather's old office, James's study now." I had noticed that the door to that room was closed as we came down the hall. "But we haven't figured out what to do for a closet in this room. The old wardrobe is so shabby . . . but I reckon you won't mind, will you? There are even some of your own things still in it! You'll want to wash up. I'll get you an ashtray."

"This is fine." I picked up a clumsy terra-cotta dish I had sent to Gramp one Christmas. I turned it in my fingers as though it might hide a secret greeting from him, while Alison fussed for a moment with the fluffy towels on the vanity.

She seemed to want to say something more, but when she caught my eye in the mirror she turned away. "I'll just go along to the kitchen, then. What would you like, tea or a drink? James will be another hour or so, and then we'll have dinner."

"Tea, I'd love some. I'm not much of a drinker." I didn't add, 'anymore.' Maybe she never knew how nearly drowned in vodka I was when she and James came to New York on their honeymoon three years ago. Behind me now, all that, and Cooper Newton and his diamond, my bushy hair, and the dark smudges under my eyes.

At least I look healthy again! The worst of ivory white skin and black hair is that it looks tragic so easily, and violet blue eyes under high-arched eyebrows look so ridiculously vulnerable, so innocent and scrutable. I smiled at my reflection in the mirror. All I need now is a good night's sleep!

As I left the room I trailed my fingers along the mantelpiece. The cracked blue bottle was still there, with the eagle's feather Perk had found and identified for me. Dusty, now, the talisman of that last summer. I ran the feather through my fingers, smoothed and cleaned it, replaced it, and went out, through the cold dining room, to the kitchen.

"What do you feed him?" Alison asked when I found her there with Hector at her feet. "I didn't get him anything but these little bone biscuits. I've never had a dog, and I don't know much about them."

Hector was well aware of this, wolfing one after another of the little bone biscuits she doled out to him in exchange for the appeal in his round eyes. He scarcely noticed me as I came in, so enchanted was he with this largesse.

"He's a beggar! He'll eat the whole box if you'll give them to him! I just feed him kibble." And I jiggled the sack at her again. "This should last 'til Monday."

She gave a little toss of her head. "I didn't mean—"

"No problem! No harm! He'll be your slave. Give him another while I go find the water bucket."

She closed the box of biscuits and put them on a high shelf. "I think James left one out on the back porch."

It was the same rumpled tin bucket I had carried a thousand times from the cistern to the shady side of the house, water splashing around my skinny legs, for the dog of the moment. As I scrubbed cobwebs and mud wasp nests out of it, a roster of the dogs passed in review in my mind, not surprisingly all of them field dogs of one breed or another. Old Pete had been there longest, ancient and fat, devoted to James but lazily tolerant of us visitors.

It had been old Pete in the last summer of his life who had found James wandering through a crashing thunderstorm one night, drunk and half out of his mind with pain from a bullet hole in his leg. I never learned exactly what happened, but I know Dad confiscated all the guns on the place that summer and put a new lock on the cupboard where he kept his bourbon and Susan's sherry. There were long, quiet conversations among the adults, to which Perk and James were finally admitted, but I was never told . . .

As I scrubbed I asked Alison, "Does James still hunt?"

"I won't let him," she said with surprising sharpness. "We've had the whole farm posted. The last time he hunted was with Perk when he came down just before he went to Vietnam."

I wasn't ready to talk about Perk. "I won't have to worry about hunters up there in the woods, then, will I?"

"Don't be too sure. There's always someone banging away up there, mainly soldiers from Fort Harrington, I believe."

I filled Hector's bowl with kibble and shrugged into my parka. "Does the fort make much difference around here?"

"A lot. We have to lock doors now, and the big guns rattle the windows, and the helicopter noise is a real nuisance. But it's not all bad. It's brought a lot of money into the area. You'll notice when you go to town."

Alison opened the back door for me, and I started through it with the water bucket in one hand, the dish of kibble in the other. We were already an untidy knot of confusion in the corner of the kitchen when the swinging door to the dining room burst open and caught the bucket broadside, and there was James.

There were all of us, crammed into a space about five feet square, with a leaping barking dog, a splashing bucket of water, kibble rolling under foot, and the doors, as always, were hooked together.

James backed into the dining room with a few hells and damns and something like "Same old Joanie, I see."

I quelled Hector and made a scrambling, ungraceful exit while Alison went for the mop.

I took my time putting Hector to bed, pulling the hay loose from the bale, finding a safe place for the water and the blanket I had brought along to make him feel at home. With a firm hand and voice I told him to "stay" and "settle right down" and then, feeling a little as though I had abandoned a trusted ally, I latched the door and went back to the kitchen to face James.

He was leaning against the refrigerator, drink in hand, his trousers changed, watching Alison pour batter into the old iron muffin pans. He put his glass down—for safety, I suppose—and we exchanged cousinly kisses without much enthusiasm. Then we stood apart and inspected one another.

I had forgotten how very tall he was! A little heavier now, more 'Big James' than ever—no one ever called him 'Jim'—but still dark and hard-looking. The early grey in his black hair was a familiar Brandon trait (I had some myself), and the sea-colored, deeply shadowed eyes showed a familiar mix of storm and challenge. His long thin lips finally curved up in a grudging smile. "You're prettier than you were," he said, "but you haven't grown up much." I pulled my five-four as tall as I could and thought how like James it was to give with one hand and take away with the other, and that with a characteristic smirk of satisfaction. "And always teetering on the brink of disaster!"

I smiled sweetly at him. "Sorry about your trousers, James, dear, But you *were* awfully sudden."

His smile became less grudging. "You should put on a little weight, though," he went on. "You look like a scarecrow made out of a hand grenade in that outfit."

"James!" gasped Alison.

I brushed some hayseeds off my sleeve. "You might have opened the bale for me," I said, still smiling because it was all so familiar. "I guess I'd better go clean up a little."

"Why don't you bring Joan's suitcase in for her, James? She may want to change, too."

"I'd better go with you—"

"Surely you can trust me to find a suitcase in that little kiddie car of yours."

"But it's a dog crate. I mean, that's what I packed in."

"You *what*?"

I started to explain to him that it's a matter of principle to take a crate with the dog when you travel and that there

11

wasn't a lot of room in Dad's Volkswagen, but he shot one disdainful glance at me as he disappeared through the swinging door.

"You may have to kind of wrestle it out of the car," I said as I trotted along behind him. "It's a kind of big—"

"I'll get the damned thing if I have to use a can opener." He slammed the front door before I could catch up with him.

Something had to give, I thought as I watched through the glass. He certainly hasn't learned patience. The crate gave, of course. It was only plastic. He kicked the car shut behind him, and I opened the front door and stood out of the way while he maneuvered it into the hall.

"Repellent thing," he growled and strode off to my room with it. He barked his knuckles on the door jamb there, and I thought he might drop it in his rage.

"Careful! There're pots in there!"

"There're *what*?"

"Pots. Ceramic vases I made for Alison and Ellen."

"I thought you painted," he said as he put the crate gently enough on the cedar chest under the window.

"I did! I do! and I do pottery, too. I do all sorts of things!"

"You do for a fact. I just hope acting like a lady is one of them if you're planning on going places with us this Christmas."

"I won't disgrace you, James. Now go away and let me change."

"I hope you own a skirt," he said not very hopefully as he closed the door behind him.

I did, but I was not going to wear it tonight. I took my heather blue tweed suit out of the crate and shook the wrinkles out of the long creamy white wool skirt I had bought in New York when I still expected to be the wife of Cooper Newton, and hung them away in the old wardrobe. I finished unpacking my other jeans and the dress slacks Susan had insisted on buying for me, "for the times when your suit is too dressy and jeans not dressy enough." Dear Susan, always concerned for me, always smoothing my way. Well, I wouldn't disgrace her, or Dad, either. I changed into tan cords, dumped hayseeds out of my shoes, brushed my hair, and went back to the kitchen.

James was not there.

"I hope you don't mind eating out here," said Alison, with her eyebrows up. "We don't try to heat the dining room when it's this cold. It isn't insulated and electricity is so high."

"Oh, no. This is nice and cozy. Let me help." I set places on the quilted chintz mats that matched the curtains she had pulled across the tall narrow windows. The room looked almost quaint, if such a thing could be said of the severe angularity of the old farm kitchen with its smoky beige walls and twelve-foot ceilings. There were chintz cushions on the oak chairs that I knew from experience were miserably inhospitable to young bodies. Folksy pottery dishes replaced the odds and ends we used to use in this room. I enjoyed the mix of old and new, but I had something more important to say to Alison than that I liked the chintz.

"I hope you don't misunderstand the way James and I squabble. We always have, you know, but it's nothing really serious. I just hope it isn't unpleasant for you."

"Oh, you don't need to worry about me! You and James have known one another too long for me to tell you how to behave."

She stirred something on the stove. "He's glad to have the diversion just now, in fact. We have—" She visibly abandoned one train of thought for another. "I think—I *know* it will do him good to have you here," she said firmly and pushed the pot off the flame.

"Oh, he looks just fine. I'm glad he's gained a little weight, and I can see why if you always cook things that smell that good."

She smiled a little. "I cook mainly for myself. James

13

doesn't care. He would live on hamburgers and too much coffee."

"Or good bourbon."

I jumped at the sound of James's voice so close behind my shoulder. I had forgotten that nasty little trick of his. I shivered a little and went on setting the table.

"What are you drinking, Joan? Can I fix you something?"

"Nothing, thanks. It would put me right to sleep."

"You've had a long day—" began Alison.

"Where'd you spend last night?" James asked.

"Roanoke."

His eyebrows shot up. "You must drive like a bat out of hell."

"It was easy. The interstates are great."

"They sure are changing the landscape around here. The Perkins farm got cut in half."

"Grampa Perkins? How awful! What did they do?"

"Uncle Leland tried to farm both halves and finally sold out to developers. And the Prentisses sold Fairlawn a while back. For a fortune, I might add. A lot of the old families are selling now, and getting fantastic prices. Shearerville is really getting some mainstream money at last. Did you come through town?"

"No, I caught Carter's Lane. Is it much changed?"

"You won't know the place. A lot of one-way streets, and condominiums down along the river. . . ."

A moment later I asked, "Who is working the Hilliard farm, James? I saw a truck—"

"Dunstan. The younger one. Worst kind of trouble-maker. We don't have anything to do with him."

"He looked—I thought—he seemed to recognize me. What kind of trouble does he make?"

He and Alison exchanged glances clearly labelled *don't tell her.* "Come along, you two," Alison said firmly as she put a bubbling casserole on the table. "You can gossip over dinner."

We served ourselves, and I waited and wondered

whether James would say grace the way Gramp always did, even at breakfast. James didn't. He evidently didn't even wonder whether I wondered. So much for old customs, I thought, and sent a little shrug to any ghosts who may have been watching. I expect they had either gotten used to James and his ways or moved out.

"How's your family?" James asked as he raised his fork. "Your stepmother well again?"

"What did Susan have, Joan, pneumonia?"

"Mostly a nasty virus on top of fatigue. But she's fine now. She and Dad should be in Saint Thomas tonight."

"I know she was glad to have you home this fall to help with the youngsters."

"I thought you were going to be married this winter," said James. "How'd what's-his-name get out of it?"

"Cooper Newton, James, and I'm the one who broke it off. I never should have started it, as a matter of fact."

"But he seemed so perfect, from what Ellen told us," said Alison. "Good family, a lawyer . . ."

"Too perfect, I guess. I just didn't feel right about it."

"Not good enough for him?" James asked, his eyebrows up.

"Not nearly!" I laughed. "He's a paragon of all the virtues, and as you have often told me, I'm *not!*" I smiled again as I remembered the relief I had felt after that final meeting with Cooper Newton, the eminently eligible Cooper Newton in his last triumphant year at Columbia Law.

For a year I had tried to live up to him, and all I accomplished was to destroy my self-confidence. In the end I was sick and tired of telling him what I wanted to do and then listening to him tell me why I couldn't, or shouldn't, or how I ought to. I had just enough sense to realize that whatever there was between us may have been sex, but it certainly was not love.

"I gave him back his ring just before Susan got sick," I said to Alison and James. "Smartest thing I ever did."

"How did Uncle Phil like your being back in the fold?"

"Dad said he was glad I could be Joan again," I said proudly.

"Well, that's good," said Alison. "You're too young to rush into marriage. Have some jam on your muffin."

I was mulling that over when James asked suddenly, "Did you stop and see Perk when you came through Maryland?"

It was time to tell them. "Yes, I saw him."

"Sorry he got so badly hurt," James went on. "But what the hell was he doing in Vietnam, anyhow? Uncle Phil should have stopped him."

"Stopped him? Dad would have gone with him if he could!"

"So . . . well, I hate to say dumb, but—"

"Then don't! It's so tiresome. We've heard it so much!"

"But they admit it was stupid. Even that lyin' bas—"

"*James!*" shrieked Alison.

I had swallowed his bait. "Not Nixon only, for heaven's sake. There was Johnson before that, if you recall. What about him?"

"I'm talking about Watergate."

"Yeah, well I'm not. I'm talking about the war. At least now there's some hope of getting our troops out of there in good order. That's at least one point in his favor."

Alison stepped in again, her voice firm. "Now, Joan, you haven't said. How *is* Perk? Everyone here has been so concerned."

"He says he should be able to walk again with . . . help." I refused to say the word "prosthesis." "But he . . . I don't know exactly. He . . . we didn't say much about it." We didn't say much of anything, in fact. There was a wall between us, a strange intangible, impenetrable wall.

"Couldn't they save his arm?"

"Not his hand or wrist."

"That's awful, Joanie. I'm so sorry."

"It really is tough," said James. "How's he holding up?"

"Not . . . too well. He's too patient about it, somehow. He just seems resigned. He just *bears* it!"

16

"I reckon it takes a long time—" began Alison.

"I'm really sorry, Joan," said James, and I knew he meant it. "We've had our differences . . ."

I looked at the white scar on his lip, where Perk's fist had cut it open the day he caught James starting to decapitate a turtle I had found. Perk had landed in the horse trough a few seconds later, but it's James who bears the scar.

"But I hate to think of him not fighting back, being despondent. It's not like him," James continued.

I took a sip of water to drown the scalding grief in my throat. "That's just it. It's not at all like him." I tried desperately to think of something cheerful to say to break the silence, but my mind was glued shut.

"Will you be going back to New York?" asked James abruptly.

"I hope not. I may go to Philadelphia. I have an offer from a really good graphic art studio down there. I don't really know."

We went on from there to exchange information about every member of the family we could think of, my twin half brothers, Pip and Jim, and half sisters Cynthia and Sidney, as well as the many cousins here who were so eager to welcome me back into the fold I would run my legs off if I kept all the provisional engagements Alison made for me. I felt tired again just thinking about it.

"I told them I couldn't make any promises for you," she said. "You'll want to see Ellen—"

"Oh, yes! Tomorrow, first thing!" I sat up straight again.

"You'd better call, then. She said something about going to Nashville for dinner with Shirley's intended."

"Shirley Perkins engaged? Who is he? Anyone I know?"

"Hayley Milton, or Hilton," said James, with obvious contempt.

"Wilton," said Alison, ignoring James. "I haven't met him, but Ellen says he's very nice."

"Damned hippie," said James, clattering his spoon around in his dessert glass so he couldn't possibly be ignored.

"James!"

I laughed as I got the picture. Of course James would dislike a cousin of his marrying a hippie. James is so totally conventional, with his short hair and clean-shaven face and necktie. Poor James! No wonder he's worried about my having a skirt to wear!

"Before you fall off your chair in wild hysterics," he said, "how about a glass of wine to drink my health?"

"Why? What's the matter with your health?" I was either closer to hysterics than I thought, or stupid with fatigue.

"Nothing! But I've had a birthday." He got a bottle of champagne from the refrigerator and popped the cork. "A special birthday."

"Why, so you have. December fifth, wasn't it? And, ah, let's see, you're six years older than I am so you're—"

"Thirty, and—"

"Happy birthday!" I raised my glass. "The first of us over the hill!"

"And free!"

"Free?"

"Of that trusteeship." He touched his glass to mine and then to Alison's. "I'm of age where the farm is concerned—at last!"

"So you are! I had forgotten."

"You can bet I hadn't. Oh, Fitch has been fine, never interfered, anything like that. But I can do as I please now, without reporting to him. Here's to freedom!"

"And your good health," I said cheerfully.

A few minutes later Alison put her hand on my arm and said "Tomorrow's another day, Joan. Why don't you run along to bed?"

I pulled myself erect again. "I have to call Scarsdale. I promised Grandma Cox and the halflings—"

"You can use the phone in my study, if you want to."

There will be ghosts in there. "I'll just use this one, thanks. I don't have to be private."

Chapter Two

THE TALL WINDOWS were velvety dark and not even star-shine illuminated the sheds in the yard when I woke. All I could hear was thin scratchy-chewing from a mouse in the wall and not a sound from Hector. I had no choice but to try to go back to sleep. When Alison said good night, she added with a definite glint in her eye, "Now be sure to sleep late, honey. There's no need for you to get up early."

I'm no good at sleeping late!

The sun was up by now in New Hampshire, shining pink-gold under the wings of gulls, gilding the tops of pine trees, glancing around the corner of the big white empty farm-house, caught on the roof of my limpet where I painted New York out of my system in huge grey-green canvases that are rolled and stuffed in the rafters like cast-off snake-skins. If I'm lucky, I'll never have to look at them again.

I uncurled my fingers and pressed them flat against the cold sheets. To avoid thinking about Perk I thought about James, poor motherless, fatherless, loveless James, who is loved at last!

It began when my mother, Sidonia, accepted Dad to be her husband, and his twin brother, James, left Woodsedge in a fit of sullen, deep-hurting jealousy. He joined the Royal Canadian Air Force and never returned, not to the States, let alone to the farm, but a year or so later his wife Lydia came to live at Woodsedge to have her baby.

Dad by then was stationed at Pearl Harbor, his bride childless, and then he was on a destroyer in the Pacific fighting the Japanese, and Sidonia, not the least bit pregnant, joined the Waves. In the best picture I have of her she is standing proud and straight in her uniform. . . .

The news of Uncle James's death "somewhere over Germany" was received when our James was less than a month old. Aunt Lydia was young and energetic and there was a war on. She, too, cleared out, leaving her baby behind, and joined the nurse corps. She died on Guam, and Gramp had to be a father again. He told us often, always in front of James, that he hated every minute of it. I don't know what Grandmother thought, that tall severe lady who had lost a son and a daughter and whose last child was engaged in naval warfare half the world away. She never said and probably was never asked. All I know is that she had snow white hair and hummed tunelessly and endlessly while she worked.

Then the war was over and Dad returned unscathed. After a proper time Perk was born, and Dad decided to go north to academia. Gramp, who had become notoriously hateful to everyone except my mother, strongly opposed Dad's decision, but Dad went anyway. That was bad enough, but when I was born and Sidonia died, Gramp flatly blamed Dad for her death.

"Don't know why you wanted to go kitin' off up there," Gramp would mutter, glaring fiercely at anyone in sight.

"That's where my work is. You know that."

"Them Yankee doctors ain't no good."

"Just among the best in the world . . . Sir!"

It became a ritual between them, Gramp bitterly accusing Dad and Dad patiently defending himself every summer. From the very beginning I knew it was painful for Dad to come here, but he came, and brought all of us with him, not only out of a sense of duty to his parents, or even to James, but because he loved Woodsedge. His roots, too, were here.

It would have been a miracle if James had liked his Yankee cousins. We outnumbered him six to one, four to one if you discount the girls, who never seemed to be real people to James. He just stepped over them or got out of their way. No part of our annual invasion could have been easy for James, and I don't suppose things were any more comfortable after we left in August and he had Gramp and his complaints and commands all to himself again—Gramp with his sly tricks and hurtful machinations.

One turbulent summer, in a grand display of power and arrogance after a particularly bitter exchange with Dad, Gramp wrote a new will. From then on he pulled that blue covered document out of his locked desk drawer to wave at us like a captured battle flag any time he thought we were "out of line." We youngsters found it silly and strangely embarrassing, but that didn't stop Gramp. He wanted us all to know to our endless sorrow that he had made James Tarleton Brandon his sole heir. Our father, he announced, his milky blue eyes glaring, had been "written off" with a gift of a dollar. (Sometimes it was "ten dollars," sometimes "a hundred." Whatever his portion, Dad never blinked an eye.) None of us Yankee brats was mentioned at all, Gramp said. My cousin James, from the time he was twelve years old, was led to believe he was sole heir to Woodsedge.

But before that summer was over Gramp began to hint that I might be an exception, that I might, if I charmed him enough, tempt him to write a new will. I was very young. I loved being his favorite, loved being allowed to sit on his lap, loved being told special stories about my mother, loved being pampered with secret gifts of candy or a fine arrowhead or a brass from an old harness.

I deliberately set out to charm him, and from then on James was slyly but undoubtedly my enemy. If it hadn't been for Perk . . .

But Perk had always been there. Until now.

But now we are grown up!

The last summer we visited here, James wanted to be friends with me, but Gramp kept the hostilities raging, happily playing his private game of God. That winter, a month or so before he died, Gramp told Dad he had written a new will that yoked James and me together in joint ownership of Woodsedge.

I was never told how James reacted to this bombshell. Until yesterday I had never set foot on Woodsedge after Gramp died, and the only time I saw James was when he and Alison came to New York on their honeymoon, and we were all, for our own reasons, on our best behavior. I don't know what he felt when Gramp died. He was of age then, working in Shearerville and living at the farm. He simply stayed there and refused even to spend holidays with us. Always secretive, our James. I still didn't know whether he cared a rap about Woodsedge, whether it was a joy to him or a burden, a habit or a downright curse. He never said, never hinted—

A whimper? A faint lonely-puppy cry!

I was up and dressed and out of there within seconds.

I closed the back door as quietly as I could, but Hector's voice changed from a forlorn howl to hopeful yelps. "Coming, pup!" The yelps changed to cries of joy, and I heard him leaping against the brooder house door. I kept our reunion as quiet as I could, but we woke everything up, including the sun from the rising mists across the fields.

Hector tried to go in all directions at once. He bounced into a pile of leaves at a corner of the hen house, and when a rabbit scurried out he turned in midair and hurled himself back to safety between my feet. "Only a rabbit, silly!" I flung out my hand. "Gittim!" But the rabbit had hightailed around the shed, and Hector cocked his head at me in wonder. He skidded to a classy point when the next one jumped out of the frozen grass, and I encouraged him again with a "Hunt in there," even though I knew the twins would disapprove of my sending him after a rabbit. He obediently got his nose down and found a third quarry down by the pecan tree, and this one got properly chased before it escaped through some planks in the grain shed.

I followed slowly behind him. The buildings near the house seemed sturdy enough, in need of whitewash perhaps, but their roofs were straight, their doors latched, and their windows, dingy with cobwebs and dust, were whole. At the far corner stood the red cabin, its chimney bent like a storybook cottage and its porch sagging, but secure enough to have a padlock on its door, the cabin evidently used by James for storage of some kind. The leafless old pecan tree beside it didn't quite block the view from the back porch of the house to the copse half a mile down the farm road to the west.

I wanted to open every door, look in every window, but the sounds from the paddock were becoming urgent. I hurried across the farm road to the grain shed, where Hector stood panting in puzzled frustration, his tongue lolling, his ears alert, his eyes red rimmed as he looked for a sign of his quarry.

When I opened the shed door it came away at the bottom hinge and hung, a dead weight, in my hands. Half lifting, half pulling, I got it open and peered in. All murky darkness, this place where we had gone for corn to feed the last lonely survivor of the Woodsedge teams so many years ago. It was alive now with a sudden scurry of little rat feet, and a cardinal flew in panic at the dingy window and beat against it for a few seconds before it found a broken pane and disappeared into the day. Hector made a quick tour of the rotting plank floor and went out again. I left the door sagging and followed him into the main barn.

The dirt floor was dry and dusty, and the great polished tree trunks that held the loft were as firm as ever. I looked up at that place we had been allowed to go into only with special permission. The rafters and planks were hidden under festoons of cobwebs hanging from a fragile network of straw. There would be ghosts up there, too, ghosts of children on a rainy day . . . ghosts of hidden litters of kittens. . . .

Ducks taking off from the pond behind the barn pulled me back to the present, and I whistled Hector in. He was only a little muddy when he came to me, a happy grin on his face, and eager for his breakfast.

I wished a few minutes later that providing my own

breakfast were as simple as providing Hector's, but after half-a-dozen distractions while I explored the all-new pantry—with a passing sigh for the old one—I gave up looking for cereal and settled for two leftover muffins and instant coffee with my breakfast cigarette. I was sweeping up the last of the crumbs when Alison appeared at the dining room door.

I forgot all about my muffin crumbs and cigarette in an urge to paint her, just as she was, standing there in the doorway, tall, almost Grecian in her statuesque grace, her golden hair still tousled from sleep, one long white hand resting lightly on the dark wood of the old swinging door, the other lifting her red velvet robe that curved to the floor. The expression on her face was vague and questing, almost as though she were lost, as though she had walked through a looking glass. . . .

I realized as she walked toward me she that she hadn't put in her contacts yet. "Up so early! Did you sleep well?"

"Beautifully, thanks, but I hope Hector and I didn't wake you. I'm afraid I do get up awfully early."

"I know. James warned me." She laughed, but I wasn't quite sure she was amused. "What would you like for breakfast, some hot cakes, or eggs and bacon?"

I finally convinced her that the two leftover muffins were all I wanted and offered to scramble some eggs for her.

"Oh, we just have coffee in the morning, and toast." She made a wry face at the jar of instant coffee. "But I do draw the line at that stuff."

"I didn't dare try to work the percolator."

"It's a cranky old thing. You have to wiggle the plug just right, until it catches." She wiggled it just right and then sat with me at the long white table. "I meant to be up earlier," she said. "I set the alarm but I never heard it."

"*Please* don't get up on my account. I don't need any waiting on. I don't want to be company—I mean, a visitor. You know! I wouldn't know how to act!"

"I reckon you do know your way around here," she said

24

with little or no enthusiasm. She raised her head from the knife blade she was caressing between her fingers. "You must tell me what to get for you, cereal or anything like that."

"I thought I might make a cake for us," I said dreamily. There had always been one on the shelf in Grandmother's pantry, one of my most cherished memories. "I won't guarantee the results, though. I'm really just learning to cook."

Her high-arched brows flew up in surprise. "I thought you kept an apartment in New York. Did you just eat out all the time? It must have been terribly expensive."

"You don't have to cook sunflower seeds or bananas," I said with a laugh. I saw no point in telling her that Cooper Newton wouldn't allow me to cook for him in the apartment we shared until last fall. One of the first things on his list for After Marriage was to send me to cooking school, I could take my choice of which one. "But I learned a lot from Susan this summer, even making jam and things—and cakes, the notorious Brandon weakness."

"A cake would be nice. We haven't had one in a long time." She looked around with a kind of owlish curiosity. "There are eggs but we'll need milk—oh, and butter. We'll make a list. Your grandmother's cookbooks are still in the second drawer."

To my delight, there they were—the same old oil-stained notebooks Grandmother wrote her "receipts" in. "I'm . . . apt to get carried away sometimes," I began, as I turned the first few pages, and then I closed the drawer again. "I mean, maybe I'd better not start on this until I know what you want to do today. You said something about the Dexters, I think?"

"That's tomorrow. The Hendersons are having a bridge buffet this evening."

"The Hendersons? I don't know them, do I?"

"I'm sure you don't. They're business associates who came here with the Pettyjohns eight years ago."

"Isn't Mr. Pettyjohn James's partner? I'm sure I've never met him. Or Mrs. Pettyjohn. Ah, I assume there *is* a Mrs. Pettyjohn."

"Lucile. We play bridge together on Wednesdays . . . usually."

"And all the little Pettyjohns?"

"Only one," she said, with a little grit in her voice. "Myra's in high school. She'll be at your luncheon on Monday. Lucile sent regrets. I'm not sure why, except that we don't do a lot of things together—except play bridge on Wednesdays."

"I don't know what Pettyjohn, Brandon, and Associates do, as a matter of fact. Aren't they brokers or something?"

"Yes, something like that. But they're involved in politics just now. He's running for mayor."

"James?"

She laughed lightly. "James knows better. He just keeps the office and helps at meetings and things. Branch Pettyjohn does the running. He's been right successful at it, too. You'll meet him Christmas Eve. He can charm the paper off a wall!"

"Do you help? With the politics, I mean?"

"I stay as far away from it as I can." There was something defiant about the set of her chin. She stood up and began to arrange a coffee tray. "I'm no better at it than James is. I just try not to . . . sabotage. . . ." She pulled a pair of gold-rimmed glasses out of her pocket and seemed more comfortable when she put them on. "Bridge is my game," she said firmly. "In winter, at least. I'd play golf the year 'round if they would just keep the course open!"

"Bridge," I said thoughtfully. "I'm pretty bad at bridge, I'm afraid." Another strike out with Cooper Newton! "Like you with politics, I stay as far away from it as I can."

"Oh. Well, if you really don't like to play . . . and our group takes it pretty seriously . . ." She gave me a forgiving smile. "I'm glad you told me. I can get substitutes for us."

"Oh, no! Oh, please don't do that! If you and James have

engagements for bridge, just leave me behind. I promise you I won't mind! And I don't even know the Hendersons. They won't miss me at all."

"Oh, they'll miss you! But . . . well, Polly wasn't going to play—so you could, you know."

I finally convinced her I would be perfectly happy at Woodsedge alone. I mentioned snapshot albums, the trunk full of mementos to look through, sketches to make. . . . The look of serenity returned at last when she was convinced I didn't need—or want—to be entertained. I thanked her with a smile and opened the door so she could carry her tray of coffee in to James.

She paused in the doorway. "Oh, if the phone rings it will probably be Ellen, so answer it if you like. She called after you went to bed and said she'd call this morning."

As I stirred my cup I wished I had a handsome husband to share coffee with in the sunshine of a Sunday morning. There had never been sunlight in our New York apartment, just a view of yellow bricks and a canyon full of noise and traffic.

A sudden wave of excitement—or dread—chilled me as the question of my future intruded on my thoughts again. Quickly I dashed it aside, and then sighed because I had nothing to replace it with, no handsome husband in sight, no hopeful prospect on which to build my own rose garden.

Forsaken now, that once-lovely rose garden between me and the morning sun. There was a ruined vestige of the arbor where Aunt Caroline had stood on her wedding day, poor Aunt Caroline, who years ago gambled away her inheritance and her husband's, and then, in remorse, took her own life. The garden seemed still to be in mourning. Lifeless stalks of rose bushes bent over the dark border of frozen marigolds and zinnias and long, weary grass—an ugly frozen wasteland.

If it were mine . . .

But it wasn't really mine. The house and yard belonged to James. That, too, was in Gramp's will. We owned the farm in common, but the house was James's home. Alison needn't have been so defensive about the changes she has made. I didn't buy any of the paint, let alone the carpet!

Maybe I imagined that she was defensive about it. Maybe all she really wanted was my approval of the fashionable new look she has given the place. I sighed again. Maybe I could fix up the red cabin or, better still, Two-Great's log cabin down by the woods! I could build a studio and get Perk to come—

The phone rang, and I pushed my dreams aside as I greeted Ellen, wife of Dad's first cousin, Fitch Perkins, and long-ago confidante of my mother. She had been a friend to me since my life began, and was not the least of the reasons I had made my midwinter journey. Two years ago she spent a weekend with me in New York. I know she must have hated the stuffy little room I lived in, the reeky old building, the sharp smell of turpentine, my bushy hair. But she never disparaged any of it. She was cordial to my friends and politely puzzled over my paintings until I told her not to worry about them, that they, too, were temporary aberrations. She understood, possibly better than I did myself. When she left she said gently and softly, as is her way, "Come home when you can, Joanie."

I didn't really understand what she meant by it until last fall. I understood much better, now!

The pleasure in Ellen's voice dropped away when she spoke of Shirley and her intended. I picked up a pencil and started sketching a hippie face on the notepad by the phone and listened encouragingly. I would know more when Ellen and I talked over lunch. I gave him a handsome full beard and luxurious black hair.

"Come as early as you like. I have some things to do at church about three. Shirley will be in Nashville and Fitch has to be in Frankfort, and the girls will still be in school, so there will just be you and me. We can have a good visit if that storm holds off."

"A storm? A blizzard?" I said happily as I put a blizzard cloud behind the hippie head.

She laughed. "Don't sound so happy about it! They don't predict a blizzard, just a few inches, and it may stay north of us, but even a little snow makes the roads slippery for a few days. I do hope you won't try to get to town if it's bad. We can visit over the phone."

"I'll be careful. Dad made me promise—"

James interrupted us by picking up the phone in the den. His "sorry" was so plainly grumbled that Ellen laughed. "Let's let him have it. It will be lovely to see you tomorrow."

Perfect, I thought, as I hung up and pulled my hippie scribble off the pad to throw it away. That will give me plenty of time to go to the Co-op after lunch and get some dog food and still be back in time to walk to Corn Crib Woods before dark.

There was an odd pattern of light in the blizzard cloud I had drawn. I tipped it to look again, turned it over. . . . Someone had pressed hard on a pencil when he—or she—wrote "Blair Hound, 3:30." A new breed of hound? I never heard of a Blair hound, but maybe they are special here—for foxes or quail. I threw the scrap in the wastebasket and went on to my room.

Chapter Three

SOME TIME LATER James stopped at my door, looking at his watch to prove he was behind schedule. "Sorry I have to rush off, Joanie. I thought we might go to Shiloh like we did in the old days, but I have a meeting in town. Glad you're here, though." He gave me a kind of salute with a flip of his hand and was gone. And I had forgotten to ask him where I could put my car.

I forgot to ask Alison, too. She had a phone call soon after James left, and came bustling into my room, pulling tight the belt of her fur-lined trench coat. "Gina Burden wants to go to the hospital," she said. "I'm going to drive her in—"

"Oh, dear! Something wrong? Anything I can do?" Gina Burden was the wife of Boyd Burden, who had done the actual farming at Woodsedge ever since Gramp retired thirty years ago.

"It's not an emergency, just a new grandbaby and her car's laid up. I'll get the groceries while she visits." She seemed to have a sudden inspiration. "Oh, and if you can spare me, I'll stop and see Patsy Reeve on the way back. Will you be able to get your lunch if I stay there awhile? She's been quite sick and maybe I can help. I'll call her from town. . . ." Her voice faded as she eyed me hopefully.

"No problem. I have a thousand things I want to do."

"But your lunch? The casserole—"

"A sandwich will be fine, ah, peanut butter and jelly?"

She laughed. "I don't think there's been peanut butter in this house since I moved in. How about tuna?"

I spent an hour or so over my tuna sandwich, browsing through Grandmother's cookbooks and the dusty, wrinkled clippings that had migrated over the years to the back of the second drawer. It was early afternoon before I surfaced, shook the cobwebs out of my head, and went to take Hector to the barn to find a shelter for Dad's car, as I had promised him I would.

The wagon shed on the eastern side of the barn was empty, but a fresh oil spot on the ground in the first space indicated that it was used as a garage. Three spaces farther down, rusted machine parts and rolls of fencing looked reasonably moveable, so I set to work to clear that space for my use.

It wasn't easy. Bits of wire rammed their way through my mittens and gouged my hands. A lumpy piece of iron wobbled out of my arms and smashed my foot. I pulled and hauled in vain at a length of pipe I thought was six inches or so under the dirt and finally had to find a pick to clear the last five feet of it before I could pull it out. I shed my parka and sweater and was working in my tee shirt and wiping sweat off my face before I finished, but finish I did, and my self-satisfaction was immense.

I whistled Hector in from his excavation of groundhog holes and went to get the Volkswagen. He sat on the seat beside me as we bumped and thumped across the ruts of the farm road that divided the house from the barnyard. "As long as we have snow and not rain, this should be just fine," I told him.

I was backing, just turning into my space, when a jeep came with a roar around the green plastic partition at the far end of the shed on a crash course with my right side. To stop would be dumb, I thought, so I gunned my engine to make the turn quicker and get out of the way. Of course my engine stalled, and there I sat, a lifeless lump to be rammed broadside by that fierce little tramp. But the driver braked and swerved in the nick of time, and I recognized my cousin under the furry trooper's hat and huge sheepskin coat.

I was glad I couldn't hear what he was saying.

I sat there a moment, blowing out my breath in relief, my forehead on the steering wheel. He would have made mincemeat out of us, and Hector first. I hugged my dog to me and looked over to James, ready to call out whatever I could in the way of explanation and apology, but James was paying no attention to me at all. He got out of his jeep and, without a glance in my direction, stamped off toward the house in what I assumed was a rage.

Feeling limp and shaken, I started my car again and backed cautiously into the space I had cleared. I would have been just as happy to go somewhere else, but I had nowhere else to go and it was Hector's suppertime. I had no choice but to find James, beard him in his den, and explain, if I could, why I was where I had been, doing what I had been doing. I wanted to get it over. "Eat it while it's hot," as Perk used to say.

James was not in the kitchen. I fed Hector and then went briskly through the swinging doors and down the hall to the front of the house. The door to the study was closed. There was no reply to my knock. Naturally, dressed as he was, he wouldn't be in the parlor, so he must be in his room. I paused at his door, heard the shower going, and hastily retreated to my own end of the hall.

I was busily sanding the track of a cantankerous bureau drawer when I saw Alison drive up to the porch, and went to help her unload her groceries. "James not in?" she asked as she handed me a sack.

"Oh, yes. Changing, I think."

"But his car's not in—"

"Joe's bringing it," James said from behind my shoulder.

He had the nerve to grin at me when I flinched, but I stuck my chin up and began my set speech, standing in front of him with my arms around the sack of groceries, feeling like a delinquent child as he towered over me. "I'm sorry. I know I should have checked with you about moving that stuff, but you weren't here and there was no point in leaving Dad's car out in a storm, and you might have offered me a space somewhere! And how did I know you were going to come roaring around the corner in a jeep, of all things?"

He grinned some more at my confusion and patted my shoulder with his huge paw. He might just as well have said "Tut-tut, little girl," but actually it was, "Don't give it a thought. I should have expected you to be there, or in some other ridiculous place. Glad I didn't run you down, is all." He shrugged himself back into his sheepskin coat. "I just have to carry Joe home," he said, and was gone.

I explained to Alison what happened as we went to the kitchen with the groceries. She didn't say anything at all for a moment, and I wondered whether she heard me. But then, with an almost visible effort, she pulled her thoughts back from wherever they had been wandering and was almost too apologetic about not having had a place ready for me to use for Dad's car.

It was time to change the subject! "Who's Joe?" I asked.

"Joe? Oh, that's Joe Burden. Boyd's youngest."

"Ah! And Joe's a new uncle! But he's just a baby himself!"

"Fifteen, honey, and all grown up!" She laughed a little. "I don't know what we'd do without Joe. He's jack-of-all-trades around the house—and around the office . . . too. . . ."

Did her voice really fade as she said those things? End in a kind of question as though she were not really sure? "Joe doesn't go to school, then?" I asked.

"Oh, I reckon he does when James or Branch doesn't need him. The Burdens are all good workers, you know."

We chatted on about the Burdens and the farm work that evidently was more interesting to me than to her. She drifted away into her own thoughts almost in midsentence, came back long enough to satisfy herself that I would have a good dinner of leftover casserole if I would make a salad to go with it—I kept my thoughts on that subject to myself—and finally she wandered off to dress for the bridge party at the Hendersons.

When I locked the front door behind them, I stood for a moment at the door, my senses at full pitch, trying to recapture the gut-crunching eagerness, the feeling of being home at last, being exactly where I belonged, that engulfed me every summer when first I stood on this spot. I inhaled deeply, tried hard to detect a vestige of the odor of Grandfather's pipe that had triggered so many exciting experiences for me, but I failed to find the slightest hint of anything but James's cigars. Alison's beige wall-to-wall carpet hid not only the mouse-shaped gouge in the hard pine floor, but also the mustiness from the cellar. The old whatnot was now a Christmas tree, the dark green wall with the brownish water stain shaped like a map of Florida was fresh wallpaper, and the black varnished woodwork was fresh ivory paint.

So be it. So much for the hall.

The door to James's study that used to be Gramp's office and was of all the places in the house the most precious to me, was closed. With a fast-beating heart I turned the knob and the door swung open on noiseless hinges. It was all new, shockingly new—a picture-perfect gentleman's retreat. Perfectly perfect. Perfectly picture book. Not a hair out of place. I crossed the handsome oriental rug to the antique walnut desk, admired the old leather-bound blotter, the elegant cut glass inkstand, and the long fountain pen—undoubtedly gold—that stood in an onyx holder beside it. Such riches! And then I realized, of course, that these things must have come from Alison's mother's family of South Carolina planters and statesmen. Alison's heritage.

There was nothing there that had belonged to Gramp. I closed the door and crossed the hall.

I flicked on the lights in the parlor, that grown-up sanctuary where we children had come only when bidden, all clean and subdued, to meet some elderly caller. I wandered over to the old rosewood piano by the window, exactly where it had always been, not surprised that it was now only an elegant surface on which Alison displayed a pair of beautiful Georgian candlesticks and a gathering of formal family photographs in their silver frames. We had the same photographs in New Hampshire; there were no special memories to be found among these.

But the rosewood was well polished, and the handsome scrolls of the legs gleamed with care. I ran my fingers around their contours and over the three-tiered bevels of the top and then opened the lid, a thing I would never have dreamed of doing in the old days. The ivory keys were pale yellow, and where the ivory was missing, the grey wood underneath showed like stubs of teeth. Not a pretty sight. Not a pretty sound, either. Tinny and thin. It would be no pleasure even to hear the juvenile tunes I knew.

I closed the lid again. There were no ghosts there, either.

With a little shrug of regret I crossed to the fireplace, where the oak mantel had been stripped of its black varnish and polished to a golden glow. I ran my hands up one of the tall pilasters that held the overmantel, up to the capital a foot or more above my head. I was surprised to discover that it was not Corinthian, as I had supposed. It was not even pretending to be! I looked up into a tiny gnome face peering slyly at me through a tangle of grape leaves in the plaster overlay.

I wondered whether Grandfather knew these satyrs had been grinning down at his Christian hypocrisy for so many years. Surely Grandmother did not, or she would have had "taken steps." Either the little heathens would have left immediately or she would have!

It would be fun to know whether Perk ever noticed. . . .

With a frustrated sigh I opened the heavy chased silver box on the mantel and helped myself to one of James's cigarettes. If the satyrs could desecrate the parlor, so could I, I thought as I blew a cloud of smoke at them and at the photographs on the piano. Whatever ghosts may have been lurking ran for their lives, and I turned out the gas log and went down the hall to the kitchen.

But first I stopped in the dining room and picked a certain plate off the plate rail. It had been above my reach but in my line of vision on those summer evenings when I sat at the table at Gramp's right hand. I had always known about the red fox prowling there in the wintry landscape, but I had never before seen the rabbit cowering under a bush, its ears folded back in fear and desperate hope, watching for the next step—a step the predator would never take. The rabbit would never have to flee for its life. The fox would never pounce. They were frozen for all time, suspended on this glassy apex of hope and fear. Frozen . . . Unchangeable and unresolved. . . .

Was that what I had been looking for? Woodsedge unchanged, life frozen, waiting for me to return and break the spell? How selfish of me! How childish! Of course it had changed! How could it not! And there were no ghosts, not even one, to show me the way back. I propped the plate back on the shelf and went on through the swinging doors.

I was setting my place at the table when the phone rang.

"Mops Brandon? Bethesda calling."

Mops!!! No one on earth calls me Mops except Perk!

"PERK," I shrieked into the phone.

"One minute, please. Two seventy-five for three minutes."

I shrieked his name again in spite of the operator and heard the coins ding into the slots while Perk said, "Easy, easy now. It's just me," through the racket.

"Reverse it, reverse it, Perk, for God's sake!"

"This one's on me," he said, this time loud and clear. "A celebration, old Mops. I did it!"

"Oh, Perk. Did what?"

"Went out to dinner—"

"You did?" I could see him there in that hideous orange

lounge I had visited, where the pay phone hung against the wall, see him through a sudden mist of tears.

He went on quickly. "Got Shanghaied by an Amazon—a nurse. Can you believe it? She said if I didn't go home for dinner with her she would carry me bodily. Could have, too!"

"So you went—"

"I did. It was something else. Pizza, of all things, with half-a-dozen little black kids running around."

"Black kids," I repeated stupidly.

"It was great."

"Tell!"

"I've turned a corner, Mops. There's light at the end of this . . . tunnel, after all."

"Oh, Perk! I—Oh, thank God! I'm so glad! What can I say?"

He laughed, a rough echo of his own laugh. "That about says it all, doesn't it?" He was silent for a breath, and his voice was controlled again when he went on. "So. Ah, how's everything down there? Big James behaving himself?"

"So far, so good! God, I wish you were here!"

"Is he bullying you?" The straight question! The old Perk!

I gave him a straight answer. "Not at all. True!"

I heard a better laugh at that last word, the one we used between us as the absolute, the certification. "Well, you watch him, hear? Leave if he gets mean. Just come on up here."

"I will if he gets mean. But I think he's getting civilized at last! Alison is taming him. I just wish you were here because I miss you everywhere. Nothing is the same."

"Of course it isn't, Mops. How could it be?"

"Well, it's only for two weeks, and I'll stop by and see you on the way north."

"Unless I get home by then—"

"What?" There was noise behind him, a clamor of voices drowning his. Or had I heard him? "What?" I asked again, louder.

I heard him say something over his shoulder and then, more clearly, "Sorry, Mops. Some bas—uh, there's a line—"

"Did I hear you say you might get up home?"

"You did. I might. I . . . I have a lot to learn about this . . . It's a new hand, Mops. It's . . . well, I'm working on it. And I can do that just as well in Boston. I think I can get transferred up there. Oh, one more thing. Genevieve said I should tell you, give you full credit."

"Credit? What? Who's Genevieve?"

"That nurse. She said you looked as though you'd been hit by a truck when you left here the other day, and she said I should be ashamed of myself for shutting you out. Gave me quite a lecture, as a matter of fact."

"Oh, Perk, it wasn't . . . you didn't . . . you never . . ."

He laughed again, and the laugh was still a little rusty but it was Perk's. "It was, and I did—But I'm working on it!"

At that moment the operator cut in with her routine about three minutes being up and signal when you're finished. "Call me again, Perk. Collect, for heaven's sake!"

"I will. On Christmas Day. Take care, Mops!" And the line went dead.

Chapter Four

I WAS THINKING about Perk when I got lost in Shearerville the next morning. I had spread my glad tidings far and wide, told James before he left for his office, caught the twins in Scarsdale before they left for a day's skiing. There was no way I could tell Dad and Susan unless they called me, but when I told them they would rejoice as I rejoiced.

Rejoice? It's too tame a word! I sang! I carolled!

And I got lost.

I had expected to follow the familiar route to Ellen Perkins's house, but the road divided suddenly and I was shunted into a network of one-way streets, where a profusion of little red brick houses, trim, pleasant enough, but featureless, homogenized, bustling with children and cars and Christmas lights, confused and disoriented me. I searched for something I knew and had almost given up when I arrived at what should have been Caitlin Prentiss's back door.

It took me a moment to realize that the red brick houses were standing on what had been the Prentiss farm. I was in a new suburb, and the fine old house lay in the middle of it, surrounded like Gulliver by the Lilliputians, with as little privacy and dignity. "Fairlawn Retirement Home," a green sign over the porch said. There was a van at the door marked "Deliveries," and a young woman in white stood at a window. I was not at the back door of the Prentiss house, I was in the parking lot of a nursing home!

Poor Cat! She had been disgustingly smug about living in the largest, oldest, most elegant and hospitable house in town, the natural gathering place for family celebrations. Probably she would have preferred to have the house bulldozed into the cellar hole than to see it become an institution.

I backed out and turned in what I knew was the right direction for Main Street.

"I only got lost once," I told Ellen as we hugged each other at her front door fifteen minutes later. "I drove up to the back door of Fairlawn Retirement Home."

"I'm sorry! I should have warned you. Never mind. You're here. How well you look! So like your mother, I can't tell you. Ah, Joanie, it's so good to see you!" When I told her about Perk tears of relief and thankfulness spilled over and ran slowly, gently down her cheeks. "We have all missed him, prayed for him, but I know it's been especially terrible for you."

She hit the nail on the head, and I was not surprised. She had always known and understood the special bond between Perk and me, the bond that was forged in the first days of my life and that set us apart together in some subtle way from the rest of Dad's family. That kind of understanding, that knowing where the pain was and putting a gentle healing finger exactly on the spot, was Ellen's special gift.

"I thought we'd have lunch on the porch," she began, when the phone interrupted her. "That will be Fitch to be sure you're here. Browse on through the library if you like. . . . Excuse me. . . ." And she was off, a small, round figure trotting down the hall.

I wandered through the huge lawyer's library that Ellen had made cheerful with strategically placed mirrors and polished brass lamps, and arrived at the glassed-in porch with gaily cushioned wrought iron furniture overlooking the garden, neatly tucked in for the winter. The windows were hung with plants, and on the shelves below them arrangements of candles and greens waiting for the Perkinses' traditional Christmas Eve open house.

Ellen had set our lunch on a glass-topped table in the pale

sunshine. "It's a handsome old house," I said when she joined me.

"Thank you, my dear, but it's a chore to keep up—full of surprises! We pray a lot!"

We talked briefly about her visit with Hayley's family, but the subject she seemed most interested in was my broken engagement to Cooper Newton. It didn't take long to convince her that my heart was not severely damaged, and her face brightened considerably. It brightened so much, in fact, that her smile seemed to have a kind of secret excitement. I suppose my face registered my question, but she only acknowledged it with a broader smile and laid her hand on my arm and changed the subject to Susan and Dad and their Caribbean cruise.

Ellen's got something up her sleeve, I thought as I drove away. The little secret smile had reappeared several times in our two hours together, but in this season for surprises I did not pry. I knew that nothing Ellen did would ever be hurtful to me.

She drew me a little map of the route to the Co-op and back out to the county road. It was all clear enough now, and I found the place easily, the same wide porch along the front, the same collection of farm vehicles pulled up to the loading dock in the rear, the same huge bales and crates on the platform.

I had some slight hope that I could browse here as I used to when I came with Dad, explore the bins of nails and bolts, examine the shiny racks of tools, ponder the bags of chicken feed while I poked the tight sacking with a finger. I had a slight hope that the farmers would ignore me now as they did then, let me walk among them and listen to their soft voices saying whatever it was they said in an accent I could never quite understand, much less imitate. I knew full well how they treated the stray grown woman who came in there. I had watched with childish fascination the way they cast down their eyes, examined the cracks in the worn wooden floor, and waited silently until Mrs. Who-

41

ever-she-was had been waited on and left the store, taking the silence with her.

And now I was that stray grown women myself.

I hadn't taken three steps in the door, hadn't even had a chance to look at the coal grates and pokers piled there, when a handsome young man with soft brown eyes came up to me and asked what he could do for me, ma'am. Dead silence from the back of the store, where a knot of denim-clad shoulders and bright billed caps indicated that the cracks in the floor were under close scrutiny.

"May I look around a bit?" I asked with a final hope.

The young man stepped back a pace or two and pretended to busy himself rearranging a display. I went over to an archway hung with broad brimmed hats over a pyramid of splendid high-heeled boots to examine a leather vest, and the young man came right along behind me. I finally asked him if he had that vest in my size.

"Oh, yes, ma'am. I'm just sure we do." He disappeared behind a door and came back a few seconds later with exactly the vest I wanted. It couldn't have been lovelier: lambskin, creamy and thick, with the wool turned inward and the skin, soft and sueded, outward. I wanted it! And then I looked at the price tag and knew I had better not even try it on. With a sigh I handed it back and asked about percolators.

As I turned to follow him into that section of the store I almost collided with a small towheaded girl who was standing there, holding her doll and watching me with the largest softest blue eyes it has even been my pleasure to see. I touched her shoulder to steady her as she stepped back, almost falling over the display of boots.

"Excuse me, darling," I said, and I *never* call strangers darling. But she was . . . absolutely darling. I gave her a warm smile and got one in return, but not a word. She lowered her eyes quickly and turned to scamper off to the back of the store, where her brother was moving toward her to rescue her from this outlander who was about to run her down, while her father kept watch over them both. I recognized him immediately as the man who had been at Carter's store last Saturday—the younger Dunstan—the troublemaker!

Red-gold hair he had, and a weathered, rugged face. A bulky denim jacket hung from broad shoulders. His glance caught mine as he reached down for his child, caught her up in his arms and . . . for one brief instant I felt a quick surge of jealousy—it could not have been anything else—and then such a strange sense of loneliness and abandonment that I grabbed a corner of my lip between my teeth as I stared at him.

But when he raised his head to look at me again I swung swiftly around before his eyes could meet mine. I hauled myself back into the real world and briskly finished my shopping. A few minutes later I led the way for the clerk carrying the sack of Hector's kibble out into the wind and pale sunshine to my car.

The bright-haired man was just driving out of the parking lot in his battered green truck with "Hilliard-Dunstan" painted on the door. Our eyes met again and he tipped his hat politely. These southern men have a way of making even strange women feel appreciated, I thought, as I smiled at him and nodded. Surely there could be no trouble in that!

Chapter Five

I WAS GLAD the wind was at my back when Hector and I started our walk to Corn Crib Woods a full hour later than I would have chosen. There was nothing, not even a fence, to slow the icy gusts howling at us. A wide milky halo veiled the sun, and steel grey clouds rolled and churned over the horizon.

I almost didn't go. I almost turned back when I realized the storm would almost certainly catch us somewhere on the open fields between the woods and home.

It was Hector, leaping and cavorting with joyful abandon, that egged me on. His sturdy white legs flashed in exuberant caprioles and flying changes of lead as he started across the soybean field, and I pulled the hood of my parka tight and shoved my hands, in their fat woolly mittens, deep in my pockets as I watched him. It was easy enough walking, but when my shadow no longer walked beside me I quickened my pace, and fifteen minutes later I turned the corner of the woods and heard the wind, frustrated at not blowing me down, howling in the treetops.

Corn Crib Woods we called it, and it hardly seemed the same place I had last seen twelve years ago. "It can't be the same," Perk had said, and it certainly wasn't. Some huge old oaks looked familiar, but along the edge of the woods a pile of full-grown trees had been bulldozed into a crazy tangled heap, their bare roots clutching huge clods of red-brown earth as tightly as a hand might hold its last grasp on life. I stood for an instant, staring at the wreckage, wondering whether two or three more acres of soybeans were really worth such devastation.

We reached the top of the woods before I saw things that looked familiar. Here, stretching east and south, was a huge field undulating like the torso of a sleeping giant in rough beige tweed, ragged and windswept, with the woods on my left his unkempt hair, his twisted belt the ribbon of Blair Road along which a red-and-silver truck was creeping toward that bus-stop, filling-station, country-store intersection where we went in Gramp's old Buick when all Grandmother needed was baking powder or some other trivial necessity.

A hawk banking the rough wind high overhead was the only sign of life. I stood for a moment in the shelter of the old corn crib, now almost totally obliterated under a thick growth of honeysuckle and bread-and-butter vines, and tried to translate what I saw into what I remembered of the place. Except for the old wooden structure itself there was little here of those summers when we worked like inspired beavers to build and furnish a tree house up here, a hidden retreat for children only, of which I could find no trace at all.

I had known it couldn't be the same, but there should have been a lingering wisp of the companionship we shared as we worked or read or talked or dreamed for hours on end, while the trees shaded and fanned us and the squirrels scolded us. . . .

But there was nothing at all, nothing but the sleeping-giant field and the trees tossing their tops in the wind. It was too cold to linger. The wind was growing colder and sharper, stronger and snow laden.

I started on, had taken a few steps past the corn crib, when I was nearly bowled over by Hector, who, with hackles up and making a sound between a whimper and a growl, flung himself to his sanctuary between my feet.

"Well, what is it," I asked him. "What's in there?"

45

He rolled questioning eyes up to mine, plainly wanting me to find out. He stayed an inch or two behind my boots as I made my way into the thicket of honeysuckle that bordered the woods out of which he had come. Not far in. A few feet.

They say artists see things other people would miss. Perhaps that is so, but I can hardly believe that anyone walking into that thicket, watching where he was going, which was hardly a matter of choice after all, would have missed the shocking pink spot caught in the honeysuckle. It was absolutely foreign and unnatural. No bird or flower in these woods was ever such a color.

I stooped to look more closely.

It was a scarf, a gaudy pink satin scarf. And under it . . .

Under it was a woman's face. I stared stupidly for a moment before my mind would admit that it was a woman's face, a young, pretty woman's strangely distorted face, her eyes grey with frost crystals. Dead eyes. Obviously dead.

I knew she was dead. I had no experience at all with death, but there was no mistaking it. Dead and very cold. There was no possible way I could help her. I touched one arm with some idea of making her more comfortable, more natural looking, but it was as stiff as a board. There was no way I could move it without moving her whole body, and I knew I could not. I hung onto a small dogwood covered with dead honeysuckle while I traced the shape of her body through the leaves and vines that seemed to have been pulled and hauled on purpose to cover it. Her legs in blue and green plaid slacks twisted away out of sight under deeper brush.

I think I screamed. Hector crept away, whimpering with distress. I suddenly had to clutch my ice cold hands over my mouth when I felt my stomach heave. The coldness somehow restored my equilibrium, and I rubbed my icy mittens roughly over my cheeks. Hector came crawling back, and I sank to my knees to hug him while he licked my face.

I don't know how long we huddled miserably there beside the dead woman before my wits began to return. It couldn't have been more than a few seconds before Hector squirmed out of my arms and hopped away a few feet, questioning with yelps and pounces what the point was in remaining immobilized in this frozen, miserable place. The sweat of shock was chilling where the wind plastered my clothes to my back, and I knew action was absolutely necessary. In the time it took me to stagger to my feet I realized I couldn't do anything at all except get home as fast as I could and get some kind of help. Help for whom, I wondered as I stood over that small wretched heap. Nothing in all the world will help her. For me then, or I might just as well lie down beside her, and there will be two of us for someone else to find.

Dear God, I thought as I struggled out of the thicket, I've got to keep my head. If I get lost . . . or fall and break a leg . . . I flapped my arms across my chest until I felt warmth sting my fingers. Then with some sort of cry to Hector that I could have saved because he was tight at my heels, I started the long walk home, back across the frozen fields, the way we had come.

Tears streamed from my eyes and froze on my face, and the wind whipped crystals of them into my cheeks until they were numb. Time and time again I rubbed them with my mittens as I stumbled across what seemed an endless space. But I didn't fall. I kept my feet moving and headed for the clump of buildings that was a fading shadow in the whirling greyness of snow. The frozen body slipped out of my thoughts and I didn't notice. I didn't even try to keep an eye on Hector. I moved automatically, plodding on, one foot in front of the other, until at last I got home, back to the place of warm live human beings upon whom I could unload the whole burden of horror.

But there was no one there. Neither car was in the garage, and there was no light on in the house. There was no live human to wrap me in comforting warmth while I gasped out the horrible news that was beating in my head. With Hector still at my side I went through to the front hall, calling and searching, although I knew there was no one there.

Shivering, my teeth chattering and the muscles in my face twitching uncontrollably, I went back to the kitchen and poured some of James's bourbon into a glass, splashed water in with it, and spilling only a little, gulped it down—and followed it with another.

Sheer desolation seemed to engulf me—sheer desolation. I sank to the floor, flung my arms around my dog, and cried.

That sort of behavior may be normal to a human, even consoling, but it was totally upsetting to my dog. Hector squirmed in protest and after a few seconds squirted out of my arms and began to do his leaps and pounces around me. His cavorting was more distracting than comforting, but after a moment the shivers became spasmodic and I began to recover my wits.

I desperately needed someone to talk to. I wanted Dad, but of course I couldn't have him. Perk? I picked up the phonebook, and as I looked for the area code for Maryland, I realized I would have to go through half a dozen exchanges and desks before I could hope to speak to him, and even then . . . I shook my head. I couldn't lay this kind of thing on Perk. Not at such a distance and at such a time. I was about to call James when the boldfaced numbers in the front of the phonebook gave me my answer. The right thing to do was call the police.

I made myself speak as calmly as I could, and I don't know what the woman who answered could understand of my story, but she understood clearly enough to tell me that I lived outside the city limits and would have to call the county sheriff. She gave me his number, and I wrote it down.

It took some minutes before I could get through to him. Earsplitting static was whizzing and crackling on the line, and I remembered that the country phones are in trouble more often than not in stormy weather, but I persevered. When he finally answered, we had to shout at one another like raving maniacs.

"What did you say?"

"She is dead!"

"I can't hear you, ma'am. Can you speak a little louder please."

It was a nightmare of confusion, but I stuck to my guns, and he finally repeated the gist of it back to me and said he would come out as soon as he could. There was a tree down across Blair Road, and he couldn't say how long that would be.

Relieved that at least he understood where I was and what I was talking about, I hung up.

And then I called James.

For a long moment there was dead silence. I heard my voice echo through the pulsating space and wondered whether the lines had finally gone down, whether he was still there, or had ever been. I was ready to shout the words against the void for a second time, when I heard him.

He was laughing at me. I couldn't believe it! "It was a woman, James. She is dead! I didn't imagine it!" Suddenly I was angry, warmly, eagerly, almost happily angry. What he heard, I suppose, was the leading edge of hysteria, and he began to be soothing.

"All right, all right. I heard you. Let me think. You said you called the county sheriff? Dennis? All right. I'll talk to him. Is Alison back yet?"

"No. Wait—yes! I think she just drove in!"

"Well, that's good. You tell her all about it. Tell her I said not to worry. No need for you all to get upset. I'll be home in a little while. I'll call Dennis right away. Now, just don't worry about it." And without another word he hung up.

Easy to say don't worry about it. Easy to say!

Alison was shocked and horrified. I stood leaning against the sink and she against the table, a huge rain scarf covering her new hairdo, total mouth-open concentration on her face, while I poured out the story. She didn't interrupt me, and at the end, when the tears were again sluicing down my cheeks, she took me in her arms and hugged me to her lovely, warm, alive heart.

"Poor baby," she said, over and over until the shudders finally stopped choking me. "I'll make us some tea."

I choked back a giggle. That's what Alison is, I thought, a dear nanny. A make-us-some-tea nanny. Nothing could be nicer than her loving sympathy or more consoling than her tea. She insisted upon my eating one of the sticky buns she had brought home while she called the Dexters. By that time the snow was thick and blowing and she didn't have to use my distress as an excuse not to go play bridge tonight.

When the reaction to shock and warm tea set in, she wouldn't let me fight the sudden drowsiness that engulfed me. She sent me to bed. It was not yet six o'clock, and she actually sent me to bed! So much for nannies, I thought, as I curled tightly under my quilts. I had made her promise to wake me the minute James came in. "We'll have to go up there," I said. "We can't leave her out there all night." Alison just kissed me, turned off my light, and closed my door. I thought I heard her talking to someone on the phone as the shivers dwindled into sleep.

But I slept only fitfully before the haunting image of the dead woman woke me. Feeling dazed and dull I went back to the kitchen and faced the husky cheeseburger Alison made for me. "You need lots of protein, honey, after a shock like that." I ate most of the hamburger and fairly wolfed down a huge slice of cake. Then we drank coffee and smoked one cigarette after the other, while a vicious wind rattled every joint in the old house and howled through every crack.

With questions and murmurs of sympathy Alison encouraged me to go through the whole story again and again, reciting every detail. "Oh, I'm so sorry, so sorry. The poor thing," she kept saying. "I wonder who she can be."

And how could I answer? I described the women yet

again. "Very pretty, young . . ." I remember long eyelashes that fringed strangely opaque eyes with grey-white pupils, eyes that were frozen open, and I wondered why I hadn't thought to close them the way they do in movies when someone dies. Then I realized that I probably wouldn't have been able to, and I was glad I hadn't tried.

I described her clothes again and saw in my mind the fur-trimmed hood of the jacket, tangled and stained with oak leaves, which made a fringe behind her head like a small dirty animal curled there. As I repeated all these things aloud to Alison they became more familiar and easier to bear.

It was nearly ten o'clock before James startled us almost out of our wits noisily stamping snow off his feet on the back porch. We hadn't heard him drive up while we were talking, and the house was protesting the onslaught of the wind. He wrestled the door closed behind him. "What a night!" There was that certain edge of excitement in his voice that belongs to someone who has made it safely home through a violent storm. Balancing on one foot and then the other, he turned chunks of slush out of his trouser cuffs and dug it out of his shoe tops. "Should have worn overshoes," he went on. "Hey, Joanie, you should have warned me! You Yankees are supposed to be so smart about these things!"

"Now, James," began Alison, "you know . . ."

His glance slid quickly over my face. I would have been glad if he had offered me a hug, but he didn't. "I'm sorry, Joan. I shouldn't tease you when you must be feeling just awful." His sympathy sounded false, as though he were playing a part. He turned away with a little shrug to fix himself a drink, and his voice became more natural. "I talked to the sheriff and he says there's not a thing he can do tonight. He can't even get out the Blair Road until they get a tree out of the way. But he'll come along first thing in the morning, and we'll go up there and see what it is you found."

"Oh, James, can't we go now? Right away? Get your warmest, driest things on, and you and I can go up—"

"Are you out of your mind?" His voice was quiet and surprisingly detached, as though he had not yet focused clearly on my suggestion.

"We can take the jeep," I persisted.

But James settled more deeply in the old rocker and gave me a glance over the top of his glass that should have been a warning.

My dander—as Dad called it—got up. "Well, all right, sit there, then! I just wish I hadn't waited for you." I turned to the huge iron hall tree by the back door and pulled my scarf free. "I'll take the jeep up there myself, and you can just stay here all warm and snug until hell freezes over!"

That put a lighted match to his fuse at last. He jerked his head up and glared at me as though I were threatening him with a loaded gun. His eyes went straight lidded and ice cold, and his words were laced with venom. "You *are* out of your mind! In the first place, there's no gas in the jeep. You'd have to take your own car. In the second place, you know as well as I do that people who find bodies aren't supposed to touch them until the police arrive. You've seen enough cop shows on TV to know that. And you probably couldn't find the place in all that snow that's blowin' around out there, anyway, and you'd dump your stupid little Volkswagen down a sinkhole and we wouldn't find you 'til spring—if ever—which might be just as well." His eyes gloated with satisfaction as he took a long swallow of his drink.

I stood there with my scarf half wound around my neck and realized he was probably right on all counts, damn him! I think I could happily have killed him at that moment. And of course, being James, he had to add an extra dig to top it off. "Besides," he said, with an unpleasant grin, "I am not at all convinced there *is* a dead body up there in the woods!"

"There is! There *is!*" I was shrieking by this time and literally stamped my foot at him.

"I feel sure, James—" began Alison.

"In either case I'm damned if I'm going out again in this storm just to give you a chance to prove it." He sank more comfortably into his chair, looking absolutely immobile, monolithic, like a sphinx nestling in the sand.

I hate giving up, but over the years I've learned to do it with pretty good grace. I hung my scarf back on the hook and got myself under control. "All right, James. We'll wait." I went over to Alison, still standing by the sink, and gave her a hug. "Good night, and thank you for being so kind to me. I'm off to bed."

As the door to the dining room swung closed behind me I heard her ask him, "But why were you so late, James?"

I didn't hear his answer.

Chapter Six

OUTSIDE MY WINDOW the next morning the world was dazzling white. Wind had pasted snow on every tree and shed in the yard, drifts billowed and surged as streams of snow whipped around the corners of buildings. It was exciting, even beautiful, but there was horror in it up there on that windswept hill, where a soulless body had spent the night as still and unfeeling as a broken branch or a stone.

But she wasn't a branch or stone, not even a dead bird or beast. She was a human, one of my own sex and age, and I had left her there alone. . . .

A sheet of tin on the red cabin roof that had thrashed wildly all night made a thunderous cracking noise as a gust caught it, but through the infernal din I could hear Hector's voice. With teeth clenched against my thoughts, I hurried to dress. I was pulling boots on over extra socks when Alison came to my door.

"Oh, you're up! Sheriff Dennis called and said the roads are pretty bad but the tree is cleared from Blair Road and he can come that way. In an hour or so, he thinks."

A few minutes later I almost forgot the horror as I watched Hector in his first encounter with snow. He snorted at it, bounced in it, rolled in it, and ate it in gulps. Between us we made a shambles of the virgin drifts in the yard, and I didn't think about anything at all until a slide of snow from one of the shed roofs came down on my head.

After I took Hector his breakfast I left the pen door open. There wouldn't be any farm trucks racing up and down the lane today. The drifts across the road to the stripping shed were unsullied and unbroken. Plumes of snow curved like smoke from the drifts in the fields.

James, huge in a corduroy jacket and plaid wool trousers, was in the kitchen when I walked in, stamping snow off my boots onto the rag rug by the door. "You're sure a sight, Joanie," he said. "You look like a snow monster from the Antipodes."

"I feel like one," I said as I unwound the scarf from my neck and tried to keep the snow on the rug. "It's really great out there, but I'm afraid I'm making rather a mess of the floor."

"Should take those things off outdoors," began James.

"Now, let her be, James. You brought your share in last night, you know," said Alison as she flipped the bacon she was frying.

The smell was heavenly and I was suddenly eager for my breakfast, but not so James. "Don't cook any for me, sweetheart. I'll just have coffee."

"You *can't* resist—" I began.

Alison's voice cut across mine. "To please me," she said, "if for no other reason. You had no dinner last night and you have to go out. You can't expect Joan to go alone."

"She's not going," said James.

"I *am!*"

"Well," said Alison, not looking at either of us, "we'll see what the sheriff says about it. Meanwhile, both of you come and have breakfast."

Somewhere between the orange juice and the first bite of bacon my appetite flagged. I settled for toast and coffee and was glad before the morning was over that I had not tried to eat more.

James and the sheriff were standing in the front hall half an hour later, waiting for me. Sheriff Dennis, a moon-faced man on the far side of forty, looked immense in his dark blue nylon jacket with its hood lined with fake fur hanging across his shoulders. His leather boots were bright and unsullied by snow or mud. There were four or five footprints on the porch that led to the mat by the door, but not a single smudge had been carried in to offend Mrs. Brandon.

He took my hand in a soft embarrassed clasp, and when I gave it a shake, it fell away from mine without any returning pressure. "Fish-hand," we youngsters used to call it, and believed it proved the owner was weak and sly.

But Sheriff Dennis was straightforward enough in his work. "Let's sit down a minute, Miz Brandon," he said, "and you tell me all about what happened last evening. Up in the woods behind the old corn crib. I think you said." He tested his ball-point pen with a few squiggles in the notebook he held open on one knee.

"I found a body up there, Sheriff," I began.

"Best start before that, please, ma'am. About what time was it and what you were doing up there, that sort of thing."

"I was walking my dog."

"Wasn't it pretty cold to be walking out there?"

"Yes, it certainly was. But I don't mind the cold, you see, and I like to walk, so . . . I walked." I couldn't understand the look he was giving me. Doubting? Puzzled?

He caught my glance and looked quickly down at his pad and wrote something. "And about what time was that?"

"About three o'clock, I think. It wasn't dark and it was only a short walk, really. I must have gotten to the woods in less than half an hour. The dog—"

"Were you alone, ma'am?"

"Oh, no. Hector was with me,"

"Hector who?" He wrote the name down and kept his pen poised.

"My dog. My young springer spaniel." He drew a line through the name and wrote something short, like "dog."
"It was he who found the body, actually." Some imp in me made me give that last word a rich British flavor. James shot me a dampening look, and my imp retreated.

Sheriff Dennis looked from one to the other of us, a rather dazed expression flitting across his pudgy face. "Oh,

the dog was nosing around in the bushes and found . . .
what, ma'am?"

"He didn't know what," I said. "But it frightened him,
and so I went into the bushes in the edge of the woods to
see what it was. It was a woman's body, Sheriff Dennis," I
said firmly.

"A body? How did you know she was dead?"

I hesitated a moment before I answered. How *had* I
known? It had been so immediate I hardly recognized the
process. "By her eyes, I suppose," I said at last. "They
were frozen. Open. The pupils were . . . white." I paused to
get my voice under control and went on. "There was no
doubt. She was . . . dead and frozen." I left the words
hanging there. I had nothing to add.

"Did you try to listen to her heart or anything like that?"

I felt my chin quivering. "I tried to move her arms," I
said, "and they were as stiff as boards. I couldn't even raise
her head. It was frozen fast in the oak leaves and honeysuckle." Oh, God, I was going to cry! My throat tightened,
and I knew I couldn't say another word.

Surprisingly enough James jumped to my rescue. "From
what my cousin tells me, *and* from the obvious shock she's
had, Dennis, you'd better believe the woman was dead."

I raised my eyes from the rug, where the pattern had
grown blurred and whirling, and gave him a watery but
grateful glance.

The sheriff coughed apologetically. "All right," he said.
"Now if you'll just describe her, ma'am."

The constriction relaxed. I described as carefully as I
could her face and clothes. I told him about the pink scarf
that had caught my attention in the first place.

"Would you recognize it if you saw it again, ma'am?"

"Certainly I would. I could pick it out of a drawer full of
pink scarves." In my mind's eye there was an indelible
image of it. I could paint it, mix the color on a palette, the
alizarin crimson and cadmium yellow light, with white to
make it milky, and the darker stains, where it had been wet

and had dried tight against her face, were almost pure burnt sienna. . . . I could reproduce the scarf's band of flamingoes, evenly spaced, nose to nose and tail to tail, the necks of the pairs forming a heart-shaped pattern around the border. There was no possible way I could forget it.

I wished I had thought to move the scarf just a little, just enough to see the color of her hair, but I hadn't. I was going to tell Dennis that but he hurried on. "And then what did you do?"

I told him there was nothing I could do except come home, and I described my walk back across the fields, my finding no one here, my call to the Shearerville police and then to him.

"I see," he said. "And then what did you do?"

I had no premonition of my danger. "Had a drink of whiskey," I said.

"A drink of whiskey?" He put no emphasis anywhere. He simply put a question mark at the end of the sentence in the way he raised his pen from the notebook.

"Yes."

"How much? An ounce or two?"

"I didn't measure it. More than an ounce, I suppose."

"Before you called me?"

"Yes. As soon as I came in. I . . . was cold." I saw now, too late, much too late, what he was thinking, but worse, what James was thinking. Well, let them think what they like, I said to myself as I got up to put my parka on. There will be no denying the body.

"Just one or two more questions, please, Miz Brandon. Did you by any chance recognize this, ah, young woman?"

"No, Sheriff Dennis, I didn't. I only just got here the day before yesterday, and except for my cousin and his wife, I don't know anyone, except older people . . . and some other cousins." It all sounded silly and nervous so I just said again, "No, I didn't recognize her."

"Did you say you looked in her pockets to see if there was any identification?"

"No, I didn't look in her pockets—I didn't even try to find her pockets. There were leaves and honeysuckle all over—"

"All right, ma'am. Now, if you're ready, Mr. Brandon, we'll just mosey on up there and see what we find, shall we?"

"I'm coming too!"

They stopped in their tracks. Both men protested at once. The sheriff, looming over me, said patronizingly, "No, ma'am. There's no need for you to go out in the cold."

James, his eyelids tightened, glared a challenge. "Now Joan, that isn't necessary. Not the right thing for you to do at all. I know where the place is. You just stay—"

I could see another "I will, ya won't" argument like the one in the kitchen last night brewing in the parlor, but this time I was ready for it. "Better put boots on, James," I said sweetly. "I'll get Hector."

Now they had something legitimate to complain about. After only a brief protest I relinquished Hector with what they accepted as polite concession and dashed out to close my dog in his pen. I was in the jeep before they were.

"We can go up through the fields," James said to the sheriff, "or around by Blair Road and up the track to the top of the big field, but it's pretty rough. Let's go down here, past the stripping shed to that old log cabin, and then up behind the woods and on around."

So many choices! I would have set out the way I had walked. It was shorter and we could avoid the largest drifts, but I had said quite enough for the present. I kept still.

It was a rather pretty ride. We cut a trail through virgin snow down the farm road, past the stripping shed where the work that had been interrupted by the storm had not been resumed, down to the old log cabin where, so family tradition went, Two-Greats Grandfather had lived for over a year before he brought his young family here from Vir-

59

ginia. We turned south and followed an old track through a long arm of the woods where the trees had held the wind in check and there were no drifts at all. The snow had fallen evenly and steadily and was only about four inches deep.

We left the woods through a broken gate and turned onto the road the heavy machinery used to get to the sleeping-giant field. It was almost as smooth as pavement. I lifted my voice above the noise of the jeep. "Has anyone been reported missing, do you know?"

"Well, ma'am, we did get an APB . . . uh, you know, uh, that's an 'all points bulletin,' for a woman from Janesville. Seemed to figure she was headed for Shu'vel."

I smiled a little at his pronunciation. I had forgotten the fun we used to have trying to make a limerick out of shovel and the native pronunciation of Shearerville. My spirits were considerably lightened also by the fact that the poor woman had been missed and searched for.

"Then you must have a description. Does it seem to fit?"

"I can't rightly say, ma'am, you know, uh, until I see the body. Might be the one. Seems about the right age and all."

"Well, I hope so," I said. "I'd hate to think there were two women out in that storm all night."

James said nothing.

We left the smooth track and skirted the far edge of the woods, past the ugly place of uprooted trees, draped now in gleaming white, a huge, rather beautiful sculpture like a castle in an ice show. Then we were at the bend of the woods, and there was the corn crib, magnified and glorified in white.

"There's the old corn crib," said James. "Now, this is the place, along behind here, isn't it, Joan?"

"Yes," I said, suddenly frightened and slightly sick. I wished I hadn't come, but sitting there between my burly cousin and the round sheriff, there wasn't even room to shiver.

The jeep pulled up behind the corn crib a few yards from the spot where I had gone into the bushes. All three of us got silently out of the jeep, and they automatically let me lead the way. I recognized the oak that dominated the place, changed though it was by its coat of snow. Its shape had struck me as nearly perfect in the last few seconds before Hector bowled into me.

I led the way into the honeysuckle thicket. Wind and snow had blown fiercely here and had changed every aspect of the place. It was dark and icy on the leeward side, with only streaks of white on the exposed branches and tightly curled leaves. The windward side was a thick mass of white and treacherously disguised ropelike vines. There was no graceful way to go where we had to go. I fell headlong into one deep white tangle, and the sheriff just missed doing the same thing. James bulled his way through the vines as though they were slightly tough spider webs across his path.

We stumbled and pushed, and three times I called, "Here! This is the place!" and began to pull and tear at the vines. They came to help, and there was nothing at all but dead branches and frozen oak leaves. I had an uneasy feeling that I was yards away from the place I wanted. I was trying to get my bearings again, looking back to find the oak tree and the bent dogwood I had clutched so frantically, when the sheriff called out.

His voice was very quiet, calm, not a triumphant shout that the mission was accomplished. I thought it must be the horror that I myself had felt when I saw that miserable little heap of tragedy. I stumbled hastily over to him.

"Is that what you saw, Miz Brandon?"

"Oh, no—What? Good God, *no!* It was nothing like that!"

He had pulled up from the snow a sodden piece of newspaper, pink, a stained, terribly ugly pink advertising insert with the words in huge block letters that shouted "Thanksgi——." The rest was torn away. A remnant of it was still sticking out of a light brown plastic sack, where hills and valleys made by the rubbish inside were outlined by the snow. A pair of torn panty hose had been pulled away from it and draped obscenely over a blackberry branch, possibly by a rodent who had been prowling there during the night.

"No," I said again. "It isn't! It's *not*. We've come too far down. This isn't even the right thicket anymore."

The sheriff showed his find to James, and he stared at it for a moment in silence while Dennis held the pink paper in one hand and pointed to the sack with the other. The memory of them standing there is tied in my mind to the sickness that overwhelmed me when I realized what they were thinking.

I stumbled away from them. They let me go without a word, and I left my breakfast there in the bushes. After a moment I rubbed my face with snow and felt better, but I couldn't think. My mind refused to focus. I could only stagger to my feet, stare at the ground, and wait, leaning against a tree, dazed and docile, for whatever came next.

The sheriff, efficient and prepared, stuffed his mittens in one pocket and pulled a Polaroid camera out of another. Then he and James emerged from the woods, and James waited for me to get into the jeep.

"I'll walk," I said in a very small voice.

"Oh, don't be silly," James protested, sounding almost jovial. "Come on and get in." I did as he said. "Everybody makes mistakes," he said as we drove homeward, across the frozen fields this time, as I had gone yesterday with my burden of horror. "Don't feel bad about it. Anybody could have thought what you did, couldn't they, Dennis?"

"Yes, ma'am. I reckon it was a simple enough mistake. You didn't figure to find any trash that far from the road, and in that light, with the wind blowin' an' all, I reckon your eyes played a trick on you. A mighty mean trick."

But I knew they hadn't. I *knew*! And I wanted to shout *"no!"* To scream that they were wrong. There *was* a body. It, *she* was there, and she was still there somewhere. I felt myself on the jagged edge of panic and didn't realize I was beating my fists on my knee until James's hand grabbed mine. I tried to shake him off but gave up when his grip failed to loosen. No gentleman's consoling clasp, this. He crushed my fingers into my palm. It hurt, but the pain forced me into some kind of balance.

"All right," I said finally, in what must have seemed to him a reasonable voice. "All right," I said again when his grip finally slackened. "Maybe I was wrong. Maybe it was the light." Oh, God! I was trying to make myself believe a lie! My spirit collapsed there between those huge men, and I felt small and slumped and beaten. I didn't move a muscle. I didn't even think until the jeep stopped in the driveway in front of the house.

Chapter Seven

ALISON MET US on the porch. I listened silently while James and the sheriff reported what happened and showed her the Polaroid pictures. Her first reaction was giggly relief, and after Dennis left she glowed at James as though he were a knight in shining armor just home from vanquishing a fire-breathing, damsel-eating dragon. When she turned to me I felt like a creature from another planet, until she hid the searching look under a reassuring pat on my arm. "Well, that takes care of that, doesn't it? I know when I walk in the cold wind it brings tears to my eyes. That must be what happened. I'm so glad we don't need to be upset about it any more. I've made some chicken soup for lunch."

A kind of rage welled up in me, an acrid resentment of her easy, too-willing acceptance of the lie. I don't know what I had expected from her, but I felt cheated and bereft. I didn't want to be near her. I mumbled an excuse and fled to my room.

Is frustration a dark murky green or a gaseous yellow-grey? Whatever the color, it is entirely murky, thick, and nauseating. Like a prisoner in a labyrinth or a rat in a trap, my thoughts ran desperately in one direction after the other, and everywhere they turned there was a wall of nothing palpable and I wanted something to break or tear so that light could get through. I tried every way I could think of.

There weren't many. There was really only one. To prove myself right I had to produce a dead body, the *habeas corpus* without which there would be no official investigation. I couldn't ask James to help me look for her again. He would be indignant, or laugh at me, or voice that worst of all suspicions—that I had been drunk. I was not desperate enough to dare to risk that.

So I would have to go alone with Hector—who had found her before and had not found a sack of garbage at all—and search for her and find her. And then what? Sling her over my shoulder and carry her home? Mark the place with flags? Coax Hector to stand guard over the body while I came back for the jeep? I could siphon gas from the Volkswagen and take the jeep back up there.

I could go right now. . . .

But what if I didn't find her? What then?

And I knew I wouldn't find her because I knew she wasn't there. Not any more. I had looked. Three of us had looked carefully and had trampled the vines flat in our search. I knew she wasn't there, and finding something, a mitten or that damnable pink scarf, wouldn't help either. It could just as easily have fallen out of the sack of trash as off a woman's body. It would do nothing to make my story credible. And that was the root of my frustration. That was what made my world dark and murky and made me want to pull and tear.

I was not believed. I, Joan Brandon, who prided myself on my honor, cherished it as the most sacred and immutable fragment of me, the part of me I could control absolutely, was not believed.

Perk! I was out of my room and into the kitchen before the possibility of not being able to reach him crossed my mind. He was in my world, only a few hundred miles away. I would spend the rest of the day cutting through the tangles of wires if I had to.

But the phone was dead. Or dying. The crackling and hissing was an earsplitting, nerve-twisting barrier between us. I could not take even the first step toward him to tell him, just tell him, and know that he believed me. He would.

Perk would. I held that certainty to me as a priest might hold a crucifix, and went back to my room.

I splashed my face with icy water and brushed my hair until my arm ached, and at last the swamp of self-pity slipped behind me and I could think again. A moment later I was pacing the floor, and I began to feel that all the Brandons were pacing with me. We all pace. A really serious problem brings us all to our feet, all except Susan, who is a Cox and who sits and watches us with gentle tolerance, and the room we are in becomes a veritable parade ground of marching Brandons.

I began to feel much better. I could not only think, I could organize my thoughts. I could be logical.

I started with the knowns: She had been young and pretty and now was dead, and I had found her body in the woods. She hadn't fallen asleep there, her eyes were open. She hadn't been carefully laid there, she had been dropped or thrown down while her limbs were flexible and they had fallen every which way. I had no way of guessing how she had died. I had seen no blood or wound, but I hadn't looked for any. I had touched only one arm. I had not even seen the color of her hair.

She didn't belong where I found her; therefore she was missing from where she should be. And so was a woman from Janesville, and between me and a description of that woman was a broken phone.

So now what? Eternal frustration or gradual forgetfulness? Suppose I let it pass, let it float away into limbo and sink in a swamp of comforting palliatives: "Don't rock the boat," "It's not *your* business," "Leave well enough alone," and a thousand other platitudes and evasions that would make it easy to forget.

I'd rather forget!

But I will not!

Almost frantically I searched through my drawers, through an old box of sewing scraps, looking for something pink, anything pink, a color I seldom wore. But in the bottom of the old wardrobe I found a little knot of pink hair ribbon, not violent, tropical pink, but pink enough, and as I straightened it through my fingers I imagined James and Alison warning me to be careful, to stay away, to mind my own business. . . .

I smoothed the pink ribbon and tied it on one of the finials of an oak chair and placed it where I could see it without even coming into the room. Just walking past the door I would see it and remember. I was damned if I would let her go.

Alison was in the kitchen preparing lunch when I went in to try the phone again. She smiled sympathetically while I struggled to get a dial tone, and when I gave up and replaced the receiver she said, "It always does that when there's a bad storm. They'll have it fixed in a day or two."

"That long?" I looked at the dead apparatus and wondered how I could wait a day or two. "Surely not!"

"Well, sometimes it comes on again right away. It depends on where the trouble is. If it's near town they get right at it. We country people just have to wait." She laughed a little. "One of the prices we pay. Was it important, honey? I'm sure Joe will come. He can take a message for you or even take you to town."

"I . . . I wanted to call Perk."

"Oh." She hesitated a few seconds. "I thought you said he didn't have a phone. You couldn't call him, he had to call you, or something."

"It won't be easy. I'll have to track him down. But never mind. If the phone's out, it's out. I'll just have to be patient." Not a thing I did with any skill! I tried to decide, as I stood there watching her make sandwiches, whether it would be a good idea to beg a ride to town with Joe Burden and use Ellen's phone. I had no clear reason for wanting to be alone when I talked to Perk, but I knew there was a reason. I just couldn't get it in focus. It had something to do with being alone, being on the wrong side of a fence, being on my left foot when everyone else was on his right. It had something to do with hiding for self-preservation, like that little rabbit on the plate—cowering. I shrugged the thought aside because it was the only thing I could do with it, and pushed up my sleeves. "How may I help?" I asked Alison at last.

At lunch no one referred in any way to events of the morning. I suppose we were afraid if our minds turned in that direction we would race back to that subject like runaway horses to their barn.

I don't think James's eyes met mine a single time.

"How would it be," I asked over cigarettes and coffee, "if I made another cake this afternoon?"

They hastened to assure me that was a great idea, marvelous, just what they wanted most. James looked at me almost fondly as he asked, "You got everything you need? I'm going to try to get to town in the jeep."

A prickly chill of suspicion ran down my back, and before I stopped to think I hurled my accusations at him. "So you lied, James! There *was* gas in the jeep! We *could* have gone up to Corn Crib Woods last night, and we would have found that body ourselves before someone moved it and left that sack of trash. You just didn't *want* to go up there last night!"

Before I had gotten halfway through this tirade James was on his feet, and Alison was standing beside him. I scrambled to mine and stood facing them across the kitchen table. I ignored Alison's pleas and murmurs and heard only James. I couldn't help but hear him! His voice was rough and clear and hostile. "I gave you some damned good reasons for not going up there last night and they still hold. All of them. Joe Burden brought gas for the jeep not fifteen minutes ago because he knew I was out. He's plowing the driveway now. Is there anything more you would like to say on this subject, Miss Smart Ass?"

"*James!*"

"Sorry," he said to Alison. "But . . . she *riles* me!"

I apologized because I had to. "I'm sorry. I should have

trusted you, I suppose. Oh, all right! Of course I should have trusted you! But why the hell don't you trust me, then?"

He looked at me across the white table with its gay chintz place mats and said carefully, measuring the words with precision, "I *do* believe you saw something up there in the woods that you *thought* was a dead body. I don't know why the hell you thought so, but I believe you did think so. That's all I have to say about it. But I'm damned thankful I don't have to figure you out. You were bad enough before, but now—! Good God, the mind of a frustrated old maid sure beats the hell out of me!"

"James *Tarleton* Brandon!"

Before Alison finished rolling out her amazement I had bolted through the swinging door on a crash course for my room.

I suppose I really couldn't blame James for being "riled" by me. I had put on quite a show, if the show was what he believed it to be, romping over everyone's feelings, dragging the sheriff out of his lair on a cold snowy morning, hauling them up to the woods, and setting them tearing around like dogs on a scent, just to amuse my frustrated old-maid self—and then accused him, in front of his wife, of lying to me!

I could hardly expect him *not* to be angry, but he didn't have to be so gross and insulting!

And Alison? Was she really satisfied with her simple explanation of tears in my eyes? I would have been amazed if she had been angry, but did she really think I didn't know what I found up there in the woods? Did she think I would run home in hysterics because of a sack of garbage?

She believes it because she *wants* to believe it!

And there is nothing I can do about it.

At dinner my morale was wallowing close to the bottom of that murky green pool again, and James, maybe because he had won the luncheon round, was as jovial as a basking rattlesnake. "Now, Joan, just because your imagination has gotten you all worked up is no reason you shouldn't eat your dinner. I promise there won't be any more corpses for you to stumble over, and you need to put some meat on those bones of yours. How do you think you're ever going to catch a husband, looking all scrawny and washed out?" I succeeded in ignoring him and continued to play with my food. Later, "You've got to get your strength up if you want to convince everyone you're, you know, real healthy and strong. You really should be looking for a husband, you know," he went on. "You never should have let that guy Newton get away from you! You may not get a better chance."

I was too tired to look up, much less concern myself about catching a husband. But James in his jocular mood was a real menace, and so I tried to head him off before he got to "what will people say!" "I'll wear rouge—"

"That won't help. The last thing you want to do is doll yourself up like some kind of floozie—"

"Now hush, James," said Alison, with a worried half smile on her face.

James paid no attention. "You can't go to parties looking like a . . . a zombie, either! People will think you're . . . People will suspect . . ." He caught a warning glance from his wife and finished lamely, ". . . something is wrong with you. You won't even get anyone to dance with you!" He pretended he thought this would be a real tragedy and shook his head sadly as he slanted a glance across the table at me. I knew that sideways look. I could guess what he was thinking.

I smiled rather limply at my plate and managed to let his words wash over me without a reply. I wasn't up to his banter and refused to let him get a rise out of me. It was Alison who cut his line. In less than ten words she dashed him, utterly. "That's enough, James. You're acting like a schoolboy."

He immediately looked deflated, crushed and shocked, and Alison looked rather stunned herself. I tried to think of something bright to say to head off a domestic crisis, but my mind was too dull and tired.

The weight of the moment seemed to hang like a fog smothering us and hiding us from one another until Alison broke through it. With a warm smile and a hand laid gently on his arm she said, "Let's have some good brandy, James, in by the fire. I think we all deserve it. It's been a difficult day." She got a smile in return, thank heaven, and we began to clear the table.

The brandy was set out on the low table in front of the sofa, but James wasn't there. There were three glasses, however, so we waited for him. "Let's see what the telly has to offer," I said brightly, without much hope for anything better than glittery Christmas specials full of fake frivolity. But the public channel was well launched into *The Nutcracker,* which I thought would be reasonably diverting.

"How's this?" I turned to see whether Alison was satisfied with my selection, but she wasn't watching. She was standing staring down into the flames of the gas log. I settled myself quietly in the guest chair to let the familiar music and dance carry me along to the never-never land of fairies and snowflakes.

When James handed me my brandy a few minutes later, he said, "I'm sorry, Joanie. I know you had a rough time and I shouldn't have teased you." But he couldn't quite let it go at that. "You really are a right pretty little thing, you know, and I'll dance with you myself."

"Thank you, James," I said primly. "Pleasure will be all mine. Now, sit down and watch *The Nutcracker* with us and relax."

He cast a swift glance at the tube and snorted, "Drivel," and turned to his wife with the second glass. "Got to run into town, sweetheart, just for a little while. You girls just enjoy your show. I'll try not to be late." He swallowed his own brandy in two gulps, kissed his wife, and nodded to me, and was gone.

Just liked that.

I looked at Alison, ready to offer sympathy if she wanted it, and saw her looking after him with an expression on her face I had not seen there before, blank, resigned, vacated, as though she, too, had walked out. Might I have seen it before and read it wrong, thought it serene detachment? Was it really a carefully controlled mask she wore and tonight it didn't fit quite as neatly as usual? Or was this something new? A new crisis? One she couldn't cope with and therefore had . . . abdicated in some way?

But I was too tired, too drained to pursue it. I sipped my brandy in a kind of daze, warm and relaxed, and a few minutes later I felt Alison take my glass from my fingers. Her hand lightly touched my head, and I smiled without opening my eyes.

When I woke from my nap I felt dazed and lost. I wondered why I was alone in this strange room; the sound on the television was faint, and the figures dancing there made no sense. I battled my way through the gluey wool that held me immobile and numb, fought clear of it at last, and stumbled off to the kitchen to find Alison so I could tell her . . .

The dishes were drying and she was putting the hostess cart away in the pantry. I went to the sink and ran the good-tasting well water, so cold and with no vestige of chemicals, letting it run until it was as cold as the earth itself. I filled a glass and drank it, slowly, savoring every swallow. Then, because I wanted to, I cupped my hands under the faucet and splashed the water over my face. Do they know, I wondered, how precious this water is? How rare and wonderful? As I dried myself on a paper towel I began to feel revived, ready to tackle the problem once again.

I plunged right into the middle of it. "There *was* a body up there, you know." Then I watched while she faced the question again. I wanted her to commit herself, to tell me once and for all whether she really believed I was a silly, flighty nincompoop who couldn't tell a sack of trash from a human being—tears or no tears—or whether she thought I was a vicious troublemaker and liar with an outrageously irresponsible imagination, or that she believed there had indeed been a body there and it had been moved from that place between night and morning by person or persons unknown. I wanted her to tell me that because I am a Brandon—and Brandons don't lie—if I said there was a dead woman up in Corn Crib Woods there must have been one.

Simply, plainly, I wanted her to believe me on those grounds alone. She shouldn't need any other proof! Perk wouldn't!

I could almost see her mind grappling with the problem. Sheriff Dennis had shown her a photograph of a sack of trash with a pink newspaper sticking out of the brown plastic. He had emphasized the placement of the paper, the shadows cast on it by the honeysuckle vines. She had studied them carefully with a look of bewilderment on her face. She must have been wondering how on earth I could confuse such a mess with a dead women. She knew I had been in a state of shock, surely she knew the shock was absolutely real! She could not have mistaken it for anything else unless she thought I was drunk. Or on drugs! But surely she knows me better than that! Surely James knows me better! He must remember that I hate even to take aspirins! He can't possibly think . . .!

I wadded the paper towel into a ball as I waited for her reply. I hoped my statement would force her simply to say she believed me.

But of course it didn't. She looked at me with all the compassion I could wish for, but she said, "I don't know, honey. If it wasn't tears in your eyes that distorted what you saw . . . I just can't figure it out. It just doesn't make sense."

I knew full well it didn't. I was asking her to take me on faith, and why, after all, should she? I tossed the wad of paper towel toward the wastebasket—and missed.

"I know it doesn't. But she *was* there—and what more can I say?" I turned to pick up the towel and to keep my face averted while I swallowed the bitter lump in my throat. When you've given something your best shot, I thought wryly, you have to let it rest there. No choice. I dropped the wad in the basket, fixed a smile on my face, and looked up at her as though nothing in the world was wrong. So much for honest Joan!

"Well," I said, "maybe in time we'll have the answer. I surely hope so. Don't worry. I . . . I won't sink into a decline or anything. I promise you don't need to worry about that." I made my smile brighter. "Can I do anything here or are you all shut down for the night?"

"No, thank you. Everything's just fine. You run off to bed and get a good night's sleep. Unless you'd like a cup of tea or something?"

"Not a thing but bed. Good night."

I didn't know what woke me some time later in the night, although I had the impression that the phone had rung. I had been sleeping restlessly. My imagination, cut loose from my reason, had played a dozen "mean" tricks on me, and I had awakened not once but several times to stare into the darkness and wish I could have Hector with me, or that I could look forward to tomorrow being brighter and better. I wished I could just touch Perk, just put my hand on his arm, or Dad's. I wished I trusted James more so that I could press my head on his shoulder and feel his arms around me, holding me and comforting me with his faith and love. . . . James, who, I suppose, loves me in his way, but who would only touch me if he had to. Well, that's the way I love him, too, but if he needed comfort I would give it to him! Certainly I wouldn't tease and torment him!

Sometime later I had gotten up to get a tissue from my bathroom and heard a voice coming through the wall from

James's study. Who was it who said eavesdroppers only hear the devil talking? But it wasn't the devil, it was James. I listened shamelessly, curious and vitally concerned, immediately aware that he was talking about me. ". . . not *real* sure, of course . . . maybe she's taking something . . . No, I never heard one way or the other . . . How the hell do I know?" He slammed down the receiver with a rough snarl, and I heard Alison's voice, strangely harsh and whining, but I could make no sense of what she said. I wanted to rush down the hall to defend myself, or at least to hear what they were saying, but I literally did not have the energy. All I could do was sigh again with a kind of bitter resignation.

I might have known the whole miserable affair would be gossiped about all over Shearerville, and my using drugs would be the easiest and most plausible—not to mention the most sensational—explanation. I could imagine what people would say: "Who's this Joan Brandon, anyway?" "Oh, she used to visit here but she lives in New York, now. In the big wicked city where *everybody* uses drugs! I remember she was always skitty-witted, even as a child . . . always in trouble of some kind . . ."

Not one of them will believe I never did drugs—not even once. Not even birth control pills!

A little chill seeped up from my bare feet on the icy floor as I reminded myself that what people said—or thought—might be all over town but it could never change the facts, and I knew what the facts were . . . and they would still be there tomorrow. Like it or not, the facts would not change. The dead woman, whoever she was, wherever she was, was still dead.

I staggered back to bed, pulled my quilt over my head, and wished for the first time in years that I had one of my old stuffed toys to hug, preferably old Bootsie, worn and shapeless—or that Hector could curl up on my feet. I would almost have settled for Cooper Newton, but he would have laughed and explained—endlessly—about frustrated old maids. I could almost hear him.

Chapter Eight

I HAD TAKEN Hector for his walk and was toying with my coffee the next morning when the phone startled me.

"Hey, Mops!"

"Perk!"

"The same! Obviously I didn't catch you napping."

"I've just gotten back from a walk."

"Well, here's some good news for you—"

"I can sure use some." I murmured.

"This is our own phone. Jake's and mine. Ah, that's John Delano, lieutenant, junior grade—my roommate. Better take down the number."

As I wrote it on the notepad I wondered how I could spoil his happiness with the awful thing I had to tell him. For just one brief instant I considered not telling him at all, and then I wondered how I could get through the day . . . the next few days.

He made the decision for me. "And what have you been up to?"

"I . . . don't know where to begin."

Of course he heard the strain in my voice. "Start at the beginning," he said in his firm big-brother voice.

Grateful tears stung my eyes, and he waited patiently while I controlled my voice. Then I started at the beginning and told him the whole sad story. He interrupted me only twice, once when I wanted to fudge describing how I knew she was dead, and then, when I told him about the sack of trash, he made me repeat that it wasn't where I remembered finding the body.

"They didn't believe me, Perk, but it's true! True!"

"All right, Mops. I hear you. I know it. Take it easy!"

The weight of the murky green miasma began to drop away—but I had to be perfectly sure. "You do believe me, don't you?"

"Absolutely. You know that. James should know it, too, the idiot. What the hell is he doing thinking you'd lie about something like that? God, I'd like to wring his scrawny neck!"

"It isn't scrawny." I was almost giggling in my relief and at his readiness to attack James in my defense. It was almost as though he were here with me. I felt warm and protected again, as I had felt hundreds of times before because Perk was on my side.

But Perk was not that easily satisfied. "What's that sheriff's name again, Mops?" I told him. His next question seemed strange. "They have a lot of bridges out down there? Roads torn up or something?"

"Not that I've heard. Why?"

"Just wondered. But there has to be something going on, Mops. Dead bodies don't drop out of trees, not in Kentucky, anyhow. We can't leave it like that."

"I know. But there is some woman missing—I forgot that part. The sheriff said some woman from Janesville. They have an APB on her. The phone was out yesterday so I couldn't check."

"So that's why I couldn't get through! You're going to find out today, then?"

"As soon as I can."

"Maybe whoever put out that APB found her body up there. They may have it all worked out by now and couldn't get back to you. Let me know, Mops. Keep me posted, will you? I can't have you wrecking your vacation because some woman got mugged on Blair Road. Get that description, and if it's the same woman . . . well, at least you've told the sheriff all you can. The rest isn't really your business. The best thing for you to do is forget it. There's nothing much else you can do—or need to do, for that matter."

"Believe me, I'd like to, but there's one more nasty bit—"

"Go on."

"They . . . well, the easy *official* explanation of my finding a body that doesn't *officially* exist, is drugs. My being on them, that is." I stopped because I had said enough.

Dead silence for a long, long moment. I had to wait. I couldn't prompt him, or howl at him to side with me in this. He had to say whatever he thought. What he said was typically Perk. "And you're not." It was a simple statement. He had no doubt.

But he was entitled to confirmation. "I'm not and never have been. True."

"But that whole topic makes it damned nasty, as you say—gives them an answer before they admit there's a question. Pretty neat, really. Has anyone actually suggested that you were?"

"Maybe they won't think it. Maybe I'm just being paranoid—kind of defensive for our whole generation."

"Maybe." He was silent for another moment, and when he spoke again there was a kind of briskness in his voice that I couldn't quite understand. Not then, anyway. I should have guessed what he meant to do, but I had been out of touch with him too long. "Okay, Mops. I think probably the best thing you can do is forget about this drug thing unless someone actually accuses you. You can't run around with a sign on your back saying you're not a user, after all. I bet most of the folks down there will never think in that direction anyhow. Certainly not the family. James hasn't said anything in that line, has he?"

There never had been a way I could hide things from Perk. I told him about the phone conversation I overheard in the night.

"I think I'd like to talk to our dear cousin," he said when

I finished. "When does he get out of the sack, about noon?"

I choked a little laugh. "He's already gone. Anyway, the Mercedes isn't in the garage, so I guess he is. He's not much better at sleeping late than the rest of us Brandons."

"Okay, I'll catch him another time. Don't worry. Just get back to me about that APB when you can, okay?"

"Right. I'll let you know."

"Either way, Mops. Whether she is or isn't the woman they're looking for, I want to know, you hear? Now, tell me how Ellen is, and Fitch."

I not only told him about Ellen and Fitch but also about Shirley. He pretended to be shocked. "I thought she was waiting for me!"

"That's Sandra, silly! Sandra Hamilton, the cute redhead. I'll probably see her tonight."

"Well, give them all my love. God, it's good to be back in the world again. I didn't know how much I missed it."

"Or how much you were missed!"

After a moment he said firmly, "So much for that. Call me any time, Mops. Jake will know where I am if I'm not here, or he'll take a message. You'll like Jake."

With a wobbly sigh of relief, knowing it wasn't going to be difficult any more for us to share our thoughts, we ended our conversation, and I began a long series of attempts to call the Shearerville police, whose line was invariably busy.

When I finally got through to them, it was hardly worth the effort. The description of the missing woman from Janesville was not conclusive. "Caucasion female, age twenty-four, five feet three inches, bleached blonde hair—she had a natural blonde's skin, I thought—"One hundred thirty pounds, blue jacket—"

"Wait! Blue?"

"It says blue here," the young woman insisted in her official singsong. And then she became more human. "Oh, reversible. They don't say what the inside color is."

"Slacks?"

"They don't say slacks, just blue jeans—"

"Mittens . . . gloves?"

"They don't say. Married—a gold band with a diamond, and she was wearing a wristwatch." She couldn't tell me anymore, whether the jacket had fur on it, whether the woman had been wearing a scarf or not. Nothing more. She may have been the person I saw, or she may not have been. I couldn't be sure. But she had not been reported as found. She was still missing. Or maybe whoever found her has not seen fit to report it to the authorities. I called Perk.

"Delano."

I had forgotten the military way of answering the phone and said "Uh" a time or two, and then asked for Perk. "Uh, Lieutenant Brandon."

"Perk?" he said, and then we were off and running. "He's in therapy. Is there a message? You're not Joan, are you?"

"Yes, Joan Brandon, his sister. Will he be back soon?"

"Not unless they run him out. I mean, he's doing double-time up there. He's like crazy—"

"What? What do you mean?"

"He's tearing around like crazy. You sure you're his sister?"

"Sure I'm sure! What do you mean?"

"Well, you sure woke him up. He's killing himself up there."

"What?"

"Oh, I'm sorry. He's just trying to break records or something. They won't let him hurt himself. You don't have to worry. Ah, where'd you get a name like Mops? Your hair?"

"No. We were in a play together in grade school. He was Peter Rabbit, and he shortened Mopsey in one of his lines to me—and it cracked the audience up. He's the only person who calls me that."

I left the message that the missing lady was still missing, but the description was far short of conclusive. Jake asked if I wanted Perk to call me back. "I won't be home after four o'clock, but if he wants to call before then, I always want to talk to him. He knows that."

"Mutual, I believe. I'll tell him. Anything else?"

"No, except Merry Christmas, Jake!"

I was feeling almost normal as I dressed that evening to go partying with Alison and James. The mystery of the lost dead woman, shared with Perk, was growing pallid for lack of nourishment, and I let it drift into the back of my mind. There was at least a chance that she had been found and claimed and mourned. The police had no information to the contrary, anyway, and nothing to add to the description they gave me in the morning. I reported all this with a perfectly straight face and serene, matter-of-fact voice to Alison and James at various intervals during the day, and it seemed to lighten their attitude toward me. By midafternoon there was a truce between James and me, and by evening it became a kind of benign tolerance. They seemed willing to forget the whole miserable episode, and I saw no reason to keep reminding them of it. There was no point in going over and over the barren ground, and I was, quite honestly, tired of it.

So when I showered and washed my hair I convinced myself that I had washed the rest of the sadness away. I convinced myself that eventually we'd know what happened up there and all the fretting in the world wouldn't solve the mystery any sooner. As I put on my makeup, I practiced a few seductive smiles and flirtatious girlish grins that eventually began to feel as though they belonged to me. I added a little dab of the very expensive perfume that had been Cooper Newton's last present to me, and the sophisticated fragrance was surprisingly reassuring. It reminded me of my recovered freedom, and I gave a little shiver of excitement and pleasure that pushed the ghost in her pink scarf even further into oblivion. Tomorrow was Christmas, and there would be no room for sadness then, and by the next day there was bound to be some definite report that she had been found. And meanwhile there was no reason why I should not get on with my life!

I was fastening gold hoops in my ears and toying with the idea of nail polish when Alison signaled that it was time to leave. I picked up my polo coat and went into the parlor, where James stood by the fire, almost overwhelmingly handsome in his dark grey suit and Christmas red necktie. He made me pirouette for him while he nodded approvingly.

"Ve-r-y nice," he said. "But you need a bracelet." He turned to Alison. "Sweetheart, haven't you got one she can wear? That gold band that was Grandmother's, maybe? Or the rhinestone one with sapphires?" Alison thought the gold band would be better and went to get it. But still he wasn't satisfied. "You're not going to wear that old coat, are you? Haven't you got a fur?"

I had to laugh. "Fresh out of wild animal skins," I said smugly, and then I saw Alison's mink draped over a chair. "This is fine, James, really. Perfect for me—"

"Maybe ten years ago it was." But he helped me into it, and when I pulled on my lambskin gloves, he told me if we had a flat en route I could change it since I was already wearing work gloves and there was no reason he should get his grey pigskins dirty.

"Well, what's the order of march, ladies?" he asked when we were on the County Road headed for town. "The Perkinses' first, and then the Pettyjohns', and the Bartons' in between? You call it."

"Perkins last, I think. Joan will enjoy that so much more, and we can stay as long as we like."

We followed that plan, and after a brief stop at the Bartons', where Alison was godmother to one of several little girls, James turned up a long curving driveway and found parking not far from the richly decorated front entrance of the Pettyjohns' house. Lucile Pettyjohn met us at her door and escorted us down the hall to the green-and-gold guest room. We laid our coats on the upholstered green-and-gold bed, where my old polo coat looked like a pallid bare twig among the luxurious animal pelts that were piled there. It didn't take longer than my brief turn at the dressing table to get the impression that Lucile and Alison didn't like each other very much. They exchanged compliments on each other's appearance, and Alison admired the diamond pin that was Lucile's Christmas present from Branch, her husband, but there were no inquiries from either of them on the subjects of family or health or interests. They were like stiff-legged dogs that disliked each other, held on tight leashes.

But I knew it was important for us to be there. There was the business partnership to honor, and the business, whatever it was, provided James's Mercedes and Alison's Lincoln, the cigars and bourbon and mink. Certainly I could honor it along with them. I tucked my polo coat out of sight under Alison's fur in a silly, impulsive gesture, and followed them to the party.

The room was crowded with middle-aged or elderly people, splendidly dressed, murmuring politely, moving with dignified, almost solemn grace under a pair of enormous chandeliers hung with crystal prisms. They seemed almost to be dancing a stately pavane as they turned and bowed and spoke, tipped up their champagne glasses, and turned and bowed again. I enjoyed the mix of colors and patterns in their dance as I made my way slowly to James, who was standing beside a tall, tanned, very handsome white-haired man in front of a swagged and festooned marble mantelpiece.

When Branch Pettyjohn was introduced to me, he took my hand between his own and smiled a picture-perfect smile and told me in a warm baritone that he had been looking forward most eagerly to meeting me. I smiled back and said the kind of thing I might say to the president of the United States if ever we met—or even to the chancellor at

UNH. He smiled again, told me he was sorry his daughter Myra was not here this evening but thought I would find her at the Perkins house.

I told him how eager I was to meet his daughter Myra, and did not realize until later that I repeated his very words to me in a kind of bemused singsong. James, with a worried look on his face, offered me a cigarette, which broke the spell, and a moment later Branch Pettyjohn moved off to speak to another guest. A pleasant elderly lady came up to inquire about Dad and Susan. I concentrated on remembering names, and the hour passed quickly.

When I said good night to my host he seemed much less cordial, almost cool, and I wondered as we drove on to the Perkins house whether I had really offended him with my subconscious mimicry but decided that politicians must be used to such reactions from the people they charmed. I compared politicians and actors in my thoughts, and recalled reading somewhere that actresses train themselves to smile without crinkling their eyes. Branch Pettyjohn never crinkled his eyes, either. They flashed, shone, glittered, and even twinkled, but the muscles around them remained perfectly still—like a mask.

I was shivering a little as we turned into the Perkinses' driveway.

Chapter Nine

COUSIN FITCH MET us at the door and wrapped me in his arms, holding me close to his roundness and warmth for a moment, and then held me back to look, just as Ellen had. I had forgotten how like Dad's his eyes were, pure Perkins, they say, with long silky lashes that sweep up in a wistful, almost doll-like fringe. Those beguiling eyes glowed with welcome as he hugged me again, and I gave him a kiss on his smooth, delightfully fragrant cheek.

"So good to see you," he said. "So like Sidonia!" He sighed a little and stood straighter. "We've been waiting for you, my dear. Uncle Leland and Charles, especially, said they'd wait 'til midnight if they had to. Come in, come in. Ellen's here somewhere."

I greeted one after another of the relatives who thronged around me. When I told them about Perk I could hear a murmur of relief and pleasure go rustling through the gathering like a summer breeze through a field of wheat. They care, I thought, they really do care. I caught Ellen's eye and wiped a tear from my own.

"The youngsters are in the library," said Ellen, when the group began to disperse. "At least they were—" She looked around in a kind of bewilderment at the library which seemed full of non-family middle-agers.

"We're out on the porch, Mother." And a girl I knew could be no one but Shirley came bustling down the hall to meet me, her arms outstretched in welcome. "Cousin *Joan*," she carolled. "I'm so glad to *see* you! How *are* you?"

She's a new edition of her parents, I thought, as I tried not to sound dull because I wasn't shrieking back at her. She had been a chubby little ten-year-old when last we met, and had grown up into a compact and energetic young woman with the wistful Perkins eyes, a lovely girl with high color and small clear features.

She swung her arm through mine and pulled me close, not quite tipping me sideways. "Come on," she urged. "Everyone's so eager to see you—Cat and Sandy and Sam Dudley, you remember Sam . . . he's married—"

"Whoah! Let me take on the elders first. Are the Original Twins in sight?"

She leaned back and peered into my face. "Uncle Leland and Uncle Charles," she gasped. "Oh, God, I haven't heard them called that in *years!* They would just *die!*"

I laughed. "One of them might, but not both. Or aren't they as quarrelsome as they used to be?"

"They've mellowed a little. Uncle Leland is thinner and Uncle Charles is fatter." She swung a wide-eyed glance at me, and I remembered she used to be in awe of the bachelor uncles at the old Perkins farm. "They're in the dining room with the punch. Uncle Charles is dosing it up in direct proportion to Uncle Leland's telling him not to!"

"Is Hayley here?" I asked as we made our way through the parlor. "I'm eager to meet him."

"He'd rather die! I mean, not than meet you, of course. It's just he hates this kind of party. He'll be up after Christmas and I'll bring him out to Woodsedge." She held her hand up to me and light flashed on a platinum and diamond ring that almost swamped her short slender finger.

"Beautiful! It's official, then?"

"Well, to me it is. I keep my hand in my pocket when Daddy's around. And Kenny."

"Kenny? Oh, wait a sec! I know—Kenny Haynes, right? Is he here?" Dumb question, I thought. Alison and James had chatted about her cousin Kenny, who had vowed at the age of fifteen that he would marry Shirley or die in the attempt. Obviously he was in deep distress if he were forced to acknowledge that ring. Obviously he would not be at the Perkinses' party tonight. I would be sorry not to meet him. Even James approved of Kenny!

I lost Shirley somewhere en route, but I kept edging through the crowd and arrived at the punch bowl some minutes later, feeling a little like Kipling's Old Man Kangaroo.

"Well, my dear," said Uncle Leland, patting my hand between his long, thin, icy-cold fingers. "Let me look at you."

I held myself still for his inspection, while Uncle Charles filled a punch cup for me. I knew what the verdict would be, and of course, it was. "You look so like your dear mother! It's so nice to see you again." He let my hand go with a final delicate squeeze. "It's good to have you here."

"It's good to be here, Uncle Leland." I smiled up into the old man's milky blue eyes. "Dad will be glad when I tell him you are looking so well."

"What's this about your being engaged, Joan?" asked Uncle Charles. "Some Yankee boy getting the jump on us?"

"Not anymore, Uncles Charles. It's off."

"Now, that's what I like to hear! No need to go rushing into marriage at your age . . . ah-h, twenty-five, aren't you?"

"Twenty-four last October," I said with a smile.

"So young . . . so young," he said and slanted a rather wistful glance down at the front of my dress.

"Alison keeping peace between you and James, is she?"

"She's a real diplomat! And it helps that James and I are more grown up—at least a little."

"They said you stopped at the Pettyjohns'," said Uncle Charles. "You'd never met him, had you?"

"No, not until tonight."

Uncle Charles' bloodshot grey eyes looked dolefully into space somewhere behind my shoulder. "His girl is here."

"Frightful man," whispered Uncle Leland, looking around as though the wrong person might be listening. "Don't know how James can be such a fool as to trust—" He caught a glance from Uncle Charles, and his shoulders sagged a little as he fell silent.

"I beg your pardon, Joan." said Uncle Charles firmly, his eyes glinting sparks at Uncle Leland. "Old men like Leland and me gossip too much. We should keep our opinions to ourselves."

"Speak for yourself, Charles," said Uncle Leland, his shoulders square again. "Joan should be warned—"

"Nothing but hearsay," Uncle Charles hissed back at him. "You should know better. Gossip is all it is."

Dear Lord, I prayed silently, let it have nothing to do with dead bodies or drugs! Let me have this night in peace! I crossed my fingers in my pocket and pretended to be only politely curious.

"Where there's that much smoke I reckon someone's been playing with matches! She should know. Keep her eyes open. Right much to lose out there at Woodsedge."

"Nonsense. Rank nonsense and tattlin'. What comes from livin' in that old folks' home! You got to get shed o' that nonsense. . . ." As he ladled himself another cup of punch he muttered, "Ol' tom cats a-hollerin'. . . ."

Uncle Leland turned to me. "Don't pay any attention to Charles, my dear. He has never understood. Does a right fine job with facts and figures, but people, ah, relation-ships—"

Uncle Charles cut him short with another, more severe glint. "Rude of us old duffers to detain Joan. Young people always have to be off and doing things."

"Come now, Charles," protested Uncle Leland, putting a restraining hand on my arm.

"Nothing to run off to at the moment, Uncle Charles," I said, still wondering what they were talking about, but the subject evidently was lost in the heat of battle, and they only glared at one another. I volunteered a peace offering.

"It's nice to see the old beehives out at Woodsedge," I said to the air between them. "They're down in the orchard just as they were at Roseland."

Both old gentlemen beamed at me. "You remember our hives, do you? And helping Martha with the honey?"

"Oh, yes! How we all loved that honey! Maybe there will be some at Woodsedge next year."

We launched into talk of the old days when the Perkins farm was almost as much home to us as Woodsedge. But the old place was only a memory. Uncle Leland and Uncle Charles lived now at Fairlawn Retirement Home. "There was no way we could stay out there, my dear," said Uncle Charles when I regretted their having to sell the farm.

"Now if you had come down to keep house for us when Martha died . . ." said Uncle Leland, and I knew by the way their eyes twinkled that the old boys were far from dead.

"It's a zoo over there at Fairlawn but—"

"Very nice to be in the old house at Fairlawn, but things change. . . ."

We were still talking about the changes when Rob came in.

I was a long way from the door, but I could feel the sudden current of excitement through the room, the tug of attention toward him. "Hey, there's Rob!" on one side, and on another, "It's Rob, Chris. He's just come!"

"He did come, after all!" trilled young Chris Perkins, Ellen's middle daughter, as she came dashing in from the porch.

Even old Uncle Leland beamed toward the door with obvious delight. "Well, there's Mary's boy. Must go speak to him, my dear," and he left me standing there while he went through the throng to shake hands with Mary's boy.

I recognized him instantly, and a quick thrill of excitement, almost of shock, flickered through me. I made a swift grab for my wits before they could desert me, and looked around for the mother of his children. But he had come in alone. . . . I caught back some wildly predatory thoughts when I realized she must be home with the babies, home with the little blonde girl I almost tipped over into the boots at the Co-op.

But even so, even though I knew he was, by my standards, off limits, the room seemed brighter with him there. Even then, before I had ever spoken to him, I felt strangely exhilarated just because he was there.

His red-gold hair caught light from the sconces along the walls. His fine skin, tightly drawn over cleanly chiseled bones, had a glow of sun and wind. His mustache, more golden than his hair, stretched in a broad grin as he exchanged greetings with one after another of the people who welcomed him. One flash of blue sparks from his eyes found me, and then they crinkled almost out of sight under his thick sun-bleached eyebrows as he hugged young Christine to him with casual affection. As I watched I envied her, and then I pitied her when he let her go and hugged another girl just as warmly and carelessly.

I turned to Uncle Charles. "Who's Mary's boy? Rob who?"

Uncle Charles, who has always been a bit of a roué, twinkled knowingly at me. "Rob Dunstan," he said, and added, "You will have to stand in line for him, my dear!"

Highly unlikely, I told myself, and deliberately turned my back on Rob Dunstan to talk to Uncle Charles about Fairlawn.

There was no point in asking James or Alison about Rob Dunstan. They obviously were prejudiced against him for reasons they very carefully had refused to tell me, saying only that he was a "troublemaker."

I caught Shirley sometime later, held her by the arm to keep her still while I asked her, "Who's Rob Dunstan?"

"Rob? Oh, he's just another cousin. I thought you knew him." And she was away.

In this house full of cousins that wasn't much help. I had better luck with a conversation—if it could be called that—

with her sister Christine a few minutes later. Her fifteen-year-old chatter came thick and fast, and I had a hard time getting all the pronouns assigned to the right people, but little by little I got the essential point. It was clear that she (Chris) adored him (Rob) but he was too busy dating her (?) to ask "me" for a date, and if he (Rob, no doubt) wasn't careful, "I" (this child?) would show him (probably Rob again) what passion(!) really was, and she (the unknown rival) would wish she had never come near the place (Shearerville?). She would never know what hit her!

I tried to steer her away from her sinister designs on her archrival and back to Rob again, but we got bogged down in "that awful accident," whether one in an airplane in Texas or in a wheelchair at the Hilliard farm I wasn't sure, but another awful woman was involved, and I gathered somehow that this one was the mother of the two children I had seen with Rob at the Co-op.

I pinned her to the wall. "Rob's wife?" I asked her plainly.

"Oh, no. Rob's not married."

Did she know how my heart leaped at those words? Did she hear by breath catch? I went quickly on. "And Andy was his brother?"

"He's dead, you know. In Texas—"

"Then Andy's wife—widow—who's she?"

"You mean Henrietta. Mother won't let her in the house."

"For heaven's sake! Why not?"

And Christine was off again on the accident that I gathered involved a wheelchair and Cousin Mary, whom I identified easily enough as Ellen's cousin Mary Hilliard Dunstan, and the picture became somewhat clearer. Not my side of the family at all, but I had a vague recollection of two boys coming from the Hilliard farm to go hiking with Perk and James one summer morning; two redheaded, freckled little boys trudging off with the Brandon boys into the blaze of a summer day. The younger one, then, was

Rob? The one who had taken three quick steps to their two to keep up with them? Where was I, then, that I remembered that? On the porch with my dolls? A kitten! That was it! I was on the porch with my black kitten, Inky, and that little boy had looked at me once, just once, with bright blue eyes, and then looked quickly away. He couldn't possibly remember, then. And if we happened to meet this evening, I could challenge him about it!

Shirley's arm was tucked possessively through his when she brought him up to me half an hour later. "Christine wanted me to promise I wouldn't let him anywhere near you," she laughed, "but he made a bet with me and I lost. You've known each other a long time, so I won't bother to introduce you." She stuck the tip of her tongue out at me and turned away as I looked up at Rob.

I scarcely heard him pretending to be shocked at Shirley's lack of manners. I hardly heard him say his name to me, nor I mine to him. I put my hand in his and it closed warm and strong and gentle around mine, and some fragment of my mind clung to the real world while the rest told me that if this was falling in love it was more like falling than anything else I knew. Falling . . . as though the bottom had dropped out. . . .

I had already planned what I would say to him, and when I heard myself begin I was surprised not to hear my voice echoing up from the bottom of a well. "How nice to see you again. Do you—uh, I bet you don't remember the first time we met."

"I haven't forgotten—the first time, or the second!"

"Oh, I mean really met—only once, I'm sure."

"Twice."

"Really? It was so—Prove it, then!"

"I plan to," he said and smiled down at me, and the laughter in his eyes made me feel excited and still oddly confident and secure. "What stakes?"

"First, my hand back."

"Sorry," he said and held it fast between both of his. "You'll have to win it."

"Now, I *know* that's not the way it goes."

"You're right, of course." And he looked at my hand, turned it over in his and looked at the palm, seemed pleased with it, and closed it again in his. "That's what I get to win. You can try for a kiss, if you like."

"Now, what ever made you think of that?"

"Inspiration straight from the heart, you might say."

"Or might not! And you still have my hand!"

"I know it." And he drew it through his arm. "Let's take a turn around the garden, shall we?"

"Good grief! It's zero out there!"

He laughed. "I wouldn't notice! Let's go somewhere we can talk. Upstairs? To my car?"

"Sir!"

"Hmm? Oh, sorry. I'm rushing . . . How long will you be here?"

"About thirty seconds more, at a guess—"

"Then to my car?"

"Certainly not! Give me back my hand!"

"But I thought I had won it!"

"*Not* so fast, not so fast. You haven't! We had a bet—"

I would have been perectly content to continue this absurdity on into the night. I was feeling more than exhilarated by it, I was feeling drunk on it, like a bee in a drop of beer, but a sleek, seal brown head pushed its way under his free arm and the youngest of my Perkins cousins smiled confidently up at him.

"Hey, Widgeon, where'd you come from?" he asked her. She said something wispy I couldn't hear. "Have you met your cousin, Joan Brandon?" She shook her head and turned a pixie face with a front tooth missing to smile at me. "Miss Molly Perkins, Ellen's youngest," Rob said, and she wiggled a little closer and smiled a little wider.

I wanted to hug her, or paint her, or trade places with her, or all three, but I didn't even have a hand to offer her. I just smiled and told her I was delighted to meet her at last.

She seemed pleased too, but had something of even greater importance to say to Rob. He leaned down to listen and then turned back to me. "There's a secret I have to look at, if you'll excuse us?" He looked down at my hand, still in his, as though he couldn't decide what to do with it. Then he raised it, placed a light kiss in my palm and curled my fingers over it, and let my hand go. "I'll be back for that," he said, and they walked away.

I knew better than to take Rob Dunstan seriously, of course, but my heart was thudding as I closed my fingers around that kiss. I would find a way to give it back!

James was telling Fitch about the tobacco crop at Woodsedge when I saw Rob coming downstairs. He stopped on the bottom step and looked over the group of people. Our eyes met with another flash of lightning, and a moment later he was at my side. He took my hand and held it on his arm. "Forgive me, sir," he said to Fitch, "but I need to have a conversation with this lady." To James he gave a cool nod.

"Well, don't be long." James seemed impatient and annoyed. "It's time we were going."

I was much too interested in my own affairs to be concerned about James and the time for going. "And all without a by-your-leave to me," I murmured as we walked away. I really didn't expect him to hear me.

"All in good time, all in good time," he said as he guided me through the thinning group in the library and right on to the porch, where there was no one at all. "Let's sit right here for a bit, shall we?"

As we sat side by side on the wrought-iron sofa with its flowery chintz cushions, he carefully isolated the fourth finger of my left hand, and with the crinkle lines around his eyes deepening, he traced a light circle around my finger where Cooper Newton's diamond ring had been. His touch sent a little shiver of excitement through me as I waited for him to speak, to hear what he had to say about that broken engagement.

But he said nothing about it at all. He closed his hand over mine and held it captive on his knee, and ran his free arm along the back of the little seat behind my shoulders. I felt his fingers at the nape of my neck, and a cascade of warm pleasure trickled down my spine at the gentle sureness of his touch. He turned to study my face, quietly and purposefully, and I finally raised my eyes to his . . . and our eyes met in a crack of silent thunder, as though the very heavens had opened. It was at once a recognition and a revelation, and it was over in a split second—in a flash. . . .

Over and finished in a flash, and a kind of bereavement gripped my heart when he pulled his arm away and withdrew his eyes from mine. A shadow like a mask dropped over his face.

That, too, vanished in an instant.

With a strange sensation of having been dropped with a crash into an alien world, I looked around to see if some disapproving dowager had come out to the porch, but there was no one there. I looked at Rob questioningly, amazed, almost stunned by what had passed.

When he spoke it was as though it were all a big mistake! "I do apologize, Joan. I had no right—" He drew a deep breath. "None at all," he said, more to himself than to me. When his eyes met mine again they were bland and cool, as though he had closed a lid on something he had to hide. He lifted his hand from mine with a contrite little smile. "If you weren't so damned lovely . . . Never mind. Let's just chalk it up to Christmas and Uncle Charles's punch."

I shook my head, knowing it had nothing to do with Christmas or the punch. I placed my abandoned hand carefully in my own lap and kept my eyes fixed on it as though to hold it there, but I was at a loss to know what to say.

The silence on the little porch was beginning to have a weight of its own, when he spoke again. There was no teasing in his voice. His tone was very level, the expression on his face controlled, politely interested. "How long will you be here?"

I gave him an honest answer. "Ten days more—"

"We'd better go back," he said and got to his feet.

"Yes, I suppose so. . . ."

What else could I say? Or do? I wanted to protest, to stay where I was and coax him back to me, but I only stretched my hand up to him as though I needed help to get to my feet. I think I hoped he would pull me up to him and into his arms, but he didn't. He pulled me to my feet easily enough but moved back as I rose. There was more than enough space between our bodies to satisfy the fussiest dowager. We stood that way for a long, long moment, our eyes locked, locked as they has been before, searching, speaking. . . .

There are no words to say what our eyes said.

But once more the contact was broken. His eyes were veiled again, and with something like a sigh he started to pull my arm through to his to move toward the door and the library, back to James and our going. I wanted to drag my feet, but what I did, entirely by accident, was to catch the hem of my skirt on a bit of wrought iron settee. He reached to loosen it just as I did, and our hands met again. A simple enough gesture, but like the eye contact, it was cataclysmic. With a quick swing, his arm was around me, gently, almost cautiously, as though he were not quite sure. Then slowly, deliberately, with one finger under my chin, the twinkle back in his eyes, he lifted my face to his and gave me a delicate, sweet, not-at-all-cousinly kiss full on my lips.

When he raised his head and searched my give-away face for my reaction, I tipped it down to hide from him. "And that's the second time I've kissed you," he said with cool satisfaction.

I knew it wasn't the second time he had kissed me! I knew he hadn't so much as spoken to me on the porch. I had no trouble at all in meeting his eyes with my quick denial. "It isn't!"

He turned to walk toward the door, pulling my arm through his. "It is," he went on, as I tried not to think of his body warming mine through our clothing, "but I forgive you for forgetting. You were just a little thing, an infant mewling and—ah—cooing in your grandma's arms." I gasped in indignation, but he paid no attention. "Mother and Ellen had taken me, protesting, so they say, to Woodsedge to meet you, and they thought it would be nice if I kissed you."

"Good Lord! You didn't, did you?"

"Think it was nice? I don't remember that I did, but I surely kissed you."

"How awful! You should have run away!"

"And missed your grandma's coconut cake? Kissing you wasn't that hard!" We walked on through the library. "Gets easier with practice, in fact. I think we should try it again."

"There's James with my coat."

"I fell in love with you the second time we met," he went on with a kind of dreamy tone in his voice, walking more slowly.

"You didn't! You couldn't have! You didn't even look at me!"

"I did. Both. I looked at you and I fell in love with you. On the spot. And I can prove it." He swung around with his back to the door, hiding me from James. I saw the laughter and challenge again in his face. The shadows had passed, and I knew we were back at the playful flirtation.

"Can you, really?" I asked, with my chin high and my voice skeptical. "Prove it, then!"

"Tomorrow? About three?"

I had to laugh at the neatness of it. But I didn't know what Alison might have planned, so I caught back a quick affirmative and risked seeming coy. "Then or soon. Perhaps you'd better call."

"I will. Pleasant dreams and Merry Christmas, my dear, dear Joan!" And he dropped the lightest kiss imaginable, a polite cousinly kiss, on my forehead, and left me.

Chapter Ten

A MIRACLE! IT can't be anything but a miracle! There is he and there am I and we are here together in this tiny fraction of the world in this tiny instant of time and it's nothing but a miracle!

And falling in love isn't falling at all, it's soaring. It's up in a balloon in a crazy wind, and it's all brand new. It's a new world with a new sun in a new sky, and even the ground under my feet is new. The smells and sounds and tastes are new. I am new!

I scooped up a mittenful of clean white snow and tasted it, and for the sheer pleasure of it, rubbed it over my face and caught the drops of it on my tongue as it melted against my skin and dripped off my cheeks. I laughed aloud with the pleasure of it. I've never been in love before! I never knew it could be like this! New! All so clean and new and exciting! Diamonds and opals were burning in the snow!

And out of the glitter came the ghost of the dead woman in her pink scarf! She tried to keep me, tried to pull me back to the worries and frustrations again, but I kicked her aside with a thrust of my boot through a drift and watched the sun catch in the crystals as they floated in the bright cold air. Hector came to help me, and for another fifteen minutes we chased one another around our tracks in a childish game of tag in which Hector broke all the rules, and I finally gave up trying to catch him from sheer lack of breath. Still laughing with my newfound joy, I gave Hector his breakfast and went to get ready for church.

It was Christmas . . . and in all the world there was only Rob . . . Rob . . . Rob . . .

I had hugged my love to myself privately and happily in the backseat of the Lincoln when James drove it out of the jumble of cars at the Perkins house last night. Alison was full of chatter, who had been there and what they said and what the ladies wore and on and on. I at least made an effort to be polite to her, which was more than James did.

"Did you meet Myra Pettyjohn, dear," she asked. "She wanted to talk to you about keeping horses at Woodsedge."

"A stocky girl with black hair? She was with Christine. . . ."

Alison burbled on about Christine and her friends. "I have trouble understanding them," she said cheerfully. "They talk so fast, you know. Just fifteen, aren't they, James? They seem to be so excited about everything!"

I had drifted off on my own thoughts when James's voice came out of the blue, cutting strongly across whatever Alison was saying. "I thought I told you not to have anything to do with Rob Dunstan, Joan."

That woke me up! "But you have never said why!" I made no effort to hide my indignation.

"Damn troublemaker," he snarled. "You steer clear of him!"

"Not good enough, James," I said flatly. "You have to give me a better reason than that."

"I'm sure he means it for your own good, Joanie," Alison chimed in. "They are . . . Henrietta is . . . difficult."

"Difficult? James expects me to . . . to steer clear of Rob because his sister-in-law is . . . difficult?" I snorted a rude laugh at her choice of adjective. "She's got nothing at all to do with . . . anything!" I tackled James again. "And where the hell do you get off laying down rules?"

"For your own good, damn it! That wild body-in-the-woods thing was bad enough, but if you get involved with Henrietta Dunstan, well, I wash my hands of you and that's fair warning!"

I could get nothing more out of either of them. They seemed to think the matter was closed!

I was no closer this morning than I was last night to

knowing anything more than that Henrietta was . . . difficult! And, for some reason, that made Rob . . . dangerous!

It was not James who got in the way of my thoughts of Rob as I showered and dressed for church Christmas morning, it was Cooper Newton. I thought I had been in love with him. A year ago I thought I knew what love was all about, and then, little by little, I had known I didn't know.

How do I know now? An hour's flirtation, two kisses—or three. What do those things prove about love?

Once the dam was broken, doubts flooded in. I remembered the traditional warnings about flirtatious southern boys, their charm that seems so honest and personal that a girl happily wades deeper and deeper into a veritable sea of marshmallow fluff, all frosting and laughter, never ever to be taken seriously.

Did I fall into that famous trap they set for Yankee girls? Am I so hungry for love I took the bait?

But it wasn't all foolishness! It wasn't all Christmas and Uncle Charles's punch, either! There was something else, some kind of bond in that instant of revelation when our eyes met . . . something almost mystic . . . a kind of recognition . . . I shook my head with wonder . . .

And fell back to earth. Perhaps it had been a dream. . . .

But my mind wouldn't leave it at that. What did Christine say? There had been some kind of tragedy. Was that the cause of that swift shadow across his face, the sudden tension around his mouth? Was it tragedy that held him back from me until, almost against his will, he kissed me?

I corrected myself quickly. Tragedy and sorrow might be against his will, kissing me certainly was not. I had never been more deliberately, thoughtfully, and carefully kissed in my life!

What had Uncle Charles meant with his "you'll have to stand in line for him"? Or Caitlin Prentiss when she stood between me and the door in Shirley's room and said "Watch out for him, sweetie! He's on the prowl!"

What a hideous expression! So like Cat!

And Shirley, not much interested in Rob, listless and tired at the end of the evening when I helped her take empty glasses and plates to the kitchen, saying, "Mamma says he's been carrying a torch for a long time. I think there's a girl in California and he'll go back there, maybe to stay, when Cousin Mary dies."

"What? His mother?"

"She's got some terrible arthritic disease. It's very sad." Shirley said no more, drifting away into her own thoughts that seemed to be giving her very little pleasure, and I went back to the parlor. Could that be what James meant by trouble, his mother's illness? But no, he connected Rob with Henrietta—and Christine said Ellen wouldn't let "that awful Henrietta in the house." And who is this Henrietta? Does she have some kind of hold over Rob . . . that goes with her evil reputation? I don't understand!

The question kept churning in my mind as I dressed for church. When I looked in my mirror to put on makeup I was shocked. Pale and wan? Good grief, so soon? And not an hour ago I was flying into the treetops? Is love an illness, then, and what I have an acute attack, possibly fatal?

I needed a reference, an encyclopedia, a chart, or a compass—even a fixed star would help! I pulled Sidonia's old Shakespeare off the bookcase, and the volume fell open in the midst of Romeo and Juliet. It was like an omen. I was tempted to skip church and wallow in it, but Alison knocked on my door at just that moment. Feeling strangely guilty I replaced the book and invited her in.

"I've brought you a little boutonniere," she said and pinned the twinkling little ornament to the lapel of my suit. "Kind of wish I had said I'd go with you after all."

"It's not too late to change your mind! I'll help you dress."

She kissed me lightly. "Thanks, but . . . not this time. There's so much . . ." Her voice trailed away in a little sigh, and her eyes drifted to the window.

I couldn't insist. I put my polo coat around my shoulders like a cape and silently added her name to the long list of prayers I wanted to make. "Don't you and James wait for me if you want to open your presents. The service will be a long one."

"We'll be happy to wait. James said to tell you Merry Christmas. He's on the phone—" She pulled her thoughts back to me with a visible effort. "Now, drive carefully. Are you sure you don't want to take the Lincoln?"

"I'm sure. I know where the icy spots are. I'll be careful."

I didn't pretend even to myself that I was going to church this Christmas morning because of any great piety or religious fervor. I went because that's what we Brandons usually do on Sundays, and always on Christmas and Easter. We brought what reverence we had and didn't worry about what we hadn't. I tried other churches in New York, went with a friend to one of her exotic "religious experience" meetings and felt cheated. Then I tried doing without church entirely and felt lonely and abandoned. So I sampled every church within walking distance of my apartment and was looking around for more when Cooper Newton came along. He suggested agnosticism and gave me a list of books to read. I sighed with relief when I dropped the last of them at the Public Library before I left the city, and went happily back to my family's Episcopal church with them.

I liked going. Liked the familiar service and having Christianity fed to me in eloquent sermons surrounded by poetry and music. But mostly I liked the feeling of belonging.

I liked being part of a herd.

I knew it last night, there at the Perkinses', even before Rob came in. It warmed me and filled some need in me that nothing in New York ever did. I am a member of this herd, and our territory is here in Brandon County. This is where I belong.

Now if I can just get the rest of my life together . . . Rob . . .

Rob! It all begins and ends with Rob! Amazing. Yesterday I didn't know he existed, and this morning I can't see the snow sparkling on the fields without thinking of him. Without him, it wouldn't sparkle! It would be the same old world with the same old problems, the same pleasures and sorrows, certainties and doubts. But now all those things are new, all waiting to be discovered and learned and lived with and shared with . . . Rob!

I was driving too fast. I remembered the ice and slowed and lit a cigarette so I could think . . . dream. . . .

Of course I was late. The parking lot was full, but I found a small space not too close to a fire hydrant and slipped neatly into it, mentally crossing my fingers that I would be able to slip as neatly out again. I left my polo coat on the seat and hurried across the street to the church.

The service had already started. The choir was passing the porch door in the midst of their festival procession, and I stood there, waiting and watching. The air smelled of incense, and the familiar hymns shook the wreaths of ivy and pine and made the candles on the altar tremble. As the choir boys marched past me, one little fake-angel with a beautiful soprano voice dug his elbow into another, and mayhem was narrowly averted when a larger boy behind them bopped the nudger on the head with his hymnal. Then came the girls' choir, and they broke into giggles back there where they thought no one was watching. I winked at one, and she immediately sobered to round-eyed innocence and marched sedately on. The adult voices thrilled me with their richness, and I knew I was one of the faithful they bade to come, and I wouldn't have traded places with a soul on earth.

I had plenty of time to say all my prayers, some of them twice over, before my turn came to go forward to receive communion. It was indeed a long service, and I was feeling a little guilty for having delayed Christmas dinner for James and Alison, when it was finally over, but one advantage of being last in is being first out. I shook the rector's hand politely at the door but made no effort to introduce myself to him. He's used to strangers at Christmas, of course, and the name Joan Brandon would not mean anything to him. He was not the same old gentleman who had been rector here twelve years ago, and probably no Brandon had been to this church since we came that long-ago summer.

I knew Fitch and Ellen had come to the eight o'clock service—"Not as pretty, but we like to avoid the crush"— so I answered friendly smiles of the strangers greeting one another out front with a quick smile of my own and hurried on across the street to the corner where my car was parked.

And there, leaning against it, the sun glinting in his hair, was Rob. The little towheaded girl of the Co-op was hugged in front of him, only her face and legs unhidden by the flaps of his sheepskin coat. I guess my mouth dropped open. My half brother Pip says it always does when I'm taken by surprise, and how I expect to grow up to be cool and sophisticated he doesn't know! I changed the gape to a grin quickly enough and greeted them with all the pleasure I felt, as Rob introduced the children to me.

"My niece, Anne Dunstan," he said, and the little girl gave me her shy smile and snuggled back closer to her uncle. "And nephew, Andrew, Chip for short."

"Miz Brandon," he said and offered me his hand.

"Master Dunstan," I replied and solemnly shook it.

"But how did you know it was my car?" I asked Rob when the formalities were finished.

"It wasn't hard. Note the outlandish license plates"—I had to admit our New Hampshire plates, exhorting "Live Free or Die," were a little outlandish—"your college parking sticker"—I murmured that Dad teaches at UNH—"and last but not least, the coat on the front seat."

"Very good! You're a detective, then. A private eye!"

"Not so," said he. "But I do have a pretty good look-and-see ratio. Do you have to hurry?"

"I should, I suppose. They're waiting for me—"

"I'll just see you off your patch of ice, then."

Chip pulled his head away from the window, where he was peering in at my mini dashboard. "We're going skating this afternoon and you can come if you want."

"What a good idea," said Rob. "Will you?"

"I . . . really don't know. I . . . forgot to ask Alison about her plans." My flightly thoughts had come home to roost! I felt myself blushing, and I looked back toward the church to hide it. "How did you get out here so quickly?"

"Ah-ha! A secret passage!"

"No!"

"Well, fairly secret. Through the choir door."

"But I didn't know . . . I didn't see you—"

"You were busy praying, and I was looking for you."

"How . . . ? We didn't . . ." And suddenly I knew. Only one person could have told him I might be at this church this morning. "Ellen! You're in cahoots with Ellen!"

"Right! We're conspiring!"

"Oh, dear! I . . . uh, oh dear. . . ." It was suddenly crystal clear. I have an ally! We both do because we're headed in the same direction! But where to? Where to so fast?

I felt a quick tug of excitement pulling me forward and it was almost frightening, as though I were running across a lawn in the dark and the ground started to slope down, steeper and steeper. . . . But then it wasn't frightening because the smile on his face was a warm mixture of tenderness and concern, and I felt secure again until instinct jumped ahead of reason, the girlish instinct for more time, more time! Don't rush me so fast! Don't surround me so quickly! A flush mounted to my cheeks again, and I didn't know where to look or what to say; he was watching me like a hawk, and I knew he saw every bit of my confusion and was enjoying it—loving it! His head tilted as he watched. The crinkles in the corners of his eyes deepened as imps of mischief danced in his eyes. If we had been alone . . .

105

But people were swarming down the sidewalk now, calling greetings to one another, and cars were turning the corner. His smile widened, and I knew he knew what I was wishing. I found my car keys easily enough—too quickly—and was very cool and collected as I started the engine and remembered to give it a minute to warm up.

"I'll call you about three," he said, and with him watching and Chip prepared to push if necessary, I moved neatly off my patch of ice and headed back to Woodsedge.

Chapter Eleven

WHEN I BROUGHT my happiness into the parlor it was as though I brought life itself, as though they were puppets sitting with their strings dangling, waiting for me to pull them alive. I more than surprised them, I galvanized them.

James, leaning against the mantel, staring into the flames of the gas log, jerked to attention and pulled a grin across his mouth that was sad in its falseness. Alison sat in front of the tea cart arranged for lunch, staring at it as though it had dropped from outer space. When she saw me she smiled as though her face would break.

"I'm sorry," I said. "I didn't mean to frighten you."

James laughed roughly. "Just didn't hear you, is all. You got the little Christ Child all safe in his manger?"

"Now, James," began Alison. "Don't you talk like that . . . don't you . . ." She choked a little and started again. "I bet it was real pretty. I should have gone with you. Are you ready for lunch? I've got some soup here, and some sandwiches. I thought that might be nice after all the fancy things last night, and there's that dinner at the Johnstons' tonight. Victoria is a wonderful cook, you know."

I had forgotten the engagement with Alison's sister and her family! I had even forgotten that their name was Johnston! I secretly resolved that I would back out if it conflicted with my skating party. "What time are we supposed to go?"

"About eight. It's an open house and buffet."

When it was time to open Christmas presents the atmosphere was almost relaxed and pleasant. James tossed the scarf I gave him around his neck over his big white sweater and looked for all the world like a dashing football hero. Alison modelled the cherry red satin negligee he gave her, fluffing the marabou collar around her face like a confection out of a girlie magazine. They stood side by side, their arms around each other, and gave me a box to open in my turn.

"How did you know?" I shrieked when I took the lambskin vest out of its box. "You couldn't have known!" I hugged the fleece against my neck. "How *did* you know?"

"Clairvoyant," said James smugly.

"It wasn't really hard, honey," said Alison. "Kenny Haynes waited on you at the Co-op. You couldn't have known, but he recognized you when he took that sack of dog food out to your car. His mother and I had been talking about you, you see." She laughed. "I don't suppose you know you were the topic of so much talk, but that's the way it is down here. He dropped it off at the Perkinses' yesterday afternoon. I think he used it as an excuse to see Shirley, as a matter of fact."

"Then it served two useful purposes," said James, giving Alison a glance halfway between a smile and frown. "I wish he'd just kidnap her and save us all a lot of pain."

"Now, James, you haven't spoken ten words to Hayley. You may like him better than you think."

"A hundred times zero is still zero," said James flatly.

I rooted for Kenny Haynes myself to keep peace in the family and thanked them again for the lovely bit of luxury they had given me.

We slipped onto thin ice a few minutes later when I made a perfectly innocent remark about gambling. James mentioned one of the football games he wanted to see on New Year's Day, and I leaped in with the gratuitous information that Pip had bet a hundred dollars on it. "He's forever getting into jams like that, and where he expects to get the money to pay off I can't imagine, so the least I can do is root for his team . . ." I was babbling, and I babbled on because no one stopped me. "Did you know gambling kind of runs in our family, Alison? Our Aunt Caroline lost her whole inheritance and her husband's too just on . . . the roll of . . . the dice . . ." My words drifted off into embarrassed silence as Alison's face went as white as paste and James whirled to clutch the mantelpiece and stare at the gas log. I debated swiftly and silently whether to apologize or just to pretend it hadn't happened, when Alison spoke cooly and with immense dignity.

"I never knew your Aunt Caroline," she said, "but I certainly have heard her story. It's all very sad but I don't believe it's an inheritable tendency. James, did you see the really lovely place mat set Victoria gave us? It will look so perfect this summer if we get that wrought iron set for the terrace."

"Then all we need is a terrace," said James with a gritty little laugh. Our grandparents had never understood our annual efforts to find a level spot for our charcoal grill on the rough brick area at the back porch. Now in the parlor on Christmas day we each very quickly had something brilliant to remember about it, and the crisis passed.

Until I spoiled it all. After we had finished our fruitcake, and were having cigarettes with our coffee, in all innocence, wanting only to be a good houseguest, I blew our peace sky high. I told James I was going to make my long distance phone calls, and that I would find out what they cost and reimburse him. He protested politely. "Oh, there's no need for that. They're my family, too, you know. Just hope you can get a line through."

"I know. And I don't want to tie up the phone too long because Rob will call."

"Who?"

"Rob Dunstan." I stared at him in surprise. Surely he didn't need to ask! "I saw him after church."

"I thought you weren't going to have anything to do with him! I thought you understood—"

"That was your idea, not mine!" I reached for another cigarette. I lit it with a fierce click of my lighter and blew a challenging cloud of smoke toward him.

"Now, James," began Alison.

"He's nothing but an irresponsible redneck and a troublemaker, sweetheart. You know that. Tell Joan—"

"Tell me yourself, James." My anger was rising nicely, and I got to my feet to face him squarely.

He glared at me for an instant and then turned back to the fire. "Just take my word for it, the man's a bully and . . . a womanizer—or worse. There's something really ugly . . ." His voice faded for a moment and was a little less vicious when he continued. "You don't know that family as well as I do. I'm sorry for his mother but . . . there's bad blood there. You don't want to have anything to do with them."

"But I do, James! I . . . his mother is Ellen's cousin, for heaven's sake. Where's this bad blood thing you're so concerned about? You keep hinting but you never say!"

He deliberately evaded the point and tried a different tack. "You're a big girl now, and you have always done pretty much as you please, and I can't stop you. But just don't you invite him here." His voice hardened into a snarl. "That's my last word. I don't want him to set foot on this place!"

Alison looked surprised at the vehemence of his words, but was content to remain silent. Not I. Perhaps she read the warning in the flush on his face. I didn't. I put my fists on my hips and jutted my chin at him, and let him have it. "This is my farm as much as it is yours, I'd like to remind you, and I will have Rob here whenever and wherever I please, and I suggest that you prepare yourself to put up with it!"

I was going to add more of the same when he turned, his face suffused with rage, and took a step toward me. He raised one arm, hand open, as though to slap, glowering and glaring, while Alison tugged futilely at his sleeve and made soothing sounds at us both.

It couldn't have lasted more than a second or two, but it seemed an hour before he spun away with a snarl and stamped across the hall to his study, slamming the door behind him.

He left a shambles in the parlor. I was more than a little ashamed of myself. I had goaded him, I had to admit, but he had started it and kept it going, and I was absolutely right about the farm. He knew it as well as I did. There was no way he could make such an order stick, and he knew it.

I turned to Alison. Her face told me that I had wrecked her happiness and her peace of mind. Her face was nothing less than blasted with distress.

But she didn't seem to want or to hear my apology. She was not interested in it or in me. Her attention was clamped on the door across the hall. Her voice was expressionless, almost mechanical, when she said, "Why don't you just go on to the kitchen and make your phone calls?"

There was nothing I could do but go.

No circuits were available for my call to Scarsdale or to Perk. I was debating whether to call the Shearerville police for an update about the missing woman when I heard the front door slam and seconds later heard the Mercedes bursting out of the driveway. I was at the dining room door when Alison came rolling her hostess cart to the kitchen, the anguish still on her face. Worse than before, in fact. She looked positively distraught.

Damn James! Surely this was out of proportion! Surely the Dunstans' dirt farm and rednecks, if such they had, were no excuse for inflicting this kind of pain. Nor was my telling him, reminding him, that we own the farm in equal shares. He knows it as well as I do! He had been perfectly cheerful when we talked about it just last night with Fitch.

"Damn James anyway," I said, not exactly under my breath.

"Oh, no. No. It's not his fault, really." Her voice was strained, high and tight as she strove to control herself.

"But of course it is! Whose else? Here, let me take those

things. You look so . . ." I pushed the tea cart out of the way as she slumped down in a chair. She looked so lonely and miserable that I sat beside her, and when she looked at me I forgot about trying to understand. I forgot about everything except that devastating loneliness I had felt myself just a few days ago. Here it was again, smeared across Alison's classic features like the blundering destruction of a cranky child. I put my arm around her, and she leaned stiffly against my shoulder.

I fully expected her to break down and have a good cry, but she was rigid with self-control. Stiff as a wooden doll, she looked toward the window, where the Mercedes had disappeared down the lane toward the county road. I heard her whisper through clenched teeth, "I should have stopped him but I couldn't . . . I couldn't. . . ." She made one more effort to pull herself together, to force the trouble and pain aside. She squared her shoulders and straightened herself in her chair. "I'll be all right," she said through white lips. "I don't mean to upset you—"

"You don't! You don't," I cried. "Tell me what it is. Let me help you. You helped me! Let me at least try to help you!"

She laughed then, an awful laugh, entirely mirthless, joyless, worse than a sneer, worse than derision. It was like laughing when you have been clutching the last straw and it has fallen apart and you are left holding the short end in your hand, laughing at yourself for being such a fool as to think it might save you. A bitter laugh at the cruelty of fate.

"You can't, you can't . . ." she said when her breath caught again. "That's the worst of it. I can't tell you so . . . so you can't help! It's . . . hell, just . . . hell!"

The last words came choking out in a cry, and I had her cuddled to me when the tears began. Great sobs shuddered through her, and for a few minutes I was frightened by them, afraid this anguish was beyond help, that it would burst the dams of reason and carry this poor soul into heaven-only-knew what kind of maelstrom. I prayed for help, for whatever I could get of some kind of relief for her. It had to stop, and slowly, almost imperceptibly, it did, until at last it was only a tired child's sobs, while I stroked her shoulders and murmured at her, soothing her as Susan had soothed me during those unthinkable hours when we believed Perk had been killed.

"Don't talk. Don't talk yet. Just be still," I said when I heard her draw in a shuddering breath. "It will be all right. I know it will." I handed her a tissue from the box on the table. She took it gratefully and was dabbing her eyes with it when the clock in the hall struck three . . . and the phone rang.

And rang again. I knew it was Rob, knew it beyond a doubt, but what I could say to him I did not know. I just sat still and gazed stupidly at it.

"Answer it, Joan. I'll . . . be all right. . . ."

So I did.

What did he hear in my voice? I don't know. I tried to make it sound as normal as I could when I told him I was sorry but I couldn't get away. I tried not to sound distressed, or even unduly disappointed. Just sorry, not today, but call me again . . . please.

"I will." A pause, and then, "Are you all right?"

"Yes. Oh, yes. I'm just fine—really. It's just something here I can't leave. Please call me again."

And I hung up. Cut him off. Put the receiver on the hook and let him go—let the love of my life slip away perhaps forever—and turned my attention again to Alison.

"Oh, I'm sorry, Joan. You shouldn't have done that. You should have kept your date."

"You're more important right now. This is. I couldn't possibly leave you. Surely not!"

"I'll be all right." Her voice sounded better, steadier and stronger, and she helped herself to another tissue.

"I know you will, but you look awfully pale."

"I reckon. I feel awfully pale!" She laughed a little and wiped her eyes again, and when she looked at me I saw a new kind of glow in her smile, breaking through the pain, a look of secret excitement I had seen once or twice before. "I should tell you, Joan," she began tremulously, "you surely have a right to know. You see, I'm going to have a baby . . . next summer . . . and—"

"Oh, I'm so glad! How really fine! I had hoped—" I hugged her again. "But you should be more careful! You shouldn't—James shouldn't—"

"But that accounts for my being upset so easily, you see. It's nothing to worry about. Dr. Peters says I'm in wonderful shape. I'm really very strong, you know."

"But you're still shaking! I can feel it! I think you had better go and lie down awhile."

"Perhaps I should, at that," she said with a shaky little sigh. "Just as soon as I do up these things—"

"Oh, no. No way will you do these dishes! You just run along out of here, and if you're not asleep when I've finished, I'll come and sing you a lullaby. How would you like that?"

"I'd like it fine." Her smile was more relaxed, and color was coming back into her cheeks. I watched her move toward the door, satisfied that she was steady again and in control of herself.

Well, that does put a different light on things, I thought, as I went to work at the sink. James to be a father! What a lot of changes that will make! A real switch for him to have a family of his own to love and cherish!

But other thoughts quickly displaced those pleasant sentimental ones. Not nice thoughts, sinister ones as I wondered whether the prospect of fatherhood might account for James's present tension, whether perhaps he was afraid he would not be a good father, or even that he might be a bad one.

James certainly had no firsthand experience of a loving father. All he had was a tyrannical grandfather and a sympathetic uncle whose time and energy were spread pretty thinly among his own offspring. For a man like James, who was impatient by nature and leaned toward cruelty rather than compassion, learning to be a good father might be a real challenge.

But James could learn! He could take a course!

I smiled to myself as I recognized my professorial father's daughter. But it might be the perfect answer. I decided to see if I could find a book for pregnant daddies at the after-Christmas sales the next day with Alison.

"I should have stopped him, but I couldn't," Alison had said, and the tone of her fear and frustration rang clearer in my memory than the tone of her happiness when she made her announcement about her baby. She should have stopped him from what, for goodness sake? From going where? "It's just hell," she said, and added that she couldn't tell me more. And James accuses *Rob* of being a bully! What are you up to James, that your lady is in such distress? You should protect her from that kind of trouble, you idiot, not cause it! And why did you rush out of the parlor in a raging temper just because I mentioned Rob's name? How can I understand such childish accusations when you won't tell me what Rob has ever done to you?

For another fifteen minutes I pondered the problem, searched for the answers in every direction I could think of. I even went so far as to imagine that the baby might not be James's at all. That it might even (Good God!) be Rob's! But that thought was totally untenable, and I pushed it firmly out of my mind, or at least as firmly as I could. It was amazing how tenacious an untenable thought could be!

I needed an antidote. I had an empty afternoon and a whole series of questions without answers, and I still couldn't get a line to the people I wanted to talk to in the East.

I cut myself another piece of cake and took it with me to my room, listening at Alison's door as I passed to be satisfied that she was at least breathing peacefully if not actually asleep. Then I pulled the thick old volume of Shakespeare off the shelf, draped my quilt around my shoulders, and started *Romeo and Juliet*.

Within half an hour my antidote failed me completely! I managed to get safely through the soliloquy in the orchard, but I couldn't face the nurse coming in with her terrible news. I put the book back in its place and took my inflamed senses out to get Hector and go on a nice cooling walk.

I'm no Juliet. I'm less innocent and a lot more disillusioned with this business of the world well lost for love. That kind of passion is all very well in stories, but it doesn't solve any real problems, not for long, anyway.

Just most, said Cooper Newton's voice in my thoughts.

False! A lie! I admit that bed was the most honest part of our relationship, but it didn't solve a single problem. It only made them go up in smoke—to choke us later! We never looked for solutions because we never talked! Never exchanged ideas. You lectured and I listened—until I got tired of it!

Cooper Newton muttered that bed should have been enough. . . .

It isn't! It isn't! Not for me, anyway. I want more. More than bed, Rob! That and more!

What more? Rob's voice now, no sexier than Cooper Newton's but more direct, as though he were asking me, not an imaginary audience from an invisible stage, as though he really cared what I thought. Really wanted to know what more I wanted.

So I answered Rob in my mind: The caring, for one thing. The "Are you all right" that sounded so . . . truly concerned.

And I said, "just fine" but I'm not just fine. I'm in love and I'm lonely and I never should have touched that damned book!

The western sky was glowing through the old pecan tree in the corner of the yard, silhouetting the branches that arched in mocking parody of our New England elms. The beauty of it did nothing positive for my mood. I kicked up some of last fall's nuts and sent them bouncing like tiny footballs across the windswept frozen ground, where they buried themselves in a fat snow drift at the corner of the red cabin, and then I played hide and seek with a squirrel around the trunk of the tree until Hector started barking impatiently at us. I walked on, scuffling idly through the snow on what used to be the kitchen garden, and was just turning into the farm road to walk to the copse when I caught a glimpse of a truck coming down the lane toward the driveway.

A few steps toward the barn and I could see more clearly. A battered green truck . . . And, oh God! On a collision course with Rob came James from Blair, and I had a vision of them ramming together at the driveway like wild sheep on a mountaintop.

And there was nothing I could do to stop them.

But Rob in the truck waited politely at the end of the driveway while James drove on into his garage. I waited to see what route Rob would take. I wanted to be there when he stopped, to beat James if I had to run. I had some idea that James might try to order him off or, as Pip might say, take a poke at him. In either case, he would have to deal with me first, damn him!

Rob stopped the truck nose to nose with the Volkswagen at the shed, and I had time to call a greeting to him before James got across the farm road, and I was standing beside him, telling him how glad I was that he had come, when James walked up, his hand extended. "Hey there, Rob," he said as though they were old friends. "You all finished strippin' over at your place?"

"Not yet," said Rob as he shook hands with my cousin. "But we're right on schedule."

Watching them standing there facing one another, their eyes locked for a moment in some sort of duel I could not understand at all, my mind recorded one of those camera-flash mental images that grow brighter and more fixed with

117

time. James, six inches taller and probably thirty pounds heavier, made Rob seem small and light and oddly menaced by James's dark swarthiness. But there was something of the brightness of a hero in Rob's golden hair and sunlit fair skin, something of gallantry in the straight tautness of his body. His eyes, the blue of a summer sky when he looked at me, were clear and cold as winter ice as they battled James's smokey grey ones.

In that brief instant I knew with perfect certainty that there was no need for me to fight Rob's battles for him. I knew that he was more than a match for James.

James turned to me. "Sorry about running out on you like that, Joanie. I didn't mean to be rude, you know."

"That's all right, James. Don't give it a thought." I looked him in the eye to let him know he'd better give it a thought or two. "Alison is having a nap, I believe. For about the past hour. She should be feeling better now."

He threw a questioning glance at me, but I had nothing to add. He could find out for himself why his pregnant wife felt ill!

Just then Hector came bounding up to where we stood, his hackles raised, obviously trying to decide whether to hide behind me at the sight of this stranger or to bite him in the leg, or to let it all go and just be friendly. In true spaniel fashion, he decided on the last and fairly fawned when Rob reached down to fluff one long brown ear.

James left us there. He and Hector barely acknowledged one another's existence.

Chapter Twelve

ROB LOUNGED AGAINST his truck, his hands in the warm-up pockets of his green goosedown jacket, his long legs in nicely faded Sunday jeans, his head cocked slightly as he watched me watching James walk away. He seemed relaxed and content, but there was more than a hint of mischief in his eyes.

I suddenly realized we were really alone together for the first time and it disconcerted me! I saw his mustache start to twitch and I knew he knew what I was thinking. I looked away from him, tried to think of something to say, wished he would say something, wondered why I was so tongue-tied when I had spent the past twenty hours having imaginary conversations with him. . . .

You want him to kiss you!

The falling sensation threatened to overwhelm me again, and I ducked my face aside and saw Hector starting his walk alone. I pulled myself together and looked at Rob with as much confidence as I could manage. "Will you come for a walk with Hector and me, or shall we go in and find a beer?"

"Wherever," he replied, his eyes crinkling even more, and he pushed himself erect, ready to go wherever, as he said. Wherever I went? Wherever our whims take us? Or the law allows? There seemed to be no limit to wherever. It goes on without end in any direction. We started walking along the farm road toward the copse half a mile away, following a wide-ranging springer pup.

The track was wide, and the snow piled on the leeward

side of the ruts were fluffy and clean. The air was as sparkling as champagne, and within ten paces my hand was with his in the pocket of his jacket, and I didn't care if wherever was a hundred years away.

We talked in phrases and half-sentences, sending the words back and forth with scarcely a pause. "Have you a dog?" I asked.

"Two. A collie, a nice old guy named Terhune."

"Terhune?" The name rang a bell somewhere, and suddenly I had it. "Ah! For Albert Payson!"

"The same." He slanted a warm look of appreciation at me. "He and Grandfather were boyhood friends. All our collies have been Terhunes."

"And the other?"

"A basset named Cobb."

"For corn?"

"Irvin S."

I laughed with delight. The homage to the jowly Kentuckian was amusing enough, but it was pure joy to learn I had struck still another vein of gold! The man I loved was literate! "I should have known," I said. "How is he on rabbits?"

"Lazy . . . but cheerful!" Which, of course was ridiculous, and I laughed again. Our walk was full of laughter, and if we cast shadows, I never saw them.

"What made you come over?"

"I couldn't see you over the phone."

I tightened my fingers around his. I hadn't been able to see him, either. A few paces farther I said, rather timorously, "James says you're a troublemaker."

He sighed lightly. "He probably thinks I am."

"But why, for heaven's sake?"

"We've . . . ah, had words."

"What about?"

"I . . . can't tell you."

A moment of silence. I repeated softly, "Can't?"

"I beg your pardon," he said quickly. "We've had words about my sister-in-law. I should have saved my breath."

"About Henrietta? James . . . Alison says she's difficult but they wouldn't say how . . . or why. What does she do—or say—that's so awful?"

He kicked a pebble from his path and sighed deeply, and the shadow was on his face again. "I want to tell you," he said, after a moment's silence, "but . . . this isn't the best possible time or place. It's too . . . bright! Let's just say for now that James is right. Henrietta is certainly difficult!"

At least now I knew what caused the shadow! With a quick squeeze of my arm against his I pushed Henrietta aside. "Right," I said, and turned the subject. "Why did we see you only that one summer?"

"You mean that summer I fell in love with you?"

"As you say." There was suddenly more than a glint of mischief in his eyes under those thick sandy lashes. "Wait! Why?"

"Why only that one? We always came for Christmas, except that once. How old were you that year, five?"

"More. Almost seven, I think. And you?"

"Nine-going-on-ten—an awful age."

"Why?"

"I wasn't big enough. I had to spend all my time running to get somewhere."

"Where did you want to go?"

"Wherever I wasn't."

"Exhausting, I should think. Little girls are much too grown up for such foolishness."

"So what do little girls do?"

"Dream a lot."

"How about big girls?"

"They dream a lot, too," I said, caught off guard because I was dreaming.

"Do you?"

"I won't tell you!"

121

He laughed again. "You don't need to!"

My hand felt warm in his. I felt warm from head to foot, warm with a mixture of excitement and security, a kind of joyful arrival at the place I've always longed to be. I hugged it tight to me for a moment before I thought of something else I wanted to know. "Where did you come from?"

"Near Asheville, North Carolina. Up in the mountains."

"What did your dad do?"

I wasn't sure why he was laughing at me again, but his answer was prompt enough. "Wholesale groceries and golf. He was a Scot, you know."

My turn to laugh. "I thought it possible! And that accounts for your red hair."

"And my red hair accounts for my terrible temper."

"Oh, sure! And I bet your middle name is Roy."

"You want to bet on that, do you?"

"Give me a clue, then. What's the initial?"

"M—"

"For all the Macs in the book!" He didn't blink an eye. "How about MacLeod?" I remembered a school friend named Jessie MacLeod with red-gold hair. I thought it a pretty good guess.

"Two," he said. "Take care, lass. This could cost ye!"

"I'm notoriously careless," I said carelessly.

He laughed and twirled his mustache like a comic villain, but said nothing.

"MacPherson?" I had known a handsome redhead of that name in art class who drew marvelous pictures of warriors in kilts. I had high hopes.

Rob shook his head and sighed elaborately. "Perhaps I ought to warn you there's no Mac in it."

"Malcolm," I said with a little skip of joy.

"Four!"

"How many do I get?"

"As many as you like."

I should have been warned by the dancing glint of mischief in his eyes, but I wasn't. I should have guessed he was not to be trusted. At very least I should have wondered why he had dropped my hand and was energetically throwing snowballs for Hector, who just as energetically ran off to find them in the copse and returned for another a moment later.

"Give me another hint."

"Oh, no. Think of all the ones I wiped out with the Macs."

The copse, a small woods originally used as a loiter for grazing cattle, was aglow with late afternoon light, sunset light that cast violet shadows across virgin drifts piled high where the wind had whipped the snow through the gaps among the trees. We rounded the northernmost corner, where a smooth bank of snow was tinted warm and golden with the light; and the sun, like an actor reluctant to leave the stage, was taking curtain calls through a bank of rosy clouds.

Rob threw another snowball into the woods, and when Hector went crashing in after it, a rabbit came out the other side and started a mad dash across the field, Hector in hot pursuit.

I was innocently wondering whether the hawk circling overhead was taking careful note of the rabbit's route to his burrow and glanced at Rob to share this speculation with him, when I saw the blue sparks in his eyes and the unmistakable grin.

I thought I would get away but a few seconds later we were kicking up a storm of snow, laughing and wrestling there. I had quite a lot of practice with this sort of rough-house with my brothers and I almost wriggled free, but Rob grabbed my hands and held them over my head, and I lay there, flat on my back, and laughed up at him.

"Stop laughing," he said sternly.

"Why?"

And then, of course, I knew. You can't kiss a girl who is laughing. Not that way, anyhow. He counted them off slowly, at his leisure, until Hector came bounding in to join the fun and all three of us lay back in the snow, exhausted and panting.

"Oh, God, you do me good," gasped Rob. "I haven't had that much fun in years."

"You poor little thing, you!"

"Be careful!"

"Not likely!"

But he was wiping snow off his wristwatch. "I'll put that on your account," he said. "I've got to run—"

"What?"

"Literally, unless you'll let me use your phone."

"Of course," I said as he pulled me to my feet and started brushing snow off me. "But why?"

"They worry."

"Who?"

"Mainly Anne. She's a classic worrier. Pure Scot."

"But, ah, Henrietta. . . ?"

"She's in Chicago."

I brushed the snow off his jacket, careful not to get it down his neck. He obviously meant it when he said he had to hurry if the youngsters were alone and it was growing dark. We started down the track toward home, the evening creeping in around us.

"Will I like Henrietta, do you think?"

"No. Not at all."

"That bad, eh?"

"At least. let's not talk about it."

"Sorry," I said.

"Don't you know if you're in love you're not supposed to say you're sorry?"

"What twaddle!"

And we laughed together again, talked about twaddle, and forgot about Henrietta. "Your hands are cold," he said a minute later. "Let's jog a bit."

So jog we did, side by side, and jumped the ruts in unison, Hector gamboling along with us.

"Mother wants to meet you," he said, without the slightest sign of heavy breathing.

Damn the cigarettes, I thought, trying to hide my panting and puffing. "I'd like . . . to meet . . . her."

He slowed to a walk. "Tomorrow evening? I'm pretty well boxed in tonight."

"I am, too. Tomorrow will be great."

"Shall I come pick you up about five? You can read the kids a bedtime story, and then we'll go to dinner and find some place to dance. I like holding you."

"Sir!"

"Well, I do. Is five all right?"

"Perfect." I smiled invitingly at him while I silently regretted tonight. I wanted to be held! Immediately and tightly! I could feel threadlike bonds of attraction growing stronger and stronger between us, weaving us together, pulling me toward him, my body toward his, powerful elastic bands . . . I brushed against him deliberately as we went into the kitchen. He knew why! His hand on my arm and the gleam in his eyes told me he knew! If Alison had not been standing there . . .

But she was.

I fed Hector while Rob made his phone call in what he considered the nick of time. He was alone in the kitchen when I returned. "Hold out your hand," he said. "I've been saving this for you."

"What. . . ? Oh! What is it?" I turned the little cream-colored stone over in my fingers. It was worn smooth, vaguely the shape of a heart, and would have fit on a fifty-cent piece. There were some crude scratches on one side.

"Just a pebble I found up at Fox Cave that day I went hiking with your brother and mine, the day I fell in love with you."

My breath caught in my throat and my voice was a whisper. "What are these marks on it?"

"Your name. It's been a kind of talisman—"

"A lucky charm? How can you part with it?"

"I have to. You can throw it away if you want to. It has to be my own luck now, you see. Not pretend magic. I can't put my faith in a stone!"

"Rob," I began, but I didn't quite know what to say, how to continue, so I just said, "Thank you!" and was rubbing it with my fingers, still puzzled to know how to take it, when he surprised me again.

"Don't come out. You'll get chilled and catch a cold and then I won't have time."

"Time for what?"

"To make you fall in love with me, silly girl!" He kissed me then, sweetly, warmly. Before I could catch my breath he was gone.

When I called Perk later that afternoon, I was full of Rob. I poured out all the laughter and excitement for him to share, which he very amiably and patiently did, until I wound down enough to get back to earth.

"You haven't forgotten to call about that APB, have you?"

"What? Oh, that. Well, I called yesterday."

"They may have an update by now."

"But—tomorrow will be soon enough, surely."

"When's tomorrow, Mops? Call now. I'll stand by. Call 'em and call me right back. I'll keep the line open for . . . exactly five minutes. That should give you time enough. Get right back to me, no matter what they say. There's no point in putting it off."

"All right. Five minutes, then. But I don't like this."

"No more do I. But that's no reason to put it off."

It was less than five minutes later that I was talking to Perk again, disappointment heavy in my voice. "The woman from Janesville turned up—alive and well—in Nashville, Perk. Last night." He could hear my despair at the renewed entanglement with the dead woman in Corn

Crib Woods, coming as it did after the high plateau of the afternoon.

"So you're back in it, Mops? God, I'm sorry."

"The worst of it is I don't care so much! I don't want to! I want to just let her go! I can't mix these things! I can't live with . . . with love and death, Perk. I feel like a damned yo-yo!"

Of course he heard the catch in my voice. "Hang on, Mops. I hear you! God, I wish I were there." A brief silence. "Let me talk to James. The least he can do is give you some help—you shouldn't have to put up with all this alone. Put him on and I'll knock some sense into him." There was a catch in his own voice as the futility of that statement came home to him. "Hell," he said, and the tone of his voice closed the book on that frustration, but frustration couldn't keep him down for long. Not any more. "You've got other brothers! What are we saving them for! Call Jim and Pip. Get them down there. No, wait. I'll call 'em! Have you told them what's going on?"

"No, nothing. Nor about Rob, either. They're so busy rushing around—and it's so new. It's, well, not quite ready for bandying. Does that make sense?"

"It's fragile still?"

"Not that so much. It's pretty tough, really, but, well, I just haven't gotten used to it myself, yet."

"Tough but tender, eh? Well; you should be able to do what you please with it, you and your Rob. How old is he, Mops? I can't quite place him."

"One year and two months younger than you, dear brother. Just exactly right!"

"I seem to remember he was a little guy—"

"He just hadn't started growing that summer you all went on your hike to Fox Cave. He's six feet even—"

"And just exactly right!" We laughed together.

"You see, Perk? You see how easy it is to forget her?"

"Yeah, it's pretty easy." He was silent for a moment.

127

"Ah, tell you what, Mops. You can't do anything about that woman—tonight, anyway, if ever you can. So you just go off with James and Alison wherever you're planning to go, and I'll put my marvelous mind to work on this missing-woman problem. See what I can come up with. I think you've made it pretty clear—if I can remember all you told me. Oh, one thing—run down the list of people you told that you had found that body up there, right after you got home."

"Well, there was the woman who answered the phone at the Shearerville Police Department. I told her about it before she told me it was out of their jurisdiction. Then there was Sheriff Dennis at the Brandon County headquarters at Blair. He was the one who answered the phone, anyway. I have no way of knowing who may have been there and heard us shouting back and forth. Then Alison, and last of all, James. That's all."

"All you know about, right?"

"Yes. I didn't talk to anyone else about it."

"Right. Oh, how about Jake? Do you mind if I bounce this around with him? He's pretty sharp."

"Not at all. He seems awfully nice."

"He's that. Okay. You just go on—and call me in the morning if you hear anything that may help. Wait. I'll be in therapy. Call about noon, your time. Are you going to share this with your friend Rob? He should at least give you some sympathy."

"I don't know. Probably not just yet, anyhow. I don't want him thinking I'm totally skitty-witted, much less hallucinating. I'm not on very firm ice where this disappearing mystery woman is concerned, you know."

"No, I guess not. And I think it may be just as well not to pressure James about it, either, if you think you can bear to fight this out alone."

"But I'm not alone, Perk. There's you."

"You're right. There's me. So don't goof off next time. Just grab it and pass it on like a hot potato, you hear?"

"Yes, sir," I said meekly.

Of course he knew I had been goofing off, I thought as I went back to my room to get ready for the dinner at the Johnstons. I had deliberately put off calling the Shearerville police to inquire about that APB because I didn't want to know the Janesville woman had turned up alive and well and was therefore not the woman in the pink scarf. As long as there was the chance that she was, police in six counties would be looking for her. Even Sheriff Dennis would eventually have to admit she had been seen, dead, in Corn Crib Woods.

You do have a way of getting things done, dear brother, I thought, but you can't do a thing about that woman who is dead because no one admits she ever existed except you and me and a guy named Jake. And all you can do is bounce it around, and how that will identify her or find her body I do not know.

There should be some notice of her somewhere—if she's still missing. But she may not be. She may have been found that same night, in the snowstorm, by whoever missed her. They found her body and took it home. So there will be an obituary. I can check that, surely. "Found dead on Blair Road, murdered by person or persons unknown." Mugged, as Perk put it, and hidden, and then found. Soldiers from the fort? Vagrants? A hitchhiker? Someone hunting in Corn Crib Woods in spite of James's signs?

If she was mugged and left and then found and taken back to her people, why the sack of garbage? Was it purposely left to confuse Sheriff Dennis and James and me, or could it have been there all along? Hector didn't go down that far past the oak tree, and I don't know that he's interested in garbage, anyway.

It could be coincidence, I suppose, that pink newspaper sticking out of a tan plastic sack. It could be . . . but I can't believe it!

I wanted to howl! Simply throw my head back like an animal and howl with the frustration of it!

And what earthly good would that do?

I took the little heart-shaped stone out of my jacket pocket and put it gently, tenderly, on the mantelpiece next to the cracked blue bottle that held the eagle's feather. Tokens of my life, I thought, as I broke the rest of my cigarettes into fragments and dumped them in my wastebasket.

Then I went to take my shower.

Chapter Thirteen

THE NEXT MORNING I used every excuse I could think of until Alison finally went off to town without me. Then, trying not to want a cigarette, I got ready to begin the paintings I wanted to do of Woodsedge. I wanted to indulge my memories with some frankly nostalgic little water-colors, misty and fragile, like the memories themselves. I was eager to start and said so to James when he knocked on my door and asked me to come to his study for a moment.

"Won't take a minute, but it's important. I have to get on to town, so come as soon as you can."

If I had had the slightest idea of the course this meeting would take, I would have run like a hare. But I didn't. I was thinking of my work. I opened a new block of hot press, scrubbed my palette, even changed the nibs on my pens. A fine line was wanted here, I thought, a gentle, flexible line that would float off into nothingness the way dreams and memories do. . . .

When everything was ready to begin, I remembered James, and feeling a little guilty, I went to his study.

He was standing in front of the red damask draperies, his hands caught behind his back, obviously tense with impatience. His heavy brows were tightly drawn, and his eyes were dark, almost black, under their shadows. I waved him a flippant salute. "At your service, James. Better late than never, you know!"

He was not amused. "Well, at least you're here." He moved toward the elegant walnut desk, where several sheets of paper were spread, picked up the long, slender, gold fountain pen from its onyx holder and offered it to me. "This won't take a minute. You could have gone back. Here. All you have to do is put your dainty little John Hancock right here on each of these papers, right here below mine. That's all there is to it."

"All right. Let's have a look." I reached for the nearest sheet, to pick it up and read it. I will never know why he didn't expect me to do exactly as I did, but my gesture surprised him. His hand came down on the sheet of paper, holding it on the desk top for one split second, but that was all I needed. The message was loud and clear. For an instant our eyes clashed violently, and I felt my heart skip a beat as his maleness and sheer physical presence loomed over me.

But James was no fool. He was instantly conciliatory, disarmingly apologetic. His lips stretched into a half-smile, bland and innocent, with just a touch of chagrin and cajolery.

"Sorry, Joanie," he said. "I forgot how important these things are to you liberated women. Let me explain this to you. I really haven't time for you to sit down and read it all. It's a deal—really a great opportunity—I know you'll see it that way. I would have given these papers to you to look over on Monday but I knew how upset you were with that business up in the woods, and then going back up there . . . and all that mess. And then Christmas. So this is the first chance I've had. Probably I shouldn't have waited. It runs out on the thirty-first, so there isn't much time, what with the weekend and then New Year's—"

He knew as well as I did that he wasn't telling me anything of any real importance. I picked up one page and carried it over to the lamp by the big upholstered chair. "Hang on, James," I said without looking at him. "I'm a pretty fast reader—"

"I don't have time for that! I'll tell you—"

"You've been talking for five minutes and haven't said a word. Now give me five—"

"I don't want you to bother your pretty head—" He reached out as though to take the paper from me, and I snatched it back and put out a hand to fend him off.

"Shut up, James. I want to—"

"What!"

I looked him straight in the eye. "I said shut up, James. I want to read it!"

His face flushed, and I could feel his anger mounting. I ignored it and noticed that the document was written by a law firm that was not Harrington, Perkins, and Tarleton. The meaning of it fairly jumped off the page. There was no mistaking it. It was an agreement of sale. I reached back and picked up the other two sheets, laid there so slyly. It took me only a couple of seconds to discover the whole truth. It was an agreement to sell this place, this farm! Woodsedge!

I fairly threw the papers in his face and shouted, "Never!" and started to walk around him to the door.

His hand flashed out and grabbed my shoulder. He gave it a rough shake, and when I turned to him in amazement and hurt, in pain, he dropped his hand and turned quickly away to the desk again. His voice was rough as he stacked the papers together again. "Sorry, but you don't need to be such an idiot. It's the opportunity I've been waiting for—hoping for. Prices will never be better. Even Fitch says so. So sit down and sign the damned things. You really have no choice!" He poked the pen toward me, and it was then I should have fled.

But I'm a Brandon, too, and fleeing from my cousin was not in me. Not then. I glared back at him as he glared at me, and a pulsing barricade of dislike and distrust sprang up between us. His hand holding the pen was shaking. His whole body was vibrating with anger and frustration. I sensed that the rage was held in check, reined in tightly, and under control. I had no reason to think he could not control himself, coldly and severely. He always had! At the very last minute, sometimes, but he always had.

I lowered my voice and spoke slowly, reasonably. "Certainly I have a choice! I won't sign it, James. Nothing you can say will make me so you may as well forget it!"

The words weren't out of my mouth before the rein broke. He snarled a crude curse and flung himself away from his desk and started toward me, the gold pen clutched in his fist. But he bypassed me and slammed the door, closing me in with him.

Still I was more surprised than alarmed.

I realized that he was flaunting his physical presence to intimidate me into doing what he wanted. Memories of similar instances flashed through my mind, times when Perk had stood beside me while our cousin loomed, chin outthrust and eyes flashing, just as he was standing now. I refused to be intimidated. He should have known better than to think . . .

And I should have known he would not know better. I wasn't ready when he turned back to me and with one violent push sent me falling back against the desk. He pulled a chair around with one hand and pushed me into it with the other. I was fairly reeling with the explosion of his fury, as gaping and powerless as a rag doll, when he thrust his face down toward mine and snarled, "Now you sit there and listen to me. I've only got just so much patience, and as you see, it's wearing pretty thin."

Brandons fight back. I had my feet under me again and started up from the chair with a snarl. "You call that patience?"

He pushed me down again and held my shoulder roughly, my shoulder that was already insulted by his touch. Some thoughts of the self-defense training I had taken in New York whirled through my mind. I was making some quick choices when his tone changed again. It was a caricature of his normal voice, spread like a thin cloak over the rage again held in check. "Just listen if you can." I made no move. "I don't want to be rough with you, but I—you've got to understand. We've *got* to sell! There *is* no choice.

I've got to have money, Joan. It's that simple. Right now, and a lot. It's mine and I have a right to it—as you have to your half. Good God, it's worth more than a million dollars!"

"Sell your half, then, James, if you have to—" But leave me mine! Don't touch mine! I didn't say it aloud. I tried to keep the panic out of my voice, but I heard it rising, tightening and stretching until it cracked when it hit the air between us.

But James paid no attention to the tone of my voice. He was fighting to control his own. He pushed it down to a harsh whisper. "It doesn't work like that! The land doesn't divide, only the money does. Come on, Joan! I can't stand here and explain law to you! Just take my word for it. It can't be divided. Just sign the damned thing and get it over and done with!"

His face wasn't three feet from mine. His voice was quiet, but mine was quieter. "I will not, James."

He clutched the gold pen, point down, poised over my face for what seemed forever, as I sat, mesmerized, waiting for him to land his blow . . . where? On my face? My neck? My shoulder?

I gripped the chair seat and got ready to lean back and kick, kick him as hard as I possibly could where it would hurt the most when his upraised hand descended. The chair had its back almost touching the desk. I knew I could give a fiarly good account of myself—in the first round, anyway.

He didn't strike his blow. As I watched the color slowly, slowly drained from his face, the flush faded to a greenish pallor, as though lights had been changed on a stage, as though life were ebbing rapidly through a wound, and his eyes seemed to lose their focus, to be looking inward, seeing himself and not me.

Suddenly with an animal cry he flung the pen with all his might against a damask curtain. It hung suspended by its point for an instant while a dark smear of ink leaked into the threads of fabric. His words were only just audible. "Get

. . . out . . ." He hunched over his desk, his hands flat on the surface, supporting his weight.

His collapse frightened me more than his rage had done. I could understand the anger. I didn't understand this. I called his name. "James! James?"

His words were thick and slurred. His hands were clenched on the edge of his desk. I could see muscles bulging in his jaw and a pulse thrumming in his neck. "Go . . . damn you! Get . . . *out!*"

"No! I won't! What's wrong? Are you sick?"

The word itself seemed to revive him. Illness of any kind had always been abhorrent to him, and the idea now acted as a prod. He turned his face away from me, but he straightened himself. "No! I'm not sick! Just . . . get the hell *out!*"

I stood where I was, and in a moment I heard him say in a voice that sounded like his own, "I'm all right." And then, when I still waited, he repeated it again in a voice from which all trace of anger and anguish had disappeared. "I'm all right. Just . . . go on about your business. You had so much to do! Just go!"

There wasn't anything else I could do. "I'll be in my room if you need me," I said, and went.

I closed my door and leaned against it—if there had been a lock, I would have locked it—and stood panting as the rabbit on the plate might have panted if finally the fox stalked past and he was safe for . . . how long? An hour? A day?

I couldn't gather my thoughts. James selling Woodsedge, his sudden violence, his still more sudden collapse, my own fear and shock, and my determination not to sell Woodsedge—all those things wound themselves into a tight knot of confusion that finally settled like a lump of lead in my stomach, and I couldn't find any single strand of thought with which I could begin to untangle it.

So I paced, and—after a time—I began to think.

Was I afraid of James? Of my cousin I have known all my

life? Bully though I have always known him to be, he never struck me, only teased and harrassed, always with one eye over his shoulder watching for Dad or Perk.

But they aren't here.

So I *am* afraid of James?

I looked as clearly as I could at that question, and the answer was no, I was not afraid of James, not of the James I knew.

So who was this stranger in my cousin's body, who could threaten to strike me deliberately to force me to do something he knew was against my will?

And why didn't he? He was ready to. The adrenaline was there, the anger and the will—but he did not strike me! Oh, God, he didn't, and thank you! But what stopped him? Was it really illness? Conscience? Some sort of convulsion? Remorse? Fear?

I couldn't even guess. I had to let that end of the snarl go.

What of Woodsedge? What possessed James that he could dream of selling Woodsedge? Was this the awful worry Alison couldn't tell me about? That he promised her he would tell me and still hadn't? He only told me about the desperate need, not the reason for it. Do I have to know the reason? Before I can begin to think what I can do, or ought to do, do I need to know why?

Yes. I need to know. If Woodsedge is to be sold . . .

But there must be a way to raise money, even half-a-million dollars. I don't know. I don't know, but surely I can find out! But I must know why! And I didn't ask him. I didn't give him a chance to tell me. I simply told him "NO!" flatly, with emphasis, and enraged him.

I had slammed the door in his face and left him hanging there with the props knocked out from under him!

What on earth was there left for him to do except blow up?

Kill himself?

The thought, the whole instant memory, struck me a numbing blow. First Aunt Caroline, who killed herself, and overlaying that, the August night Dad found James, drunk and with a wound in his leg. It all happened years ago, but the memory even now was as chilling as a deluge of ice water.

I was halfway across my room, thoughts and phrases scrambling around in my head as I tried to think what I could say but determined to go to him and stay with him just in case, when I heard the crash of the front door closing. I ran back to my southerly window and watched him go toward the garage, his raincoat hunched around his shoulders and his briefcase in hand.

Had he forged my signature and gone off, triumphant, to turn those damned papers over to that unknown law firm, to that unnamed buyer? Was his problem solved and Woodsedge sold?

But there was no victory in his walk, no sign of triumph. My thoughts and emotions tumbled over themselves again as I read the answer clearly, easily. He was far from triumphant. He was in despair!

I didn't get there quickly enough. I ran to the door, shouting and waving madly, thinking he might see me and come back. I called and shouted and waved as the Mercedes turned out of the driveway. I ran toward the lane to intercept him, but I was too late, or the yew hedge was too high . . . or he was in too much pain. He didn't turn his head. He didn't see me.

Silent and alone I stood in the ruined rose garden between the house and the lane, and watched until he turned on the county road heading toward town, then I ran to the house and into his study. I found the phonebook in the center drawer of the walnut desk, its top cleared now of papers . . . but I wasn't concerned about James's papers. I was concerned about James's life.

I drummed his desk at Woodsedge with desperate impatience while the phone in his office in Shearerville rang slowly, pompously, and was answered at last. "Pettyjohn-Brandon, may I help you?"

"Oh yes! This is Joan Brandon. I know my cousin James isn't in yet but will you take a message for him, please?"

"We don't expect Mr. Brandon in today," she sang cooly, while I imagined her hugging the phone between chin and shoulder, filing immaculate fingernails—fiddling while Rome burned!

"Do you know where I can reach him? It's very urgent." I didn't attempt to disguise the near-panic in my voice.

"Just a moment, please." After a few seconds she continued, "You might try this number . . ." And the number she gave me was this one, the phone I was using.

I was just starting to ask whether Mr. Pettyjohn might be able to help me, when he spoke to me. "Can I help you, Miss Brandon?"

His voice slid over the space between us, unctuous, too melodious. But I had no time to be charmed by Branch Pettyjohn's voice. "Oh, yes? Yes, please! I'm looking for James. It's terribly important that I speak to him. Something has come up—" How could I explain? I couldn't bring myself to say I suspected James might be going to commit suicide. It stretched normalcy too far. I said the only thing I could think of. "I . . . just have to talk to him. At once. Face to face. Do you know where I can find him?"

"Well, now, I'm sure we can find him for you. I expect to see him after lunch. Can the important thing wait that long?"

"I'm afraid not. It really can't. I wonder if his secretary has a list of his appointments. Perhaps she knows where he was going this morning."

"Oh, I doubt it. She's not yet that familiar—ah, that was your own number she gave you just now, you know."

"Of course." You're wasting time, I wanted to shout, and you're not finding James! My mind raced to test alternatives. The police? Impossible! They would question . . . and what could I say except that I was frightened for my cousin? Then if they remembered the missing woman they would have to decide whether I were hysterical—and waste more time. There was no point in calling the police. Not yet, anyway.

Call Fitch? He had gone back to Frankfort. Ellen? She doesn't keep track of James. Rob? Rob, stripping tobacco . . . no phone in the shed . . . and he's twice as far from town as I am. . . .

The idea of dumping my worry squarely and honestly on Branch Pettyjohn's shoulders was, for some reason, abhorrent to me. I didn't wonder why. I hadn't time. I sighed audibly as frustration glued my mind into a soggy mash.

I suppose the sigh sounded like a sob. Branch Pettyjohn heard it and purred, "Wel-ll, perhaps there are one or two places I can call for you, or perhaps I can help you myself. Is it something you need? Your car won't start? Something like that?"

"No, nothing like that. It's just we . . . quarrelled and I . . . I don't like him to think . . . I really need to talk to him!"

"Ah-so. Ye-es. I see . . . I, ah, I see-ee." He was silent for a moment, while I wondered whether his seeing would help me find James. I wished he would just tell me what I wanted to know.

He was in no hurry. He continued to purr, his voice musing and soft. "You and James quarrelled, you say? Such a pity. There was no need at all for that. I told James he should be open with you. That you are a sensible young woman and would understand—"

"I . . . I would really like—"

He refused to be interrupted. His purr overrode my voice. "Did he tell you the deed will satisfy his obligation to me? Did he give you a sense of the size of that debt?"

I heard the word "debt," and sharp claws of apprehension wrapped around my throat. Pettyjohn droned on. I caught a few words. ". . . must bow to progress . . . I will be glad to show you our plans for Woodsedge . . . horse park . . . still top secret! A marvelous investment in our county—in our state!"

I tried to stem the flow of words. "But James . . . I need to talk to him at once, Mr. Pettyjohn. You said—"

"It's time we finalized our plans—legalities. And then we can begin raising money." His delight in the prospect was obvious.

I tried to cut my voice across his. "But I haven't signed—"

It had no effect at all. "However, it may be possible for Alison and James to continue at Woodsedge. As soon as the weather settles we will get surveyors out—"

I made my voice stronger than his. "But there is no agreement! I refused to sign it!"

He continued without a pause. "We will not start building until spring, of course, in any case—"

"Mr. Pettyjohn," I literally yelled, "Please! You don't . . . understand!" My voice faltered when I realized I had successfully gotten his attention. I hurried on to the important point. "I *must speak to James at once!* You said you knew—"

He slipped back into his overriding drawl before I could complete my sentence. In a sudden crash of cold desperate anger, I grabbed a line of attack that often worked at home. I made my voice as soft as silk and clipped my words delicately, almost sang them to him. And he stopped talking so he could hear me! "The matter of that agreement of sale will wait, ab-so-lutely, Mr. Pettyjohn, it will wait until I talk to my father. That is final. I am trying to find my cousin for another reason entirely! It has . . . nothing to do with that!" I mentally crossed my fingers when I told that lie, and forced myself to stay calm. I spoke slowly, gently, as though to a hysterical child. "You said there were one or two places you could call. Will you please give me the names of those places, Mr. Pettyjohn? At once!"

Branch Pettyjohn's voice was suddenly harsh and ugly, as rasping as a fingernail dragged across slate. "No. I will leave a message for James to call you—*if* he comes in. That is all." And he hung up.

I looked down at the receiver in my hand, listened to its buzzing, and wished I had his handsome masklike face in front of me so I could throw the phone at him.

But he wasn't there, and neither was James. The only thing left to do was go to town, immediately, and search all the streets and parking lots for the Mercedes. But first I would phone the police and ask them to do the same. On a hunch? A fear . . . And what would I use for credentials? My credibility with the local lawmen had to be zilch!

Forget the police. I would search for James and find him myself! Alone!

I raced back to my room, grabbed my parka and purse, searched frantically for my car keys, found them beside the blue glass bottle, and had my hand on the kitchen door when the phone rang.

It was Alison. There was the same tightness in her voice that had signaled her breakdown on Christmas afternoon, but her first words were reassuring—more than reassuring—and I sat quickly on the chair by the phone and held my head in my hand as she went on. "James and I are here at the Club for lunch, Joan. He says to tell you he's sorry he made you mad at him. He would have called you himself but he thought you might come have lunch with us if I asked you. Will you? We'll be glad to wait for you."

The flatness of her tone made the invitation almost insulting, and I wondered for a moment why they had bothered to call me at all if they didn't want me there. Then I understood. It was really a stroke of genius! I had been apologized to, neatly, and without any fuss or explanation. They thought I didn't know anything more about James's terrible problem that I did an hour ago, that I only knew he was sorry he had made me mad at him and that he was alive and well enough to eat lunch with his wife at the Club. And all the proprieties of good manners had been observed. I was their houseguest, first and foremost, and I must not be neglected in the matter of having my lunch.

Quickly I gave Alison a list of reasons for my not going to

town. I told her about the paintings I wanted to do, the notes I needed to write, the blouse to press, everything I could think of, including my date with Rob to get ready for.

She was easily reconciled to lunching alone with James. There was a lilt again in her voice when she told me she would be home early. "Fix yourself a nice lunch. There's still some soup . . ."

I thanked her most sincerely and hung up.

On the stroke of noon I dialed Perk, relieved beyond words that I didn't have to go into the matter of James's anger or despair, or my conversation with Branch Pettyjohn that was beginning to sound in my thoughts like the gibbering of a maniac. One glaring fact would be shocking enough. "James wants me to sign an agreement to sell Woodsedge," I said in an off-hand voice. "He told me so this morning."

"You aren't serious."

"I wish I weren't! He had papers all drawn up."

"And so—?"

"I refused to sign them and he was . . . a little angry."

"A little, eh? And then what?"

I picked up the pencil and started doodling on the notepad. "I told him to get lost and he . . . did. I had a call from town a minute ago. He's having lunch with Alison.

"Just went on to town for lunch—just like that?"

"Ah-yup!"

"Did you ask him why?"

"Why what?"

"Why he wants to sell the farm."

"He didn't say why." True, I thought. It wasn't James who told me why. "He just said he wants to—correction— *has* to realize his part of the inheritance, and prices will never be better."

Perk was silent a moment, and my mind was entangled again with Branch Pettyjohn's horse park. I drew a series of horses' heads on the notepad. When Perk went on the tone of his voice was distant, almost dreamy. "From what you tell me about the Mercedes and Lincoln, they can't be scraping the bottom of the barrel. Maybe he really wants to buy a condo in Florida or California or something. I seem to remember he liked Florida."

Idle chatter from Perk! I put bridles on my horses and murmured vaguely, "They're talking about a trip to Mexico this winter. Got brochures lying around. I think Alison really dreads the winter here on the farm."

"A trip? Not house hunting?"

"Not . . . not that I know of."

"And you turned him down? You turned down big money, Mops! I don't know what land is selling for these days—"

"He says it's worth more than a million dollars, Perk. Sounds crazy to me! I remember Gramp thought twenty-five dollars an acre was highway robbery when he bought that Fox Cave part. He cracked his knuckles for hours before he finally decided on it!"

It seemed to be the end of the speculation about selling Woodsedge. I went on to tell Perk about my futile search through the newspapers for an obituary that might refer to the woman in Corn Crib Woods, until that subject, too, seemed exhausted.

"So where are you off to tonight, Mops?"

I prattled happily on about Rob and our evening on the town, while Perk encouraged me with a nice mixture of patience and sympathy until I began repeating myself. He went back to James and Woodsedge. "Tell James I'll call him tonight, Mops. I want to talk to him about this business. He doesn't need to have the idea that just because I'm not there I'm not concerned! Tell him I'll call about eight. You're sure they aren't going out or having company?"

"I'm sure. At least, as far as I know." I wondered as I went back to my painting whether James would tell Perk about that massive debt that could cost us Woodsedge.

Chapter Fourteen

THREE YOUNG WOMEN—three harpies!—came calling, and it was all I needed to finish wrecking my day. They rolled up in a creamy Cadillac just as I was laying a delicate wash on my first painting, carefully edging it against the almost-dry ink of my drawing, tipping my paper and watching the wetness move, with that initial excitement when everything can still go perfectly.

But I put the work aside and shrieked at Shirley when she shrieked at me, and hugged her as though she were my favorite person in the world. I didn't hug Caitlin Prentiss. She and I have never been on those terms. I shook hands warmly with Janice Franklin when Shirley introduced us.

"My dearest friend," cooed Shirley. Cat gave a huff, and Shirley quickly amended it. "My *newest* dearest friend!"

I scrambled around to entertain them. In my old jeans and a faded cotton shirt I felt like a scullery maid as I turned up the gas log in the parlor and dashed off to find Alison's sherry and some crackers, while they sat like perfect ladies in their polyester suits and dainty shoes and Shirley extolled the *fantastic* changes at Woodsedge since she last visited here.

We chatted. We sipped sherry. We nibbled biscuits and chatted some more. I desperately wanted a cigarette, but I got another bottle of sherry, too sweet this time, and tried not to look at the kitchen clock. I poured sherry and passed biscuits and chatted on. And when finally it was over I had not only lost all hopes of walking my dog, much less rescuing my painting, but I had learned that Janice Franklin was Rob's steady girl.

Cat, who has always known exactly how to stir up a hornet's nest, broke a silence I hoped meant they were getting ready to leave by asking, softly but not too softly, what I was planning to wear for my date with Rob tonight. I saw Janice's head come to attention, but I didn't know why. Rob's name had not been mentioned until then, and certainly I had not told anyone about our date. Like a silly schoolgirl I asked Cat how she knew and gave her exactly the opportunity she wanted.

"An educated guess, kiddo! You're new meat and he's on the prowl!" Janice was silent, stunned, I suppose, just as I was, while Cat rocked happily back and forth in Grandmother's chair. "I know the man," she went on. "He'll break your heart if you fall for his line. He comes on like gangbusters, but he's cold as ice deep down, just totally heartless. He and that sister-in-law of his are a matched pair of . . . of heartbreakers! I wouldn't trust—" Cat's face had grown a little flushed.

"Another glass of sherry, Cat?" I interrupted her deliberately, fairly pushing the nearly empty bottle at her. "Did you say it was raining, Shirl? There goes the snow, then, and it was so pretty—"

I might as well have been talking to the wall.

Janice spoke softly and smiled sweetly, but her hand trembled when she put her glass on the table. "How sad for you, Cat, that you haven't had a chance to know him better. If you had, you would know he is far from heartless!"

"If he has one, it's made of stone!" Cat's eyes were flashing. "He's out to bed every cute girl in town, and after his mother dies he'll go back to California. He's been living with a girl out there for years. In fact, I think he's already married!"

"*Cat*," shrieked Shirley. "He's my cousin! I know better!"

Cat curled her lips sweetly. "You're a first cousin, darlin', and all you know is the tip of the iceberg—"

"Second," yelled Shirley. "We're second cousins!"

"Well, you're too bloody close, even for Rob Dunstan! You're practically his sister—"

I grabbed the back of the nearest chair to keep from slugging her. "I think I just heard Alison come in," I said loudly. "Have you met her, Janice? The wife of my cousin, James?"

The brawl ended as Alison came to greet my guests. She remarked how dark and drizzly the weather had become, and finally, finally they got up to leave.

But it was not quite over. At the door Cat, still smiling sweetly, thanked me for the lovely visit and added, with a sharp pat on my arm, "You'll get two dates with him but that will be all. That's his way. He'll break a date and send you flowers and you'll never see him again. Just don't lose your head over him, Joanie. And don't, for heaven's sake, let him seduce you! If you can stay out of his bed you'll be all right!"

Janice heard her, of course. She turned blazing green eyes from Cat to me and put out her hand, long and slim and cool. "Enjoy your date, Joan. If it's with Rob, I know you will. Of course, since you'll only be here another week, you probably won't know him well enough to learn he really does have a heart, but I promise you he does!" She didn't have to add that she thought it belonged to her. She was patronizing me because she considered me only a temporary nuisance, and a cousin at that.

Shirley had the grace to apologize when she hugged me good-bye. The others had gone, out of earshot, toward the car, their plastic rain scarves glistening over their heads.

"Forgive me, Joanie," she said. "I never should have brought them out here, or not at the same time. I should have known they'd make a scene. Cat's just scratchin' jealous, is all, because Rob is crazy about Janice. At least that's what I think. Isn't she just darlin'? Well, we'll see you Monday."

I closed the door behind them and, in a daze, went to let

Hector out—too late for even a short walk—and to get his dinner. I thought of the little stone heart on my mantelpiece and my own longing, almost breaking one, and felt the floor under my feet sinking away. Too much sherry, of course, and I desperately wanted a cigarette! Desperately!

But they were in shreds in my wastebasket, and I was glad and miserably sorry that I had found the nerve somewhere to burn my bridges. My pride would not allow me to turn back. If I could just get through the next hour . . .!

But he says he loves me!

How can he know he loves me when he doesn't even know me! I'm not still that little girl in pigtails he said he fell in love with so long ago!

Did he tell Cat he loved her? And Janice? Did he have a little stone heart for each of them, or some other token, some other special little thing that made each of them think she was . . . special?

Surely not! Surely he was sincere! Or is he—like Henrietta—a heartbreaker? Is that what makes Henrietta difficult? Is that all? How can that be bad enough for Rob not to want to talk about her? Cat said she wouldn't trust . . . and I had interrupted her. Trust who? With what?

The questions nagged at me all through a quick shower. I was almost dressed when Alison knocked at my door.

"I brought you a key, Joanie. We're going to the Dexters for that bridge game we missed the other day. We'll probably be home before you are, but just in case—"

I thanked her as I squirmed into the pale blue cashmere sweater I had hoped might be nice to hold, but when I popped my head through the neck I saw a different expression on her face than I had seen before. Her chin was high, and in her eyes there was both a warning and a challenge. "James and I were sorry you couldn't join us for lunch," she began. "He told me what happened this morning, how he upset you. He . . . he said he frightened you, and he's terribly sorry."

What could I say? As an apology, the second one, it was

perfectly satisfactory, but it didn't explain anything or improve anything between James and me. But there was nothing I could think of to say at this moment that would make any difference. Anyway, I was much more concerned about my own affairs than I was about James and his. So I smiled at Alison and told her it was okay. And then I turned away to brush my hair and put on makeup. I wished she would leave.

But she seemed to be in no hurry. She was searching for words, the look of challenge and warning replaced by a kind of longing, almost wistfulness. She began to play with the pink ribbon on the back of my chair, pleating the ends and releasing them again and again. "It just gets . . . harder to explain," she began. "He said he would tell you, but he didn't, did he?"

"Tell me what? Why he needs money? Needs to sell Woodsedge?"

She flinched as though I had struck her. "Yes," she whispered. "He couldn't, could he? Not James. It's . . . pride, of course, and . . . it's out of my hands. He made me promise. I . . . don't think I could talk about it, anyway. Not just now. There are too many things I don't under-stand—too many questions."

She looked so miserable and sad I wondered for an instant whether I should tell her I already knew, whether knowing I knew might help her, comfort her, but for the life of me I couldn't rehash that problem again. Not now. I had had enough of it for one day, and I had my own problems. A reprise of my consoling pats and murmurs of yesterday might help but I literally couldn't spare the time or the energy.

Whatever Alison read in my face as these thoughts went through my mind seemed to make her uneasy. She avoided my sympathy, as she would probably have avoided my hug, by turning quickly away to the door, saying only that she hoped I had a nice evening and that she would leave the back porch light on for me.

In a kind of puzzled frustration I looked toward the window, just as the clock on James's mantelpiece across the hall struck five, and I saw the headlights of Rob's truck turn into the driveway and come to the front porch.

"I have to go. There's Rob." I grabbed my polo coat to pull around my shoulders, dropped it again in favor of my parka because of the rain, and threw her the brightest smile I could manage as I ran past her down the hall to meet Rob.

He was coming up the steps as I pulled the door closed behind me. The porch light was bright on my face. I saw him hesitate for an instant, the look of eager greeting quickly fade into one of concern. He didn't say a word. He just took me in his arms and held me close while I clung to him. One long sob that I couldn't control, never knew was coming until it shuddered through me, shook me and passed, and I leaned against him for a moment, blinking back a rush of tears I refused to let spill over. Without raising my head from his shoulder I said at last, in a silly, giggly voice, "It's been one helluva day!"

He tipped my face up to his and lightly traced his thumbs across my forehead and down over my cheekbones. His hands trailed down to my shoulders, and I felt the strength of his fingers through my parka somehow reviving my own strength. "It's evening now," he said softly. "The day's over and done—something about Arabs folding their tents and stealing away?"

"With '. . . the cares that infest the day.' " Then, because I wanted to, I reached up and pulled his face down to mine and gently kissed his lips. "Thank you," I said.

"Any time! And you may also tell me about your helluva day as we go, if you like. Here, you'd better put your jacket on. The heater's broken and we'll have to snuggle like everything to keep warm!"

A fair amount of snuggling went on while he wrapped a blanket around my legs and got me ready for what might as well have been a ride in an open sleigh. With music. "What do you like?" He indicated a shoebox full of cassettes. "We've got choices from country to Wagner in here, even

150

some hard rock. Something for every occasion and to fit every mood."

"Wow, what wealth! Let's try this, flutes and harps with rain." I handed him a Mozart selection that slipped neatly into the background and caught itself unobtrusively in the rhythmn of the erratic windshield wipers. "How far do we go? Ah, to your house, I mean?"

I caught a glint of blue mischief from his eyes as we turned out into the lane. "Ten minutes or so . . . to my house," he said. "Over the river and through the woods, except that it's the other way around from this side."

We crossed Blair Road on a new extension of the county road that wound through a woods, dark and lonely and scary, as though wild animals prowled here and people got lost. I snuggled closer to him and slipped my arm under his.

"Have you ever smoked?" I asked, without stopping to wonder why I wanted to know.

"Who-eee, I reckon I did! There's a little patch of jungle in Vietnam that's half-an-inch deep in micronite filters!"

"You quit?"

"My reward for getting safely home."

"Was it . . . hard?"

"At first. Accounted for a lot of helluva days."

Too canny, this man, I thought, and snuggled closer still. "But worth it?"

"Ay-up."

I laughed. He had it almost right, that Down East affirmative that always got a reaction from these Kentuckians. "You need an 'h' in there," I said. "More 'ahh-yup.' " He tried it again, and we were still playing with accents when we turned up the lane to the old Hilliard farm. Lights on in the yard here, too, and I could see the long rectangle of the white house that crowned a hill. Rob blinked his headlights as we passed a smaller house that nestled almost out of sight behind a stand of trees and as we turned from the farm road into the driveway the blue yard lights ahead blinked an answer.

"Hey, neat!" I said, sounding just like one of the twins

playing with electronics. "You-all having an identity crisis?"

"That's Archie on guard. We run an armed camp here. I'll tell you all about it." He followed the driveway around to a long back wing and stopped at the porch door. "This is my end of the house and now . . . it's yours!" As he helped me out of the high cab of his truck, the pleasure in his eyes was as welcoming as his words. We crossed the porch and entered his end of the house.

While he hung my parka next to his beside the door I walked over to the fireplace, which was glowing with high-piled coals, and stood for a moment warming my hands. On the mantelpiece in front of me a clutter of tools had been shoved aside to accommodate a pile of opened Christmas presents, their bright paper and ribbons hanging in a glorious confusion of color against the slab of dark walnut. A pair of fleece-lined slippers stood on their toes in an L. L. Bean box and I knew before I read the tag that they were from his mother. A can of tennis balls still sported a red ribbon and there was a scroll of newsprint smudged at the edges with blue and green poster paint, tied again with a red ribbon that small hands had tried in vain to coax into curls.

Over the mantel was what looked like a Kentucky long rifle; under it some feathers had been tucked behind a homemade tomahawk. Hung to one side was a powder flask and shot pouch, obviously antiques, and on the other side a wooden plaque displayed a fine collection of arrowheads and an incongruous fat swag of horsehair, dark red, with the words 'Robin's tail (part)' burned into the wood. I imagined the boy who put it there, the bereaved boy, honest to a fault. When he came to join me I asked him whether his horse had lived here in Kentucky or in the mountains of North Carolina.

"Here. Andy and I spent a lot of time on horseback . . . it seems a thousand years ago!"

"And this is where you read?" I turned to warm my backside and studied the big leather chair surrounded by piles of pamphlets and magazines and books, some on the floor, some on a rickety table, all pertaining to farming. This was where he did his homework, learned to follow the footsteps of so many of his ancestors who had left only a dim, outmoded trail for him to follow. I asked him why he didn't lease his land to someone like Boyd Burden, who had years of experience, not to mention six sons and big machines to help him.

"I like getting my hands dirty," he said. "I like doing it myself. Besides, they left me the land! Without the land I would have to get a desk job in town. I'm eternally grateful to them for hanging on!"

My sigh for the fate of Woodsedge was interrupted by a polite scratch on the hall door. "There's Terhune," said Rob. "Shall we let him in," he asked with a warm, inviting hug. "Or . . . ?"

A moment later the collie escorted us through to the kitchen where a quick glance told me this house belonged to the same severe turn-of-the-century architecture as Woodsedge. We greeted the children having their supper at a long white table that might have been twin to ours. But nothing else was similar. Here there was an ancient cast-iron stove, and copper pots and pans hung in the shadows behind it against walls of smoky beige and worn red brick. In each of two tall narrow windows a crimson fuchsia bloomed with extravagant energy. Opposite the windows, in front of another open fireplace with glowing coals, stood a rocking chair on an oval rug and in the exact center of the chair seat there slept a cat, a golden cat, with its tail wrapped around to its chin and its whiskers draped over its paws.

Rob finished speaking to the children and was waiting for me, again, as so often, watching my face as I looked around.

"Who created this miracle?" I asked him as we went, Terhune in escort again, through the pantry.

"Generations of Hilliards and one small Korean lady

named Setsuko, whom you will meet," he answered as he held open the door to the dining room for me.

I had known a Korean lady once and had some experience with her firm determination to create beauty in unlikely places, like fuchsias hanging in the windows of a sooty antique kitchen. A class act, that one, I thought as I followed him.

Too fast, too fast, I wanted to say as we went through to the front of the house and I caught only glimpses of the pantry, the dining room, and the back hall en route, my head swiveling from side to side with curiosity. And then I realized that this remarkably punctual young man was in a hurry. He had a date with his mother and meant to keep it on time. I'll be back, I promised myself as I hurried along with him, leaving scenic wallpaper, pictures in heavy gold frames, and countless other items of interest, behind me.

A quick glance to my right in the front hall showed me a master bedroom with what seemed to be an Aubusson carpet on the floor. A gentle fire burned in the grate and a small woman in white with coal black hair—undoubtedly Setsuko—was turning down the sheets on the high tester bed. No more than a glance. We were at the parlor door that stood open on the left and there, near a merrily burning wood fire, sat Rob's mother, the lady I had come to meet.

How tiny she is, I thought. How delicate and fragile. And then I realized she may once have been as tall as I but was shrunk now upon herself by the ravages of her disease. She seemed almost to disappear into the plaid shawl that lay across her knees and wrapped her legs. There was little substance left of Mary Dunstan, but an indomitable spirit shone from her eyes and in the smile she gave me as she offered me her hand. I took it gently, and it felt in mine the way a bird I once held had felt, vibrating with energy that was caged in too small and too fragile a frame.

I scarcely remember what greetings we exchanged or how our conversation began, but in no time at all I forgot my almost overwhelming pity for her and heard myself describing the kind of work I had done in New York. She told me she had long ago studied painting in London, "until they made me come home because of the war. . . ." By the time the children came to join us we had a list of things to talk about at some later date, and all without a word from Rob, who stood somewhere in the background trying not to look like a cat contemplating a bowl of cream.

Anne pulled a small rocking chair up to her grandmother's side and sat quietly while we talked. Chip curled up at her feet, feeling carefully to be sure hers were safely out of his way. They listened to our adult conversation patiently enough, but I sensed that they were waiting for something else. There was a kind of eagerness held in check. Then I understood. Mary Dunstan put her gnarled hand over Anne's tiny young one and began, "Now, when I was a little girl . . ."

Her anecdote was a simple one about the way her father dressed when he went out to get honey from his bees, rob them, as she called it, and the children giggled with delight and looked at their uncle to see whether he, too, enjoyed this play on his name. A snapshot of the old gentleman in his bee bonnet and long rubber raincoat, with gloves held tight at his wrists and his trousers fastened over his high-topped shoes, was passed from hand to hand. Thus the children's great-grandfather came alive for them. He became more than a snapshot, more than a formal figure in the gold frame over the desk. He became a real live person whom bees could sting if he was not very careful! It could only have been shown in this way, with a living voice, an eyewitness account. Lucky children, to have this memory to carry with them, to share with this lady and with each other for the rest of their lives.

Setsuko was standing in the doorway when the story was finished. The visit was over. The children gently kissed their grandmother goodnight, and when I said good-night I think she knew, as I did, that there was more than one bond between us.

Anne took my hand as we went into the hall. "Come see my room," she said, and led me through a doorway under the stairs into the oldest part of the house, where the original log cabin formed a wing of its own. Compared with the rest of the house it was miniature, almost a cottage, with the old log walls, leaded diamond-paned casements and deep window seats, chintz cushions and braided rugs.

There was no light on in the first room. "Mamma's," said Anne, and she flicked on the light inside the door. Pristine, impersonal, charming, and vacant, only a pink sweater over the back of a chair showed that anyone had been there. Anne flicked the light off again. She never stepped inside.

We didn't go in the next room just yet, either. Anne said, as we stood in the open door where lights were glowing softly on the bureau, "My room," and I caught a glimpse of a ruffled bedspread on a small brass bed, where a nest of animals waited.

Next, the bathroom, steaming still from the evening wash ups. Then Chip's room. He was reading, curled under a red quilt, the bassett named Cobb at his feet. He raised his head, somewhat reluctantly, from the book.

"Go on," I said. "We won't disturb you."

He grinned his appreciation, and we went on to the room that had obviously been a playroom—and workroom—for several generations. A lovely old dollhouse occupied one long shelf, and a spaceport, still under construction, cluttered a table backed up against the log wall. I gave it wide berth in favor of the child-sized easel in the window corner. Pans of poster paint drying on the tray reminded me of my own first paints—even smelled like mine. The painting on the newsprint pad was large and childish, three figures, a mommy flanked by a boy and girl, their hands locked with scribbled circles of dark blue, the girl and mommy with butter-colored hair in spirals, with a red triangle perched on top, the boy with a man-shaped hat of bright green. There were wide, blue jack-o'-lantern smiles on the children's faces. The mother's face was still blank.

Marvelous! I wanted to praise her for it and looked around, expecting her to be waiting for my judgment as young artists are apt to do, but she was paying no attention to me. She was watching the rain slashing against the window at the far end of the room.

Surprising little girl! "It never rains in Texas," she said when I joined her there. "Not rain that sounds good."

I stood beside her and listened to the beat of the downpour against wood and glass, the obbligato of the wind in the trees, the splashing cacophony of wild streams of water punctuated at random by the drips from the eaves. To me it wasn't bedtime music, it was marching music, a rallying battle song of all the forces of nature, a wild banshee skirl of bagpipes and fifes and drums.

As we left the noise, whatever it was, behind us, I wondered why I had assumed the painting to be Anne's. But Chip would have chosen to paint airplanes, I thought, or trucks. I didn't have a chance to ask her before she opened the door on the left. "The kitchen," she said, and there was the golden cat, sitting now on Rob's lap, 'making bread,' as we Brandons called it, and purring with satisfaction. Sensible cat!

"Don't get up," I said hastily to him when he started to dump the cat. "Don't you dare get up. You're the picture of domesticity!" And he was, sitting there in a worn tweed jacket and his Sunday jeans, with the cat on his lap and the collie at his side. Setsuko was working at a table, arranging a supper tray with all the exquisite care she might bring to a flower design, a lovely bit of still life to carry to an invalid. Rob introduced us and she smiled at me, appreciating, I thought, my own appreciation of the scene.

Anne gave her uncle a warm kiss, helped him stroke the cat a moment, and then said, "You promise you'll wake me if Momma calls?"

"I promise. And if I'm not here Setsuko will."

"But you're going out—"

"Setsuko and Archie will be here—"

"Right here in the house?"

"Right here in the house, until I get home again. Promise."

The little girl turned her eyes to Setsuko for confirmation and received her nod and smile of reassurance. She sighed a little and kissed her uncle again.

The scene was repeated when Chip came to say good night, Rob adding only the admonition to him to have his light out at nine. "The book will keep until tomorrow, sport," Rob said to him. "And you said you'd help me strip. You said at eight sharp."

"Yessir. Right on. I'll be ready."

This is for me, I thought, as I went with Anne back to her room, this world of good rain and good space, where a tired man strokes a cat, where a boy can read until nine and be ready to strip tobacco next morning at eight, where there is tobacco to strip! Where there is work he can do that needs to be done, not a trumped-up job to keep him busy and out of trouble. Lucky boy! He will have no doubts about his own worth, his contribution to himself and his family, and he will have the tremendous satisfaction of having earned his daily bread.

And this child, this girl dutifully brushing her baby teeth, what of her? I sensed a sadness about her, or reserve, a kind of secretiveness. I thought about it as I waited for her and looked around the room. There was neatness and order, almost too much order. It was as though she had only one foot in the door, as though she didn't expect to stay. I remembered her words to Rob. The child is lonely for her mother! Of course! And she misses her father . . . is still grieving for him! I could only thank God that she has Rob, and that he adores her!

I arranged her menagerie of stuffed animals in a nest around her pillow and stood back to admire my handiwork, and realized suddenly that it was all wrong. All but one of the animals were fluffy and recognizable for the species they represented. That last, that different one, was mis-shapen, faded, threadbare, worn out. Should be thrown away, or at least mended and laundered, but I knew why it wasn't and I went over my handiwork again. I put the long-eared pinky grey whatever-it-was under the covers, with its head on the pillow, and waited for Anne to come to bed.

I had been almost right. The only correction she made was to move the pretty ones out of her way, lining them against the head of her bed, where they could keep watch all night but not share her warmth. Evidently they were only stuffed animals and didn't need it. She slipped down under her covers with the favored one and lay waiting for her tuck-in and good night kiss. I asked her his—or its—name, and was told "Buffer. He's my friend."

I gave him a kiss too, and turned out her light thinking how right it was, child and friend sleeping here in this protected place. "Pleasant dreams, sweetheart," I said. I would have liked to stay, talk with her a few minutes, share something of her day with her, or her hopes or fears or dreams, but she didn't ask me to. She simply said good night to me, adding nothing, not even my name, and her eyes followed me as I closed the door.

Chapter Fifteen

Rob was not in his room when I returned there and as I waited for him I took the opportunity to learn more about this man who was more interesting to me than anyone else in the world.

Obviously he likes compartments, I thought as I walked slowly past the wall-to-wall, ceiling-to-floor bookcase that separated his room from the kitchen, a bookcase with an arrangement of shelves and cabinets as intricate as a Louise Nevelson sculpture. I would come back to it.

I knew perfectly well where his bed was and what it looked like. I slept in one at Woodsedge that was almost its twin. I ran my fingers down one side of the massive walnut headboard and over a down quilt, shoved one line of thought aside and got pushed in the back by another and I think if Cat had been standing there I would have scratched her eyes out!

I walked quickly on. There was no way in the world I would risk being found by Rob contemplating his bed!

Between closet and bathroom doors stood a big oak roll-top desk, flanked on each side by file cabinets. The pigeonholes were neat and orderly, the small drawers above them were labelled with firm black printing. Pens and other utensils were lined up above a brass-cornered blotter and a pile of mail lay beside a typewriter, an ancient desk model that stood heavily on a pull-out shelf. I imagined him doing the farm business with quick efficiency and military precision while Terhune slept at his feet.

I went back to the bookcase, noted the neatly organized

music area where the components of his stereo were as austere as my brothers'. Beyond them was a cluster of silver trophies that had been awarded to Robert Melrose Dunstan, for tennis! And that took care of that!

I was bemused at the rich selection of his books, many of them favorites of my own, but others heavy engineering and scientific tomes that were to me absolutely awesome. I ran a respectful finger along their backs and hurried on to the corner by the tall narrow window in the reading area. I was enchanted and my mouth was hanging open with surprise when Rob came back into the room. He knew what I was looking at and smiled rather smugly as he walked toward me.

"Where . . . did you get that?" I pointed to the small framed painting that hung in a niche with a light arranged above it—a small watercolor of waves dashing on a rocky shore.

"Bought it one day in New York," he said, his eyes half-closed with pleasure, the blue mischief just gleaming.

"Where?" When?"

"Place they call SoHo. There was this little gypsy girl in a red skirt with a flower in her hair."

"I never knew! Why didn't you say something, tell me who you were or something!"

"There was a big blond gorilla with you, looking possessive."

I had to laugh. The description fit Cooper Newton rather well, all things considered. "You should have said you were an old friend or something if you recognized me. Did you?"

"I did. I was looking for you. But there was that four carat diamond flashing at me—"

"Just under two," I said, a little sheepishly.

"Huge! Anyway, I felt totally outclassed, so I just grabbed my painting and ran."

"I wish I had known! I . . . I wish you had said!"

What I wished didn't matter in the least to the sudden ringing of the telephone on the oak desk. With a word of apology to me and a curt "Dunstan," he answered it, listened a moment, a frown pulling his eyebrows together, and said, "Check the room number again." A moment's silence, then, "All right. Try at five-thirty in the morning. Yes . . . exactly. Let the phone ring at least ten times, and if she doesn't answer go up there and check. Yes, man! Take the house dick with you! Right! And if she's not there, call me. Call me in either case! Have you recorded this call? What? Yes, man! Log it! Make a note of it! Right." He hung up, none too gently.

I thought the spell was broken, but I didn't realize then that Rob's mind was as neatly compartmentalized as his bookcase. He closed the door on the phone call and opened his arms to me, and I stepped into his embrace and tipped my face up for our kiss. I pressed my body into his, felt the quick rise and fall of our breathing and throb of our heartbeats, the warmth of our two bodies together more than a delight, a bond, an invitation . . .

"I want to keep you here," he murmured as his kisses moved down to my throat. "I want to take you to bed. . . ."

And I heard Cat's voice! Shrieking. . . ! I heard her words, and they blasted Rob's, shattered his gentle, loving words, into glass-hard slivers of pain. I was speechless with it!

Of course he felt me stiffen. Of course he heard the shock in my quick indrawn breath. He raised his head but kept an arm tight around me, and turned my face up to his. I felt my cheeks burning as he searched for an explanation. I don't know what he saw, how much of the pain or destruction of Cat's accusations. I felt only a creeping sense of loss, a frightening hollow fear that sprouted somewhere behind my heart and threatened to pull me down into a vortex of loneliness and despair. I had to do something to stop it, and I had to do it quickly before my mind was numbed with the chill . . .

But Rob's was not! His smile was as warm as ever, his hands as firm and sure as he smoothed them across my cheeks and held me still. "Don't. Don't be distressed," he said softly. "When you're ready . . ." I would have told him I was ready—eager—but his next words put bed out of reach. "Let's go have dinner," he said. "It's forty minutes down the road and I'm hungry."

"Tell me about Anne," I began some moments later.

I don't know exactly how it happened, but somehwere between the bed and the truck, the result of Cat's malicious insinuations was sealed off in a compartment of its own, and when the blanket was wrapped around me again, I snuggled close to him to drive to Shearerville for our dinner. Somehow I was able to resist my feminine instinct to haul that last scene out again and dissect it. I wanted to know how much of Cat's vicious report had been based on fact and how much on her feline nature, but common sense came to my rescue. I knew I would have to come back to it one day . . . but not tonight . . . not tonight if I could help it. We had a precious evening to spend together, and there were a thousand other things more important to learn about one another than why I allowed myself to be deviled by Cat Prentiss.

I began with Anne because we had seen her small face at the window, watching us drive out of the yard. It was a heartwrenching sight, and I think Rob was tempted to turn around and go back, but at just that instant we saw Setsuko open Anne's door. Rob waved to the child as she waved to us before she turned back to Setsuko, and we drove on. "Tell me about Anne," I said.

"Anne is too much like me for her own good," he said as he put a cassette in the tape deck. I didn't recognize the selection, so I read the label as we drove out of the yard under the silver-blue lights. I had heard of Pierre Rampal and his flute, and I listened with interest while Rob watched the turns in the driveway through the fitful swishing of the windshield wipers tearing at the curtain of rain.

We paused at the gate while he operated some sort of gadget on the dashboard that closed it behind us. He went on. "Anne worries too much. Did you know Scots aren't really dour, they're just thinking, just worrying their thoughts around in their minds when people think they are being sullen and silent?"

"And don't give anything away until they are ready!"

"And as little as possible then!" He laughed. "Except in special circumstances, and then they have quite a lot to say. But not Anne. She worries and mulls and doesn't talk much."

"What do you and Anne find to worry about?"

"I've outgrown that kind of worry, that what-if kind. She focuses it on her mother, I'm sorry to say."

"She worries about her mother? I . . . don't understand."

"I'm not surprised. It's . . . unnatural. But, as you have heard, Henrietta worries a lot of people."

I saw a look of anger or disgust darken his face, but he slipped it off immediately when I spoke again. "How old is Anne?"

"Five last Thanksgiving. Seems older, doesn't she?"

"I know so little about the young—about the very young." The words echoed in my mind and associated themselves with another thing, a very special thing. "Does Henrietta read to them?"

"I don't think she *can* read!"

"Do you have any children's books around?"

"Boxes of 'em out in a shed. What have you in mind?"

"*Winnie the Pooh*," I said.

"Good Lord," said my love. "I haven't thought of Pooh in a hundred years! I bet all four Pooh books are in Mother's room. They'd never be put in the shed."

"Anne needs them," I said and leaned my head against his shoulder with great satisfaction as I thought of the animals on her bed and Buffer, and the pleasure ahead for Anne.

"She does," said Rob. "Hang on tight, my love! This stretch of road is like a roller coaster!"

The road suddenly dipped and turned and dropped away,

and with a thundering rattle we crossed Pretty River on a plank bridge. It roared like kettledrums in a Brahms symphony, and when we scrambled up the far side, the cab of the truck was filled with the special wetness of the air around a river in spate. A little shiver chattered through me, and since the road obligingly straightened again, Rob put his arm around me, pulled the blanket tighter, and hugged me closer.

"All straight going from here," he said. "I should have a Jaguar for you, my Joan, or a horse-drawn carriage and deep fur rugs—sable and silver fox—to wrap you in. If you catch cold I'll shoot myself!"

I laughed. "I'm not that fragile, really. I like the cold. The air is good. Please don't worry! About Henrietta . . . is this a good time . . . ?"

He was silent a moment, and I thought he would put her off again, and I was going to tell him not to talk about it since it was obviously such an unpleasant subject for him. I was beginning to wish I hadn't asked at all, when he began.

"I want you to know . . . and this is as good a time as any, here in the dark and the rain . . . with an end in sight." He took another moment, while I studied the windshield wipers and wondered idly whether the right-hand one was more nearly in time to the music than the left. I would not allow myself to speculate about Henrietta. I wanted to know about her, but only as much as Rob wanted to tell me.

It was much worse than I could have imagined.

"Henrietta is your exact opposite," he began with a short sigh. "Absolutely. Except that you are both female and beautiful. She's an insult to both those things, but they are facts and the only good I can say about her. We're at war, she and I, and the children are the prize."

There was silence again except for the engine noises and the tires on the road. I assimilated his words, which I knew had been carefully chosen, and I accepted them as the exact truth as he understood it.

He took his arm away from my shoulder to reach out and

restart the tape, but with an abrupt gesture he repudiated even that slight diversion and turned it off. "She's a bitch." For an instant the epithet hung there without modification or apology. Then, "A rabid bitch who fouls her den, the very air she breathes. She causes pain for the sake of pain—and evil. I've seen her . . . push Anne away . . . down . . ." He stopped a moment, and then, with a kind of tight surprise in his voice, he said, "God, Joan, I can't tell you!"

"Stop then, Rob."

"No. No. You wouldn't believe me anyway. You can't have any conception of such a person. I wish I didn't either, or Mother, or the children." He stopped for a breath of the clean night air, pulled it into his lungs deeply, and began again.

"It will be better if I tell you about my brother Andy. You would have liked him. He was a cheerful guy, impulsive, optimistic, always falling into scrapes, always a pushover for a beautiful woman. I didn't see him often after school. There . . . We were always passing, meeting for a day or two, places like San Diego, Saigon . . . But we wrote a lot. He told me—"

He pulled in another deep breath. The words came faster then. "He got a job with an airline after Vietnam. Flew copilot out of Chicago. He met Henrietta there. Some months later she was pregnant. She wanted an abortion, but he talked her out of it. Bribed her out of it. He wasn't really sure Chip was his child—neither was she—but he chose to believe it anyway. Fed up with killing, he said. And then, when Chip was almost a year old, they got married. More bribery. She wanted—" He shook his head. "I don't know what the hell she wanted, but he wanted her!

"I was in the States then, at Stanford, and I went to Chicago and stood up with Andy." I watched his fingers tighten and loosen on the steering wheel in a kind of desperate rhythm. He didn't look at me. "So they got married. Andy quit the airline and took her and Chip to

Texas, where he could be home more—keep an eye on things, and get in the oil business, which was what he had studied for at A.& M. And then Anne was born. You'll be glad to know she looks exactly like him."

I scarcely recognized his voice when he said those words, the tension was like a wire pulled too tight. I wanted to stop him but I needed to know. To be of any use to him, I had to know.

He went on, his voice vibrant. "For almost two years it looked as though he'd be able to swing it, make a decent sort of life for himself and his family. But she was— Henrietta was just getting things lined up. Finding her way around out there. And suddenly it was all downhill. She went off, no warning—for days, then weeks. I found out later she was selling work papers to illegal aliens—in exchange for drugs, of course. Among other things. But it was worse when she was home. She had the house full of junkies—Andy said bandits and thugs—sleeping all over the house . . . a kind of way station. Andy couldn't . . . well, I think he was having a pretty bad time with drugs by then himself, and he didn't . . . He did make one shot at getting a divorce, but he never got it together. And the kids were getting older—seeing more—and it was getting nastier. 'Sordid' was the word he used when he wrote me about it.

"Then Dad died. He'd retired and he and Mother'd been living here at the farm for a year or so. I was in Nam again, and Andy pulled himself together. He brought Henrietta and the kids back here. I reckon he thought . . . hoped . . . Well, the kids were better off. Chip started school. But for Mother it was really the pits. Henrietta never let a chance go by, tormenting—"

Suddenly he turned to me, seemed almost surprised to see me. "You okay? You . . . hanging on?"

"Yes. But stop, Rob, if you want to."

"No, I want you to know—if you can stand it." He paused a minute as though to give me time to protest.

"I can. Certainly. I just wish . . ." I wanted to share it, to take the bitter—and sordid—with the sweet joy of being part of his life. "I wish I could help somehow."

"You help! Believe me you do! But I'm afraid I'm pretty incoherent. I've never told this to anyone before, and the words get tangled up with the memories and thoughts. Ask me anything that's not clear, and I'll go back."

"All right. But for now, go on."

But he wasn't quite ready. He sidetracked. "Did you know Ellen Perkins can work miracles?"

"I suspected it!"

"She found Setsuko . . . or Setsuko found her. That's a nice romantic story I'll tell you sometime, Setsuko looking for Sgt. Archie Hilliard—Yes, love, there *is* a family connection!—in the States while Archie looked for her in Korea, whenever he could get there. A nice happy-ending story."

I had met Archie Hilliard just before we got in the truck. Rob introduced him as "my henchman," and Archie grinned, a brilliant smile on his handsome black face. I thought they looked like conspirators as they stood there talking about the security of the house, the signals and new gate locks and yard lights. I was glad Archie's story had a happy ending.

"Happy in all sorts of ways," Rob went on. "For Mother the greatest possible blessing. Setsuko and Archie came to live at the farm, and Andy took Henrietta and the kids back to Texas—away out in the desert somewhere. But it just meant she went farther and was gone longer. He found a reliable Mexican girl to live in, but then one day Maria just . . . disappeared. They found her body and put out a warrant for a pal of Henrietta's named Ramon Chivas, but they never caught him. I kept the letters Andy wrote me from then on, I'm glad to say."

His voice became hard now, and the words were cracked off in swift splinters of ice. "She's ransacked the house for 'em a couple of times. Takes me for an idiot, I reckon. Fitch has them. They'll help when we get this thing to court—which we will. She doesn't believe me. She's trying to find an apartment, a place to take the kids to in Chicago and—bottom line, Joan!—I'm damned if I will let them go! It's that simple—and that ugly. I'll fight for custody of those kids with any weapon I need. *Any* weapon!"

In the dim light of the dashboard his face was more than stern, it was harsh with hate. "And now you know something more about me, don't you? I'm not always a nice guy," he said through stiff lips. "The red-haired temper isn't always a joke, nor the Scot's stubbornness." He turned his face to look at me, and his expression began to melt and soften again. "I can't apologize for either of those things, Joan. They're part of me, and I'll just have to take my chances—"

"But you've told me so much more! Don't you see? Things about yourself! Wonderful things!" I laughed a little and wriggled closer to him. "The Scots also have a reputation for loving—fiercely, loyally. Good things like that. I expect Andy was thankful to have you on his side."

The smile he gave me wasn't the least bit fierce. I think it got sidetracked by my own fiercely loving look, and he put his arm back around my shoulders and gave me a hearty squeeze.

"Almost finished," he said. "We'll come back to that point." He was silent a moment and then continued. "Andy was desperate. He rewrote his will last winter. Left everything to the children, except a bottle of tequila to Henrietta—just for the record. He made me the executor. And he had a good lawyer write it. She's tried to break it, of course, but she'd have to prove him insane which he wasn't. He wrote me one last time, explaining the whole thing, and even had his signature witnessed when he was through. He knew a lot about her by then and knew how desperately she would want the children, just for their share of my Dad's estate, and he knew what kind of fight she'd put up until she got 'em—which she won't."

A breath of silence before he went on. "Then last spring Andy . . . said he'd given it his best shot. . . . Flew his little crop duster into a tornado. Went out looking for one. Even told me he was going to. Not in so many words, of course, but you know how brothers are. We had a sort of code, an understanding. And it was like him. He'd always let me know when he got in too big a mess and needed help to bail out. Only this time he bailed himself out and left me to take care of the kids. He knew I would. And he gave me all the tools I need. I'll make a decent life for them or . . . well, there *is* no alternative.

"And that, my lovely, sane, warmhearted, real-live-girl, is the whole bucket of worms. I'll enlarge any point you want to know. I don't want any secrets from you. But I'd as soon talk about anything else just now. Even the weather!"

Chapter Sixteen

WHAT I WANTED was a cigarette. I wanted to register my sympathy by tamping the tobacco down with short, sharp thumps, and then with a flick of my thumb light up the cab of the truck with a flash of fire. I wanted to pull the smoke deep into my lungs and exhale it through my nose like an angry bull, as an outward sign of my disgust for that woman and my vigorous partisanship with Rob.

But I had no cigarette. I dug my fingernails fiercely into the palms of my hands for an instant and then remembered the music. "How about some nice fighting music," I asked and began to rummage vigorously through the box of tapes. "How about Wagner? *Die Valkyrie* to go with the weather and dark thoughts?"

He put it on and smiled at me. "You are something else, Joan Brandon. I might have known! Are you up for a thick steak at Pal's or four courses at the Club?"

"Steak . . . and a cozy corner. Do they have one?"

"I believe it can be arranged."

It was, by a cute curvaceous headwaitress, who called Rob "Rob-darlin' " and smiled much more sweetly than was necessary. Certainly he didn't have to smile back at her or give her a very suggestive grin and raised eyebrow when he asked for a table in a cozy corner! She led the way to a secluded banquette with her hips swinging seductively, and handed us menus. I was rapping a tattoo on the table by the time she laid a much-too-familiar hand on Rob's shoulder and told us our waitress would be Ginny and she would be here in just a minute. She had the nerve to smile at me before she glided away, her voluptuous hips undulating . . .

When I met Rob's eyes he burst into laughter. "I'm sorry," he said when he got his wits back. "I should have introduced you. She's Peggy Something-or-other, my third or fourth cousin—on the Dunstan side. She just got married a few weeks ago. Her daddy is Pete Strawbridge. We did some hunting together this fall. First time I've ever hunted quail . . ."

I let him prattle on about the joys of hunting on his own farm because I loved the happiness in his voice, but my thoughts came to attention when he said Pete was the deputy sheriff of Brandon County.

"Under Sheriff Dennis?"

"Yes. Do you know our stalwart officer?"

For just an instant I wanted to tell him about my encounter with Sheriff Dennis, to pour out to him my miserable story about the body in the woods, but I caught the words back. After all, there *was* no body in the woods, not officially. Officially the dead woman was only a figment of my imagination . . . or worse. There was nothing Rob could do to change that and nothing I could gain by a recital of it. But there was a lot I could lose. I could endure Alison and James thinking whatever they thought, but I could not risk even a remote suspicion on Rob's part that drugs had played any role in that horror. That road was far too hazardous, so I held tight to my resolution to consider the matter closed. "Only slightly," I said to Rob, and to the waitress, who was standing at Rob's elbow, I said, "Rare, please." And the moment passed.

To supply a happy-ending story of my own I told him about Perk, and for a few minutes we joyfully traded memories of youthful adventures on the farm, while Henrietta drifted into the shadows. But she hung over our cozy corner like an evil genie until finally Rob was drawn back to her. He told me about her Christmas presents to the children, roller skates for Anne, and a plastic ship model, all

172

assembled, for Chip. "And she topped it off with a singing telegram, phoned at dawn on Christmas day. The poor guy had to sing it twice, once to each kid, to the tune of Jingle Bells. Some ridiculous jargon about the joys of Christmas in Chicago. We went out and had a snowball fight afterwards to clear our heads!"

I was not the stuff of the heroes who stand and wait! I could never be a passive bystander like a rag doll or a floppy animal. I put my hand on his arm. "I'm a whiz at snowball fights, Rob. Let me help."

I watched him think it over, watched his bushy eyebrows slide up and down, into a frown and out again. Then he turned to look at me, his face more serious than I expected. "No. Thank you—" He wrapped my hand warmly in his. "You already help more than you know just by listening and . . . caring. I needed to tell you about the kids and Henrietta. I need you to understand. But I can't let you get involved in it. It will be all I can do to keep the kids . . . safe." He laughed a short, mirthless laugh. "Sounds like a soap opera, doesn't it? And that's not far off the mark. You just don't know!"

"Tell me, then!"

"She fights dirty. No rules, no laws. She doesn't just break laws, she defies 'em. With her it's tooth and claw. You wouldn't believe!"

I had a quick vision of the reliable Mexican girl who disappeared. There were too many such visions in my life just then, but I may have misunderstood. "Tell me," I said again. "I need to know!"

"You do, don't you? You being you—" His eyes were searching my face again, reading whatever he found there. "Little fire-eater, that's what you are!" I thought for a moment he wouldn't take me seriously, that he would close that subject and go off to a more amusing one, but I underestimated him. He really wanted to talk to me about it. Talking helped.

He kept my hand in his and began again. "It took me

almost two weeks to get to Texas after Andy died. I had to get untangled from the army and come and check on Mother, and finally I got down there to settle up Andy's things. I didn't warn her I was coming. I just walked in on her one day. Waded my way through a mess of thugs. She was running some kind of illegal alien safe-house just then—a sideline for her deals with Ramon and the drug trafficking. Anyhow, I found the kids huddled together in a back room. Anne clinging, too scared to look up, and Chip holding her, his eyes like saucers. . . . I hope I can forget that someday." He was staring off into space. He said it softly, musingly, as though he didn't expect anyone to hear him or respond.

"You can start forgetting it right now," I said, as softly as he. "I'll remember it for you."

He put his lips in the palm of my hand for a moment. "Rare gift you have, my love," he said. "You . . . hear!"

New! It was all new! I made a difference to him! My being there, sharing his problem, listening and hearing. I *mattered!*

He went on. "I didn't let them out of my sight after that. Just tucked 'em under my arm and took them wherever I went, lawyers, court, motel, everywhere. She had us followed, which was dumb. I told her where we were going, even invited her along." He laughed that short harsh laugh again. "I ended up sleeping with a gun under my pillow, if you can believe it. She was pleased when I told her. She carried a pistol in the waistband of her skirt—note skirt, not slacks!—and a knife in a boot-top. I think she saw herself as a kind of female gang leader in the glory days of the old west. Goodness only knows what she had up her sleeves! She told me she needed the weapons as protection against rattlesnakes, and rolled her eyes at the Mexicans lounging around so I couldn't possibly mistake her meaning. That was the day before the kids and I were due to leave, to fly out of there. I invited her to come along, but when I reminded her she couldn't run around armed to the teeth

like that in Kentucky, she decided not to. I thought—
hoped—we might never see her again, but she was up here
two weeks later and said she had decided to turn her
"business" over to Ramon so she could be with her children!

"Two days later she was feeding them sleeping pills and
tranquilizers—she said to keep them quiet! So I packed her
off to town. She promised to reform, got her old job back—
at Pettyjohn-Brandon, and in another week was stirring up
trouble there." He sighed again and continued almost apologetically. "We get into the rumor area now, my love. I
don't know first hand what she's up to right now, but with
her everything has to be melodrama, high intrigue, a web of
lies and subterfuge and malicious plots, with her at the
center like a spider." He was silent for a moment, then
continued. "She's got some kind of psychosis. Paranoia
with a twist of sadism or something. I don't know much
about such things, but maybe we can get her straightened
out someday. I don't know. But the kids come first. Far and
away first. Top priority!"

Certainly the children are top priority! I thought of those
two, asleep in their rooms under the stairs, guarded by
Archie-the-henchman, under the wing of this careful, caring man, who has every intention of keeping them there.
They wanted to be told if their mother called, not hoping
she would but fearing she would, and that she would try to
take them off to a place unknown, a city apartment where
the rain is a nuisance and dogs aren't allowed, in their
minds a place of threats and dangers, of horrors unthinkable . . .

"Legally," Rob went on, "there's no way I can stop her,
not yet. Legally I'm only executor of Andy's estate, not the
children's guardian. But she always needs money, so she
needs me. Her schemes have a way of backfiring before she
gets to the payoff. She get tangled in her own webs more
often than not." He laughed and shook his head. "She's
trying to pick up where she left off when she was here

before. I don't know who's financing this Chicago venture, but I hope he's ready to lose his shirt."

"He?"

"Undoubtedly. She never deals with women, just ignores them or torments them or—" He shook another thought aside. "Her main battery is her female wiles, gathering, ah, susceptible, gullible, vulnerable men around her, and then playing them off against one another. Andy had a taste of that." He reached out for my hand and held it tight. "I told you she's an insult to her sex!"

"How can you prevent her taking the children up there? If she finds a place and gets a job, how can you stop her?"

"So far, only stumbling blocks, one at a time, strategically placed. I got a letter just this morning from an apartment manager up there saying she gave him my name for a credit reference. She handed me a neat little stumbling block that time. I was glad to tell him a few hard facts about her credit—in writing!" I thought he was enjoying the prospect of tripping her up, but then his face sobered again. "You see, to get legal custody of the kids I have to prove she's an unfit mother. On the face of it, it's a nasty thing to do, but by any decent standards she *is* an unfit mother. I can't afford to forget that or make excuses for her. That phone call a while back is an example. She's checked into the hotel she said she was going to, but she hasn't called the kids, and she promised she would. Breaking promises to those kids, after what they've been through, is pretty damned unfit in my book, and if I have to wake her at five-thirty tomorrow morning I plan to tell her so!" For a moment his fingers were almost painfully tight around mine. "I wouldn't mind, if it weren't so rough on the children," he said softly.

"Hell for them, I should think, waiting . . . worrying . . ."

"It is. I've talked to Ellen about it, ways to blunt the pain for them." He drifted off for a moment into his thoughts and then came back with a smile. "We've found a few. Truth, for one. I keep them informed about what's going on. Tell them everything they want to know. Amazing how much they understand, really. And security, basic security. The armed camp with Archie is for them. We walk a pretty tight line there because if she gets the idea it's a contest she'll try tricks like trying to snatch them away in the night. She couldn't do it, and the youngsters know it, but it's the sort of thing she and her thugs would love to try. It's the last thing we need, so we tell everybody who's concerned that the security is for Mother, that she's deathly afraid of the soldiers roaming around, which is a joke! Mother's never been afraid of anything in her life!"

"So they think they are protecting her?"

"Well, no. They know that the security is for them but they have to pretend it's for Mother. Gets pretty complicated, but they laugh about it . . . sometimes. Kids are great at games of make believe, you know. Chip is trying to talk me into getting a Doberman and Anne . . ." His voice trailed away.

"Anne—?" I urged.

"She's beginning to catch on. We've just about got trust established. She *wanted* someone to trust. They both did."

"Anne adores you." I breathed it into his ear like a soft sexy secret.

"And you?" His reaction was beautiful, all warm and hopeful, his eyes inviting.

"Someday, maybe . . ." I paused for just the lightest imaginable nip on his ear. "Someday maybe she'll adore me, too."

For a moment it was just as well our corner was not only cozy but deserted. But then Ginny brought our bill, and after a final kiss we went to get our coats.

"There's a reasonably peaceful place for dancing not far from here," he said. But in the bright lights of the foyer I could see the fatigue on his face, the shadows under his eyes and pallor behind the freckles and sunburn. I was feeling somewhat less than eager for a raucous band myself, but I wasn't expecting the clock over the cashier's desk to read well after eleven. The cashier was, in fact, yawning. I looked around at the empty tables.

They had been good to us!

I made a quick detour to find Peggy, who was helping Ginny clear our table. I put my hand on her arm. "Thank you for not running us out. I had no idea it was so late."

"That's okay," she said with a smile. "I haven't seen Rob laugh like that in a long time. Have a nice evening." And she turned back to her work.

I was still thinking about what she said when we got in the truck. "Take me home, Robert," I said as he wrapped the blanket around me. I laid my finger on his lips when he started to protest. "It's been a long day—and a lovely evening. Thank you."

We said little on the drive home, each of us wrapped in his own thoughts as the music of the flute wound softly around us and clouds scudded across the moon.

Each with his own thoughts. I could only guess at his as he sat there with his arm around me, watching the road, the county road to Woodsedge with its fat right angle turns. No ice now, only occasional puddles that might have drowned the Volkswagen but were no trouble for Rob's truck.

My own thoughts were in a turmoil. Worse. In a raging battle. I was at war with myself, my two natures fighting and raging, knocking against each other, pulling and hauling, pushing and tearing. Each truly me, truly Joan, while the body of Joan lay warm and quite in his arms.

I can't let him go! I won't!

You have to. Don't be idiotic!

An hour! I only ask an hour!

Brutal. There's a phone call at five-thirty, and Archie and Setsuko leave on their vacation at six. . . .

To be gone until Tuesday! I won't see him again! Won't have another chance . . . alone . . .

Cool it, for heaven's sake! You can't be so greedy!

But I was—utterly greedy! I wanted him! All of him!

Some sane part of me knew it wasn't fair. The better

Joan, I suppose. The children come first, that Joan said firmly.

But what about me! What about what I want? Damn Cat! I want another chance, now! Tonight! I'll go home with him—

Oh, ducky! Just fine! And greet his mother and the children at breakfast? That will be charming!

An hour, then. At Woodsedge—

Where ghosts pounce on you when you light a cigarette?

Well, I gave them that! They owe me!

You can't ask him. You can't even hint!

Why not? Why the hell not?

For his sake, you . . . ghoul! For his sake! The man's worn thin with worry! That fine skin will never learn to hide fatigue.

But if he asks—

He won't. Not at Woodsedge.

The hell with Woodsedge! Damn the ghosts. It's not fair!

There are the children—

Damn the—

Joan!

I came to my senses.

What did he hear? A sob? A sigh? I don't know. Wrapped as I was, held by his arm against his chest, my hair tickling his chin, I don't know. His arm tightened around me, and I felt his breath in my hair, felt his lips . . . But he said nothing, just drove on, into the yard at Woodsedge.

You'll have to fake it, Joan. You'll have to! You think you love him? Prove it, then! Loving is caring, isn't it? Taking care of? Protecting? Well, prove it! Prove you're a big girl!

I sat up so he could maneuver into the driveway at Woodsedge, and I searched my mind for some bright remark, to end the evening with laughter . . . somehow. Leave him laughing—somehow—while I stood alone and watched him drive away.

But what I said surprised me. I hadn't realized it was so close to the surface of my thoughts. "Rob?"

"Hmmm?"

"Who's Janice?"

"Janice Franklin?"

"Yes."

I waited for him to go on, but he said nothing more until he had pulled up to the back door, where the lights of the porch shone into the cab, and suddenly I wished he could not see me so clearly, or read my thoughts so easily. I held my face as still as I could and studied my mittens, turned them this way and that in my lap, held them up to the light, looked everywhere I could think of except at Rob.

And then, of course, I had to look at him.

His expression was serious and sweet. "Janice was my girl, the closest I had to one, anyhow, until Christmas Eve. I don't know whether we're still friends or not because I haven't asked her. There are no commitments between us, no obligations, no promises, and no strings, so she's just . . . Janice Franklin." He cocked his head at me thoughtfully for a moment. "Do I sense Cat Prentiss in this?"

My laugh was rather thin, but at least it was honest. "Shirley brought Cat and Janice out to Woodsedge this afternoon. We . . . drank too much sherry!"

"Lord love a duck! You did have a helluva day! And I bet Shirley was no help at all."

"She tried—"

"But she has too many troubles of her own. If she'd just slow down and think! But I don't know about Cat." He laughed a little wryly. "I wish I'd been a fly on the wall!"

"Oh, no you don't! You would have thought she hated you!"

"She does. I made her angry at me!"

"How?"

"Now that I can't tell you. Gentlemen don't!"

"Oh. Oh! All right. I see! It doesn't matter, really, anymore. Kiss me good night, Rob."

Chapter Seventeen

I WOKE IN the morning longing for him. Simply that. Longing for him. And in a warm, dreamy euphoria I loved longing for him. I drifted in and out of drowsy almost-satisfying dreams while the dripping roof overhead sent silver rivers sliding down my windows.

Until the ringing telephone brought me back to the real world.

When I got to the kitchen I found Alison already there, up to her elbows in flour. "Oh, I'm sorry, Joanie. I thought you were out with your dog. That was Rob. He says he'll call back at noon."

"Oh, yes, that's fine," I said, still not far from my dreams. And then I thudded back to earth. "Is James up? I'd really like to talk to him."

"Up and gone. He had a meeting with Branch." She swung around as she spoke and made a big thing about rattling utensils in a drawer.

"Did he get a call from Perk last night? I mean, before you all went to the Dexters?"

"No. No one called until Branch this morning. And Rob, of course. Was Perk planning to call?"

"Yes. He has some idea for Woodsedge. I don't know what, but he wants to talk to James. Maybe he'll catch him today. Will James be back for lunch, do you think?"

"There's no telling, I'm afraid. It's nice of Perk to call, of course, but I'm afraid there won't be anything he can do. I think . . . we really don't have any choice . . . about selling the farm, you know. There really is nothing else we can do, Joan."

I started to say what I said to James yesterday, that we always have a choice, but in view of her very firm conviction that we did not, it would have sounded like a very limp platitude or a very rude contradiction. I watched her making cream puff shells and tried in vain to think of something constructive to say. She seemed increasingly uncomfortable with me standing there. She didn't exactly say "run along and play" the way Grandmother would have, but that was the message I got. I had to let it go.

To deal with a rainy morning I took Hector for an extra long walk; well, not exactly a walk, we spent the morning prowling through the buildings in the barnyard and even went, during a break in the rain, down to Two-Great's log cabin.

Rob was never out of my thoughts.

What I want to do is marry him! I've known him four days and I want to marry him! I could say the wedding vows right this minute with total sincerity, because they are exactly what I mean. I want to be part and parcel with him. His other half, and he mine. He suits me perfectly! Perfectly!

I had to laugh. We're far from perfect, Rob and I, except perhaps for one another. Shirley says his eyes are cold, that he scares her when he looks at her with that special intensity that I love! Shirley prefers brown eyes, soft and gentle, while Rob's eyes are a blue as compelling and clear as the zenith of our northern skies. They suit me! His lean hardness suits me, his strength and grace, his hands, so sure and warm. I'll be touched by those hands . . .

I thudded to earth again, called Hector away from futile digging in the rotted floor of a cabin, and trudged homeward.

Cat's crazy if she thinks he has no heart. Obviously she has never seen him with his mother, or the children, or stroking a cat. Some girls might think he's cold, abrupt and commanding, that his gestures are too controlled or his sentences too clipped, that his eyebrows are too thick or his face too thin and craggy. His mustache soft . . .

I rubbed Hector dry and put him back in his pen, and went back to my room, my thoughts romping out of control, my breath a little short, my pulse a little fast, and began to brush my hair vigorously to get my blood back in my head where it belonged!

He has faults, of course. Liabilities. Rich, Cat said, and she should know better. A man who owns a farm has a rich potential for life-shattering debt—unless he sells out and then he isn't a farmer any more, as Cat knows perfectly well. But it's a rich way of life, space and privacy, a big old house and trees to shade it, hard work and quiet . . . We can be quiet together! With all the things we have to say and learn about one another, still we can be silent. We communicate just by breathing the same air!

You are having fun, aren't you! Go back to faults.

Well, some girls might think the children and his mother . . .

Go on.

They might resent the attention, sharing the time—

They might? And you're some kind of saint or something?

Oh, no. Never. I only wish I were!

So you admit you're resentful? Jealous? Call a spade a spade, why don't you?

All right, I admit it. But it's a fault in me, not in him.

That's interesting! Go on.

It's all part of him, part of what I love in him, that caring, that tremendous capacity for loving and caring! It has no limits! It's part of what I want to be part of!

I was standing at the kitchen phone at noon, and James's clock had not finished striking when it rang. "Saturday afternoon off," said Rob. "Will you go to the mall with us? A treat for Chip. . . ."

Three o'clock finally came, and with it came Rob and the children in the battered green truck. It was a brilliant afternoon. Wind swept boiling grey clouds across a transparent cobalt sky, that miracle color that nature can produce with the flick of a north wind, and that artists can't, not with any combination of paints in their box.

Something made a connection in my mind between the flying clouds and "A capital ship for an ocean trip," and in a few minutes we were singing "The Walloping Windowblind," chorus and verse. Rob joined in on the "blow-ow-ow" and the "play-a-aay" with a magnificent booming bass, while Chip helped me with the treble. Finally, like a little bosun's whistle, Anne piped up with the rest of us. We went from there to "The Rovin' Kind," slightly expurgated, and I was doing an impromptu verse when we passed the part of the county road that had been the scene of the battle that had raged, Joan against Joan, last night.

So this is what it's all about, I thought. His love is like the widow's cruse of oil—there's always more than enough to go around! There's enough for all of us, even for me—especially for me, his eyes said—and because I'm so rich I can share my love, too. I put my face down into Anne's sweet-smelling hair and got my reward when she sighed and snuggled closer to me.

The mall was crowded with families on outings, groups splitting off and reuniting, meeting and losing one another. The central place was a low stage with seats, where elderly people were stationed to keep the coats and an eye on the baby, and as we walked past it no one would have thought we weren't a family, too; Chip tugging at Rob, pointing at something in a shop window and Anne, with her hand in mine, her lovely hand, soft and clinging, like the first tendril of a vine reaching up. I thought, if this is how I get to wherever, it's perfectly fine with me.

Our first major stop was a bookstore. Anne was trying to choose between a book of horses beyond-nature-beautiful and one of frogs who wore marvelous formal clothes, tight pantaloons and cutaway coats that reminded me of some drawings in a childhood book, I couldn't quite remember which, when young Molly Perkins joined us. I slipped into the background to watch while they went through the books together. Another dividend of keeping the family ties intact, I thought. Anne was pleased that this older cousin would take time to say hello, much less give her attention to this weighty matter of choosing a book. A small thing, as things of this world go, but immense, really, when it is multiplied by the number of times those two will be thrown together in all the future they will share. A treasure for each of them, this feeling of comfortable relationship, this blood-in-common tolerance and concern, the security of belonging to the herd.

It was quite a herd! Chip was studying automobile books, Christine and a friend were leafing through magazines, Ellen talking with Rob near the front of the store, and Uncle Leland sitting on the podium outside, with coats piled around him, watching the crowds go by.

And suddenly Rob was not talking to Ellen, not standing relaxed and happy, but galvanized, alert, like a dog on point. I could see the tension in the poise of his head as he looked through the glass front of the store to a figure lounging there. He turned and shot a swift glance toward Chip and then to Anne, met my eyes with a flash of blue, his face cold and hard as steel. He said something to Ellen and in the next instant was out of the door, and I saw the lounging figure come to life as he turned to confront Rob.

I felt Anne's hand clutching my parka. She was looking toward the door, her body pressed into mine, trying to burrow out of sight but too fascinated by her uncle and the bushy-haired swarthy man who faced him to tear her eyes away. For an instant I wanted to hide her, to stand between her and what was obviously an animal confrontation outside, the two men, equal in height and weight, who stood toe to toe, eye to eye, beyond the glass.

And suddenly I was glad she saw. The words they spoke were inaudible, but their effect was perfectly clear. The swarthy man faded, shrank a step back from Rob, two steps, and three, trying to move away but fascinated, compelled to listen. Rob said something that jerked the man's head to attention again, and then he lowered it, swung it from side to side like a beleaguered animal, and finally, cowed and beaten, he moved away, melted quickly into the throng of shoppers, and vanished.

I had Anne in my arms when Rob came back to us and took her in his own, holding her, soothing her and loving her while she clung to him, her small body shaking, her face buried in his neck.

"Was that Ramon?" Chip asked, his face greenish white under his freckles. He tugged on Rob's arm and rolled his eyes toward the door, eyes round with such fear as a child should never know.

"It was. He's gone now, sport. He had to leave. You won't see him again."

"How—? What did you say?"

"A number of things that did not please him at all. Things he didn't want to hear." Rob laughed with a light-heartedness I couldn't believe he felt. "Some of them are even true! For example, Pete Strawbridge was standing just behind Uncle Leland over there, watching the whole thing. Pete has been expecting Ramon might show up here for quite a while, and now Ramon is very sorry he came." Rob's voice had become very matter-of-fact, as though the things he was saying were things he said every day. He took a handkerchief out of a pocket and wiped Anne's face with it as she turned to look toward the door. "Feeling better, sweetheart? That guy won't be back. Promise! So you don't need to worry any more. He's gone. He'll be lucky to get out to the parking lot before Pete catches him."

"But what if he gets away? What if Pete can't catch him?" Chip's face was flushed now and his eyes agleam with excitement.

"He'll catch him, all right. You can count on it, he and the narks. . . ."

"Narks—" breathed Chip in a kind of awe.

"Narks," said Rob firmly. "And police cars and sirens and lots of things like that. They'll catch him, no doubt about it."

Even Anne responded to the flavor of the TV-conditioned images—the good guys chasing and finally catching the bad guys. She wiggled out of Rob's arms back to the floor, gave herself a little shake, and put her hand in Rob's to lead him back to where Molly was still waiting, the books in her hands, a puzzled concerned expression on her pixie face. Anne's voice was thin and high with only one small catch in it. "Do I want the book about frogs or horses?"

There were five of us in the cab of the battered green truck when we left town for Woodsedge early in the evening. Ellen had persuaded Rob to let the children have supper with Molly at her house, and we had gone shopping for carryout pizzas. It was, on the surface, very casual and impromptu. There were even side trips into one or two other stores. Nothing was hurried or dramatic about any of it, but Anne never let go of Rob's hand and Chip was never more than a step from his side.

There had been no chance to talk alone with Rob. He obviously had no intention of rehashing that encounter in front of the children, seemed perfectly content, in fact, to forget it. But I was fairly bursting with the need to know what was going on, what he thought might come of this new development, where he hoped it might lead and how soon . . . how soon. . . .

But he was acting as though the incident had never happened!

I tried to hide my concern, but I felt bound, handcuffed and shackled, with frustration and anger. I tried to be as casual as he was, but I was choked into silence by the overt cruelty of a woman who could allow thugs to terrify her children. I thought I had managed very well to be brisk and cheerful in spite of the lingering tremors of shock, when Rob encountered me in one of Ellen's many hallways and greeted me with a swift hard hug. "I love you," he said softly, and after our kiss he hugged me again. "This all looks pretty cold-blooded, I know, but there's nothing constructive we can say about it just yet. But Ramon may be the break we need. Pete will let us know." As we turned back to the kitchen and the pizza party, he put his lips against my hair once more. "Do you think you can sing some lullabies for that crowd on the way home?"

I told him I knew one or two.

"Molly's coming with us," he said. "She can help you, can't you, Widgeon? Don't you know some lullabies?"

The little girl I had thought so shy and wispy on Christmas Eve took the pose of a lady rocking her baby in her arms and began, immediately, on the spot, singing in a lovely clear soprano the first few words of the Schubert Lullaby—in German! "I can thing the Hanthel and Grettle prayer, too," she lisped with an elfin grin, while I stood with my mouth hanging open.

"Later," said her mother firmly. "Get your things ready. Anne, help her get her things together, there's a good girl. Chip, get their coats for them, will you, please? It's time to go."

So five of us drove to Woodsedge, where they would leave me. Rob walked to the porch with me and held me close . . . close . . . before he kissed me.

"If I were Anne, I'd have nightmares," I said into his shoulder while I clung to him for another moment.

"Molly will help. They'll sleep together tonight, and Molly's not prone to horror, as you can guess."

"No. I had no idea!" I laughed. And then, because it was what I wanted to say and I saw no reason why I shouldn't, I added, "Who will sleep with you?"

He laughed a delighted soft chuckle, and his arms tightened around me. His eyes were alive with love, sparkling and dancing with it. "Soon, my love, soon! You'll see!" And he kissed me, a warm, promising kiss, before he turned to drive away.

Chapter Eighteen

THE CLUB. IT was never called anything else. When people in Shearerville said "the Club" they meant the Shearerville Country Club, and as it said on the shield-shaped sign at the gate, it was for members only.

If I wanted to start a social revolution in Shearerville I would picket the Club. The town would collapse and dry up like a beached whale because the Club was the filter through which the lifeblood of the town passed. It was the smoke-filled back room where the town politics were fabricated. It was the playing field on which the town battles were fought, and the ballroom in which the victories were celebrated. The town revolved around the Club, and if you didn't belong to it, you simply didn't belong.

It was huge, elegant, and very expensive.

It had no black membership, and precious few Jews.

It was where the people who "counted" said whatever it was they said. It was where the backbone of convention and custom and manners kept all the other bones of the community in their proper place. It was where the skeletons of the past were enshrined and nourished and worshipped.

On the surface.

But under the surface it was a dogfight. Who was it who said people are scarcely human? They were well-controlled, well-fed dogs, who never openly snarled before they bit, who challenged one another not with raised hackles and bared teeth but with raised eyebrows and knowing smiles. And the softer their voices became the more wary their listeners were.

It was as tricky as a bog and as treacherous as icy wave-washed rocks!

It scared me almost witless.

But I went there with Alison on Monday for the luncheon she gave for twenty-five or so young women to honor me, many of them cousins, others I had known since childhood, and a few, like Janice Franklin and Myra Pettyjohn, were newcomers. It was quite a party. We had a charming room to ourselves, cocktails, pink and frosty, delicate, very salty hors d'oeuvres, chicken Kiev, and an elegant fresh fruit salad. And champagne, expertly selected by James, in crystal tulip glasses. Soft music was piped in from some-where, and the table was set with sterling silver and spar-kling white damask. There were tiny bouquets of silk flowers for favors at each place. It couldn't have been lovelier.

On the surface. At first glance.

Under its polite veneer it seethed with gossip and intrigue and emotion.

Janice Franklin's greeting was cool and reserved, which I easily understood, but why Myra Pettyjohn, overladen with jewelry and exaggerated makeup, put on such a show I had no idea. She arrived late and marched straight across the crowded room, shoving other guests aside as she came, and looked me up and down as though I were a freak in a circus before she put out her thick damp hand, and then dropped mine at the first touch as though it were contaminated. If she wanted to embarrass me because my cousin owed her father a lot of money, I don't think she made her point very clear. If she hoped to demonstrate her overbearing person-ality she did a pretty good job. And she seemed fascinated by me. Every time I looked around, there she was, standing close to me, watching, hanging onto every word I spoke as though I were a prophet or celebrity. She spoke to no one else except Chrissie, and never smiled at anyone, especially not at Alison.

It wasn't until much, much later that I began to understand Myra Pettyjohn.

But it was my cousin Shirley Perkins who dropped the first, and worst, bombshell, and repercussions of it bounced around the room in a wild series of small explosive yelps of horror. She was pregnant! And Christine, her sister and the youngest guest present, hadn't been warned! The poor child ran out of the room in tears, and I couldn't blame her. Her friend of the mall went with her, and some minutes later Shirley went, too, to find and comfort her, I guess, because they all came back together a little later, tearstains hidden behind fresh makeup and brave smiles.

Alison and her sister Victoria were the only matrons present, and they tried to steer the conversation into less titillating channels, at least on the surface, but the whispers went on and on, and I wished there were some way I could do something about the bleak lost look on Chrsitine's face. I didn't know what might help, so I just gave her a hug and a kiss and whispered, "Hang in there, Chrissie. Shirley will be all right! I know she will!"

I was trying diligently to make reasonable conversation with Myra Pettyjohn, who seemed obsessed with my chin, or ears, or hair, but who, I discovered, had a tongue like an adder, when the next bomb exploded. Fortunately a much happier one. A tall dark-haired girl who was someone's houseguest for the holidays showed off a diamond ring and blushingly announced that she was engaged to Peter Tarleton, a distant cousin of ours. Everyone approved, and shrieks of pleasure took the place of wails and moans about Shirley's "secret."

There were dozens of undercurrents I never understood at all. Cat switched placecards with someone, for some reason unknown, furtively, smiling to herself, up to something, I had no doubt, but I never learned what it was.

Janice only looked at me when she had to. I was sorry. I'd like to be friends with her someday. But today she had nothing to say to me beyond hello and thanks and good-bye. I didn't blame her, either. Everyone seemed to know there was something "going on" between Rob and me, although how they came by the knowledge I had no idea, but I think if I had been in Janice's shoes I would have snubbed me. I would have left my place at the table vacant. I admired her poise in the face of it all and hoped she didn't love Rob half as much as I did! I never heard his name mentioned at all.

I had a few minutes of quiet talk with Sandra Hamilton in the ladies' room and got a private little bombshell of my own. Perk had called her three times since Christmas Eve!

"I thought I had lost him," she said. "You know . . . I mean I knew he wasn't dead, of course. We would have heard. But I didn't know where he was. After he left here that time he came down, just before he went to Vietnam, I didn't write him right away. There was . . . a reason." She blushed prettily, and I guessed the reason was another man. "And then I heard he was wounded. I wrote and wrote but he never answered my letters. Maybe he never got them. I used his old address but I guess they didn't forward them. I should have asked Alison where he was but it seemed so . . . And you were swallowed up in New York somewhere. I really . . . goofed!"

I remembered the afternoon, that last summer I was here, when Sandra and I sat side by side at the Prentisses' swimming pool (under a red brick house behind Fairlawn Retirement Home now, I suppose) and wished Perk had chosen to come with me. He hadn't. He had gone off on some affairs of his own that day, but Sandra, all of fifteen, I think, had confessed to me how much she loved him! Way back then!

I looked now at this slender girl, who knew about the missing leg and half an arm (but perhaps didn't realize it, as I didn't myself until I saw him there at Bethesda), and whose eyes shone like stars when she spoke of him. I wondered . . . I wondered . . .

I explained as well as I could why he hadn't answered her letters. He hadn't, for months, even answered mine! "He was kind of like a wounded animal," I told her. "He just wanted to crawl off and be . . . miserable . . . all by himself. Dad went out to California and finally convinced him to come East, but he still didn't want to see anyone. I . . . I just walked in on him without warning last week, and it . . . sort of changed things."

"But he's still Perk!" She gave her head a little toss, and there was a distinct challenge in her voice.

"He certainly is," I said and gave her a hug, to tell her whatever the warmth of the hug might mean to her. However it turns out, whatever the long run is for those two, a girl who loves Perk is loved by me. It follows as the night the day!

The last and most disturbing bombshell was coming into the room even as Sandra returned my hug. Her voice was clear and piercing, her meaning unmistakable. "Oh, Alison doesn't know yet! James is such an accomplished cheat! But Henrietta takes the prize! Did you know she's chasing Branch Pettyjohn, too? I mean, two men in the same office! God, what nerve!"

I didn't know the woman. She wasn't at our party and I had never laid eyes on her, but I will never forget her or the sound of her voice, brittle and sharp, as her face was, and everything else about her, right down to her gilded shoes. Her cocktail dress glittered and her hair glittered and she was enormously pleased with herself.

She didn't recognize me, of course, but the woman she was with evidently did and signaled her to hush. I felt Sandra's arms tighten around me, and I reached up and put them aside. I stood up from the little plush bench and turned to look at the woman, looked her straight in the eye. I could feel the blaze in my own and wanted only to have her feel it, too.

193

And then I knew I didn't know. I had no idea how much truth there was in what she said. There was no way I could contradict her, no statement I could make to demolish her as she had demolished me. So I said my name. With my nose high and my eyes boring into her, I said coldly, "I am Joan Brandon." There was nothing to add, but I stood there a moment longer, silent, staring hard at her.

The woman tittered something that sounded like "so sorry" and went quickly into one of the stalls, and the second woman went into another with nothing to say at all.

As Sandra and I returned to our party she whispered to me that the gilt-edged siren was Bailey Comstock. "Editor of the Women's Page of *The Sentinel*. Her mother owns it, you know. Bailey's a terrible gossip and snoop. Don't pay any attention to her. People who know her don't."

The drive back to Woodsedge with Alison seemed almost endless. She talked about Shirley, hoped she would do some careful thinking about her future, and do it quickly. I tried to show an interest in Myra Pettyjohn while Alison told me how many trophies her horses had won, but I couldn't think of anything except the remark the glittery woman had made, so I was pretty quiet. Alison seemed tired and a little jumpy when we got home, and was relieved when James phoned from town a few minutes later to say he was having dinner with the Pettyjohns.

It wasn't until I talked to Perk later in the evening that I realized I had not been in a room alone with James since we were in his study together three days before.

Chapter Nineteen

EARLY TUESDAY MORNING everything began falling apart, and by dinnertime, James, who hadn't looked me in the eye or spoken more than the merest civilities to me since Friday, was the only friend I had left. At least he took my side against Branch Pettyjohn. Alison still did not commit herself, in the odd moments, that is, when she wasn't treating me as though I had leprosy.

It was bad enough to have to confront Caitlin Prentiss, but I was cut off from Rob!

As soon as I heard his voice on the phone I knew something was wrong. "Anne has a fever," he said. "Mother says a hundred and three isn't terribly high for a child, but she's feeling miserable. Dr. Birdsal should be out about noon, and I'll know more by then. But I wanted to warn you—"

"I'm so sorry!" I grabbed the pencil by the notepad and did some heavy crosshatching through Alison's grocery list while I steadied my thoughts and voice. Sorry was only the beginning of what I felt.

"Setsuko should be back by suppertime, but that about tears our date, I'm afraid. If it's not serious maybe I can get away a little while later this evening. We'll have to see." His voice was losing its military crispness, and my heart went out to him.

"Let me come, Rob. I can read to her or something. I can help!"

But he wouldn't allow it, not until he knew whether or not it was, as he suspected, measles. "Chip's reading to her

195

now. They're well launched on Milne. You're here in spirit, anyway. And I have a token. Did you know you left one of your mittens in the truck? I have it here, a gaudy little purple-and-orange mitten, fuzzy and soft—"

I laughed a shaky little laugh. I wanted to be inside that mitten! "My color-blind sister knit it for me for Christmas. . . ."

We chatted! Rob actually chatted over the phone! I pictured him at his oak desk, fondling his token mitten while the fire in the coal grate warmed him, and he could see the little Maine coast watercolor on his bookcase. I wanted to see him! Touch him!

But it didn't last long. "They're getting too noisy in there. I'll have to go. I love you. Good-bye!"

He promised to call back after the doctor's visit, and I had a morning of loneliness ahead of me, and a mysterious encounter with Caitlin in the afternoon, Caitlin and her "something I think you ought to know!"

"About Rob?" I fired the question at her before I had time to think.

"Not Rob," she said too quickly to stop herself.

"What, then?" But she wouldn't tell me. I would have to wait.

I went to find Alison, in a crisp smock with a bandana wrapped mammy-fashion around her head, cleaning the parlor. She stopped the vacuum when she saw me but kept her toe on the switch. I told her about Anne, and she murmured something sympathetic as she looked away from me to plan her next attack on the rug. When I asked if I could help and made a move to take the ungainly hose out of her hands, you would have thought I was trying to steal her dearest treasure!

"Oh, no, no! I'm so nearly finished. There's not the slightest need—" She stopped and her frantic expression relaxed a little. "Here, I'll tell you what. Why don't you go out to the red cabin and see if you can find that marble slab we talked about. I think I know just the place for it. It was

196

always used for rolling pastry, you know. We can measure it and see if it will fit on that table between the windows in the pantry."

As a distraction it certainly worked. I had been wanting to see what was behind that padlocked door, and when Alison told me where the key was, I ran back to my room for my parka and went to get Hector.

My heart was thudding beyond all reason. I might as well admit I secretly expected to find the missing body of that young woman waiting behind the door. Ever since she had *not* been under the honeysuckle vines in Corn Crib Woods, I had been looking for her, consciously or unconsciously, as I poked around the various outbuildings at Woodsedge. It always seemed possible to me that she might have been hidden in a place like this.

But of course I knew it couldn't be here in the red storybook cabin. I remembered clearly that Hector and I made the first marks in the huge virgin snow drift in front of its door. I remembered regretting that we destroyed it before I had gotten a picture. If the body had been brought to Woodsedge on the night of the storm, it had certainly not been put in the red cabin. I would swear to it.

And still I turned the key in that padlock with a shiver of dread, and after I pushed and kicked the door to get it open, I stood aside like a craven coward and urged Hector to go in first.

He was glad to. His tail wagged wildly as he sniffed his way across the dry plank floor and among the old trunks and boxes that were stacked there. I heard a scurrying sound and knew the place was infested with mice, if not with rats. *Be brave*, I told myself bravely as I spotted the marble slab gleaming in the shadows behind the bottom section of Gramp's old oak desk. Funny that I had never bothered to ask where that desk was. I had been too distracted by the mystery in Corn Crib Woods and my romance with Rob to miss it or to care.

I ran my fingers over the surface, grey with neglect,

strips of veneer bubbling loose where dampness had softened the glue, and after one brief stab of nostalgia, it was merely an old desk, a place to store rusty nails and other hardware, a surface to stack boxes on and bits of plumbing and old flowerpots. I looked around for the rolltop desk with its ranks of drawers that had fascinated me in my childhood, and when I saw it I gasped with surprise. It was a shambles! A wreck! Someone had smashed it with an ax!

I looked more closely. Not an ax, a wrecking tool or chisel. The brass lock on every drawer had been forced open and never mind how badly gouged and scarred the wood became in the process. In my imagination I saw James attacking it, impatiently using violent force to rip the locks apart. Why? When? How soon after Gramp's death? Or before? While the old man watched?

My stomach knotted at that thought, which was immediately supplanted by another. James desperately searching for the will that made him share this farm with me! That forced him to wait until he was thirty years old before he had even half of the control of Woodsedge.

Of course James would have destroyed that will in a split second if he had found it. Obviously, then, it hadn't been in the desk. Where else had he looked? How desperately had he searched while Gramp teased and tormented him with hints and suggestions? Or was Gramp already dead and James alone at Woodsedge with time running out before Fitch came, or Dad, to take charge?

I tightened my lips as one memory after the other of Gramp's manipulation of us all, but especially of James, seethed in my mind. Gramp had never cared how much pain he caused, and James was his victim time and time again. Looking back now, knowing James better now than I ever had before, I could see the hurt deeply buried under his pride, the frustrations festering and seething and occasionally erupting in violence. It was no fault of James's that his father angered and embittered Gramp when he went off to war. No fault of his that Gramp tried, constantly, crudely and vainly, to use him and the farm as a bribe—or threat—to keep Dad at Woodsedge. No fault of his that compulsive gambling was a hereditary tendency or that his temper was short and his self-defense was secrecy. It was not really surprising that last week he had raised his hand to strike me, or that he had not struck me. And when all was said and done, it was Gramp whose game of God made it almost inevitable that Branch Pettyjohn, or someone like him, could dream of owning Woodsedge.

With these thoughts scrambling and churning in my mind, I measured the marble slab with the tape measure I had brought with me. Of course it would fit perfectly between the windows in the pantry. That was where it had come from. And Alison knew it as well as I did. She had sent me out to see that desk top because she knew I would understand how it became so savagely ruined. She wanted me to understand, in case I had forgotten, how violent James could be, how ruthlessly he could attack when he was cornered, and how deeply he had resented my sharing Woodsedge with him—from the very first!

My hands were shaking when I refastened the padlock on the cabin door.

"Walking! I didn't know you ever did, Cat."

"Lot you know about me, then! Come on! You said you go every afternoon, you and your dog. What are we waiting for?"

"Me to change my clothes, for heaven's sake! I can't go walking in this weather in a skirt!"

I don't know why I had thought I could deal more effectively with Cat if I dressed up, but I had. I even had put on makeup and she turned up in wool slacks and Bean boots. I sent her out to the pen to get Hector while I changed, and when I met her down by the barn they were fast friends.

"How long do you have?" I asked her. "I usually plan my walk according to the time I have to spend—"

"I want to go to the place you call Corn Crib Woods, and I don't care how long it takes."

I gasped with surprise, but since she was panting with cigarette smoke I don't think she heard me. "You what?"

"You heard right. I want to go up to that place where Myra Pettyjohn says you have a stash of drugs."

"What in heaven's good name are you talking about?"

"To tell you the truth, that's what I want to know. That little . . . nerd . . . is actually phoning people on purpose to tell them you're a druggie!"

"I don't believe you!"

"You'd better! She's doing it! And she proves it, so she says, with a wild story about you keeping a stash of drugs up here in some kind of corn crib and hallucinating all over the hillside. She called Shirley first and Shirl called to warn me, so when Myra called me—"

"I can't believe this—"

"—I egged her on. Listened to her whole spiel and I swear I think she's crazy."

"Tell me what she said."

"That's why I'm here. I hope you have a strong stomach."

"Like iron. Go on."

"Well, it starts with you calling the police because you freaked out on speed and thought you stumbled over a dead body hidden in the honeysuckle. She said it was a naked man at first, and then amended that to a naked woman dressed up in pink fur or something weird like that. A go-go dancer or fan dancer or something. The kid really has a fantastic imagination!"

I hardly heard what she was saying. My mind was churning with the fact, the cold hard fact, that this teenager knew something about the dead woman in the woods that I had thought no one outside of my own family and the county sheriff knew. No one else knew anything about that pink scarf. How on earth Myra Pettyjohn could have learned about it was the question that needed a quick, accurate answer.

James! It had to be James.

Could this be a scheme of his to force me to sign that contract? To betray me like that?

I could not believe it!

But believe it or not, I had to go on from there, from the realization that the woman in the woods was becoming part of terribly damaging malicious gossip that threatened not me alone, but my whole family. And if such a story got to Rob—to his mother . . .

I had to go on from there, and here was Cat to help me. "Let's by all means go and see this remarkable place," I said grimly and started briskly across the long sleeping-giant field, Hector leading the way. We hopped from clod to frosty clod like a pair of demented clowns until we got to the track that goes from the Blair Road almost straight across the field to the corn crib. The track was puddled and rutted with tire tracks I hadn't seen before, but I paid little attention to them in my hurry to see whether anything had been disturbed at the thicket behind the corn crib.

When we got to the woods it looked very much as it had before the storm. The wind and weather since James and Sheriff Dennis and I had tramped it flat looking for the woman's body had whipped the thicket back in to its normal tangle, and Hector went into it and sniffed around exactly as he had before.

I decided not to volunteer any information to Cat. I would keep as cool and quiet as I could, even though my heart was bashing itself into jelly against my ribs. I closed my teeth hard against the impulse to blurt out the whole story. I needed to know what Myra Pettyjohn knew, but I didn't intend to add an iota of information to her story. Certainly it would be idiotic to mention the sack of garbage to Cat.

Cat mentioned it to me. "Myra Pettyjohn seemed to

think there was a plastic sack up here. She said you stashed—her word—your garbage . . . her word again . . . in it in the corn crib. You say this is said corn crib?" She waved at the dilapidated mound of weathered boards held together with dormant honeysuckle vines.

I nodded. "The only one extant on the place, that I know of." I watched Cat poke among the soggy vines and underbrush that festooned the corn crib and yell a few unladylike words when a shower of icy water slid down her neck.

"What a hellish place," she said at last, but she didn't give up. "How do you get in it?"

"I don't think you can. Even as kids we never tried to. All the wood is rotten and the old corncobs are full of weevils and things. Not to mention rats. It wasn't made for getting in, you know. Just a covered wagon for carrying corn up here for the hogs—about fifty years ago."

"It looks like the hut what's-his-name lived in. You know, the guy who had to kill his dog because he drove the sheep over into a quarry."

"Farmer Oak?"

"Right. Now there was a man!"

I looked at Cat as though I had never seen her before. "One of my heavy favorites," I began, but she ignored me while she lifted up honeysuckle vines to peer into the wagon. Finally she gave it up.

"You haven't got any dope hidden in there, have you?"

Straight question, straight answer. "Never any dope hidden there or anywhere else. I don't use it. Ever."

"Not even Mary Jane?"

"Not even Mary Jane."

"I didn't think you did." She said it so calmly I wondered why she hadn't said so in the first place, why she had gone to all this trouble.

Eventually I found out why. But, of course, not easily. That was never Cat's way. With her, it was direct, vicious assault and devious, secretive retreat. As a strategy of war it was pretty effective.

As we started back to the house she asked me the question I was asking myself—shrieking at myself while my mind raced in circles like a rat in a cage trying to find an answer. "What are you going to do about Myra?"

"Oh, God, I don't know! I've never been up against anything like this! Slander . . . from a sixteen-year-old kid! What *can* I do, except deny it?"

"Wouldn't she just love that! You deny it and she keeps it going! Nice rich glop and glue for her to slurp. God, I hate that kind of slime!"

I shot her a sharp glance. Cat was the worst, most malicious gossip I ever knew. She caught my look and jutted her jaw at me. "I do not tell lies about people behind their backs! Check it out, dammit! I do not lie!"

"About Rob you did!"

"Not a lie! He *is* as cold as ice! You know it! Or you will!"

I clenched my teeth hard and dug my fingernails into the palms of my hands inside my second-best mittens until the urge to hit her had passed. "But Rob is not the subject here," I said firmly. "Let's get back to that . . . loathsome brat. What do I do about that?" I closed my mind—tight!—to the idea of telling Cat that there was some truth in the slander.

"Leave it to me. As far as she knows, you don't know anything about it, or her. I've seen the place myself and can go on from there. I have my own way of dealing with . . . slime buckets!"

"But, since it concerns me, closely, I think you should tell me if you have some plan—"

Cat laughed. "Some plan is good! I have three, at least. First place, everybody in Shearerville knows she's a pathological liar. I will remind her of that. Second, her daddy is running for mayor, as perhaps you know—"

"I do."

"Well, it won't do him a bit of good to have her mixed up in a name-calling slander suit with the prestigious Brandon-

Perkins family. Myra absolutely adores her daddy, you know."

"I . . .didn't."

Cat laughed again. "They're two of a kind—three of a kind! Her mother's the worst. They're all slime buckets!"

"Cat!"

"Sorry. James works with Branch Pettyjohn, doesn't he. I'm damned if I know why. But of course I do know why. James likes to be close to the source."

She waited silently until I tumbled neatly into her trap. "Source of what?"

"Money! What else? Branch Pettyjohn knows how to get it and how to use it, and James . . . well, James needs it—badly. He also is Pettyjohn's understudy in the art of covering his tracks."

"What on earth do you mean? Good God, Cat, you better watch out for slander yourself!"

She slanted a look of pure disdain at me and grinned wickedly. "I've shocked you, haven't I? Shocked little Miss Goody Two-Shoes! God, Joan, I wonder if you ever will wake up and join the world! I swear you would make Rob a great little wifey. He's always so pure and holy and . . . so damned stuffy! The original straight arrow! It's no wonder Henrietta refuses to stay out there with him!"

For an instant I had an almost overwhelming temptation to ask Cat to tell me everything she knew about Henrietta Dunstan, but since she was so obviously prejudiced against Rob, I pushed the temptation aside. I gave her a cold, disdainful look and dug my fingernails into my palms inside my mittens again. "This has nothing in the world to do with Rob Dunstan or his family and you will please go back to James and that insinuation you made."

"What insinuation are you talking about?"

A neat ploy. One my squirmy kid sisters use regularly. "You know perfectly well."

"What did I say?"

"Come off it, Cat. You implied that James is linked with

204

Branch Pettyjohn in some kind of money-grabbing scheme, and James being a very clever understudy—which, come to think of it, seems perfectly possible—and being secretive. . . ."

"Ah-ha! Your words, not mine! You're getting the idea!"

"Well, I don't like it much. But—" I stopped. I knew too much and too little, and to say more to Cat at this point would be like playing with firecrackers around a campfire. Anything could happen. I wasn't up for it. One more nasty shock and this day would end up with me in a heap on the floor. "Let's go back to Myra," I said more firmly than I felt. "Do you really think you can shut her up?"

"Absolutely. Immediately."

"But why? What's in it for you, Cat?" I had to ask. There had never been any altruism about Cat, and this was no time for me to think there might be. I was in deep enough trouble without having Cat slipping some noose of indebtedness around my neck. I needed to know where this frightening business was headed.

Cat gave me one of her frigid green-eyed looks, one designed to shrivel all pretensions. "I don't work for pay," she said coldly.

"I didn't mean that, for heaven's sake, Cat! Will you come down out of your tree? I simply mean why should you bother? Why care what Myra Pettyjohn says about me? You will have to go to at least a little trouble. You already have, to come out here. All I want to know is why you are going to the trouble, that's all. And it is my business, too. After all, it's me she's accusing!"

"You're family."

I dropped my mouth open in amazement. "Surely that's not the only reason!"

"Why shouldn't it be?"

The look of cold disdain would have daunted me a few years ago—a few days ago! Today I laughed at her. "All right, Cat. Don't tell me. But hear this—I appreciate your concern. I will appreciate like everything your saving me—

and the family—from disgrace. I will show my appreciation at every opportunity. I'll start right now, in fact. Will you come in for a glass of sherry and get warm? We can sit in the kitchen and have nothing to do with whoever that is parked in front of the house."

"Good God, it's Branch Pettyjohn! I'd know his big black limo anywhere! He's calling on James, I suppose. I wouldn't be caught sitting in the same house with him, let alone the same room. Thanks anyway." She slid quickly and neatly behind the wheel of the little Cobra her daddy had given her for Christmas, and rolled the window down. "If you must know, it's because I have to know what's going on. I hate not knowing and I hate being fooled. That's all. See you around, and all that." And in a spurt of gravel she backed out of the driveway. I went on to the house, carefully avoiding James and his guest.

I wondered whether Branch Pettyjohn knew what his daughter was doing, whether, in fact, he would care. I wondered whether I could really trust Caitlin Prentiss, especially since there was no denying that I had very deliberately fooled her from the moment she first mentioned the Corn Crib Woods. I wondered, too, whether I would have a good night's sleep again until I knew for certain that young Myra Pettyjohn's guns were spiked. Where she got her ammunition in the first place was a mystery I laid on Perk that evening after I had told him about my broken date with Rob, Anne's measles, and Caitlin's visit.

"Damned if I know, Mops, but I sure will try to figure it out. This could be . . . very interesting. It sounds like more than a jealous kid slandering the Brandon family."

"I asked James about it at dinner. First dinner he has had with us since last Friday, in fact. He turned pale with shock! He honestly did! He didn't even have to sputter his denial!" I imitated James's deep voice. " 'Why the hell would I want to rake that stuff up again by repeating it to anybody, let alone Branch Pettyjohn?' It was very convincing, believe me!"

"And Alison? How did she react?"

"The same way. 'Floored' describes it pretty well. James suggested Dennis might have told Pettyjohn about it, and Alison chimed in that Myra would be perfectly capable of listening at keyholes. I think they would have liked to stay home tonight and kind of mull it over, but they had another of their bridge club meetings—"

"Okay, Mops. Let Jake and me worry about it. I'll get back to you tomorrow."

It had been another helluva day, but a phone call from Rob late in the evening left me warm and comfortable. Anne was feeling better now that the spots were out, but she must be careful—Rob must be careful of her. Of course! "Chip says . . . *says* he's had 'em," he went on, "but he's not sure. Henrietta should know but of course she's not saying—anything! I don't know about Setsuko, either. They just called from Nashville. It's just a little dismal around here!"

I consoled him the best I could. We consoled one another, and except for the physical distance between us, we might almost be said to have had our date. Almost. . . .

Chapter Twenty

SOMETIME TUESDAY NIGHT warm air from the Gulf of Mexico deposited moisture on every roof and tree, every blade of grass and bit of gravel, and the cold night air froze it fast. Wednesday morning, the last morning of the old year, the world was a silver and crystal fairyland.

Because it was beautiful and because I wanted to go there again, my dog and I walked across the fields to Corn Crib Woods, leaving footprints behind us every step of the way. I thought about Cat as I went, wondered about her determination to be intimidating, wondered why she was afraid to have people like her, but I had no answer.

When I got to the woods I went past the corn crib to the far corner, as I had intended to go that first day. There was no wind, and the branches and twigs, heavy with frost, didn't stir. No squirrel risked its furry neck on the slippery trees. Only the crackling of Hector breaking his way through the tangles disturbed the silence.

A few yards beyond the corner I stopped in my tracks. The pale blanket of frost was torn across with a dark trail of wet, and my heart raced with the sudden realization that Hector and I were not alone out here. A hunter . . . hunters? I heard nothing, no footsteps, certainly no shots. My heart chilled as I remembered the deer stands the twins had talked about, the crude platform hunters built above deer trails so they could ambush. . . . I looked up in the trees, trying to ignore the pricking sensation down the back of my neck as I imagined a soldier from Fort Harrington sitting up there watching me. But there was no deer stand. There was no soldier from the Fort.

There were, however, sharp twin-toed hoofprints in the mud. I blew out my breath and laughed at my fast-beating heart as I followed the deer trail down the side of the huge ancient sinkhole, lost it when all around me the frost had melted, found it again on the crest of the depression, and with my eyes traced it until it disappeared into the farthest field.

I went down into the sinkhole, fought my way over and under slippery fallen trees and through hateful tangles of blackberry brambles, honeysuckle, and multiflora rose-bushes. I had known since earliest childhood that sinkholes were full of mystery and hazards, rusty tin and broken glass, snakes and groundhog holes that caused cave-ins, lizards and spiders . . . I had always before given them wide berth, but that had been in summer, when the creatures lurked . . . I wasn't afraid of metal or glass. I wanted to be sure. I had to see for myself.

I clambered over rusty remains of farm machines and a huge iron drill, kicked aside some wheel rims leaning against an old sewing machine, and stepped around innu-merable rusty pots and pans and buckets. I went down deeper into the depression and found in a sandy place some shards of Grandmother's lovely old Spode with the pheas-ants still bright and exotic. I forced myself to look into the cab of Gramp's old Buick as it tilted crazily on the brink of a recent slide of rocks and fallen trees, and found nothing but torn seat cushions and a crumpled pack of chewing tobacco possibly twenty years old.

But I never found anything pink—anywhere. I was al-most as sorry as I was glad.

I was also a little disoriented until I finally climbed the rim again and could see Two-Greats Grandfather's log cabin through the woods. Within minutes I was back on the broad farm road that went past the stripping shed to the house.

My heart sang with joy as I paced back up the lane. I knew at last what I wanted to do with my new year and who

I wanted to do it with. I wouldn't have changed places with a soul on earth. I was ten feet tall and queen of the universe when I went in for my breakfast.

I was queen for an hour.

Thirty seconds after Rob's truck turned into the driveway I was in his arms, held warmly there, and I knew he had been lonely, too, by the hunger of his kisses. I pressed myself against him, my length against his, as hard as I could.

But then he put me back from him, firmly, and straightened himself away from me. "I'm not being fair to you," he said, with a kind of sternness in his eyes. "Why don't you stop me?"

"I love you!" The sound of it delighted me. I said it again. "I love you!"

The sternness drowned in dancing warmth, and he caught me to him again and said, before he put his lips on mine, "I do believe you're beginning to!"

I tried to tell him beginning had nothing to do with it in the way I returned his kiss, but he raised his head from mine and carefully pulled a strand of blackberry bramble out of my hair. The look on his face was no longer stern, but it was serious when he said, "I have to go to Chicago. She won't return my calls, and I have to talk to her. School starts Monday, and I can't keep the kids wondering. I'll bring you up to date if you'll . . . just stop distracting me!" He kissed me once more, very warmly, and then set me back from him again. "I have to go to Chicago this morning. I have a reservation."

The thoughts that raced through my mind were selfish—unforgivably selfish. I couldn't meet his eyes for a moment. Finally I said the first words I wasn't ashamed of thinking. "Anne. What about Anne?"

"She's feeling much better, but she looks a sight. I just dropped her off at Ellen's. Chip, too. Setsuko got in about midnight. She hasn't had measles so I couldn't leave the kids with her. Everyone at Ellen's has had 'em, and they're glad to have the youngsters there. Glad to have a diversion."

"I have too, had measles, I mean. I'll go and read to her."

"She'll love that. They all will. Even Molly has never read Pooh! They all think you are great."

"And I can help Chip strip tobacco—"

Rob laughed at that. "Chip's laid off for now. I've got one of the Burden boys down there with his crew."

"Joe?"

"Joe's older brother, Pete. He owes me one."

"One what?"

"Favor. We were together in Vietnam. Everybody who got back from there owes somebody something. He's just paying up. I just hope Boyd can get along without him for a day or two." He was silent a minute. "We're sidetracking, aren't we, my love?" He kissed me again, gently. "I love your eyes. Did you know they say things to me that you don't say?"

I looked down at the floor. "I suspected it. About Henrietta, then—?"

"Did I tell you they caught Ramon last night? He's jabbering like a monkey, and some of what he says is probably true. I want to get her back here before he's extradited to Texas. This thing may just be coming to crisis point, and I can't miss a chance. So I have to go."

"Of course. Certainly." Something in me was already in mourning. I pressed my hands against the place that hurt, just under my heart. "Rob . . ." There was pain in his eyes, too, and a kind of searching, memorizing look that reached down to that hurting place and tugged on it. He took my hands in his, and I held on hard and whispered the words. "I'm supposed to leave . . . on Saturday . . . at dawn."

"I know it—full well. I should be back Friday. God willing. She checked out of that hotel and went to her sister's, but they've evidently gone off somewhere. Her sister doesn't answer her phone. I've got to go." He sighed as he dropped my hands and reached for the little white florist's box he had put on the table when he came in. "I picked this up in town for you."

Carefully, slowly, I slipped the silver ribbon and sprig of mistletoe off the box and uncovered a pale, almost blue orchid that nestled, delicate and pure, in the green tissue. "How . . . perfectly lovely. How dear of you, Rob!"

"I wanted it to match your eyes. I should have known even orchids don't come that color. Will you wear it? Please? Go to the Club with James and break the guys' hearts . . . and miss me, just a little?"

There was a kind of pleading in his voice and in his eyes, his head tilted as he watched my face. He was handing me what solace he could in the little white box, and I gave him what I could of a smile. "Y-yes, of course, I will." Part of me will, I thought, but not all. Not all. I felt a chill slip down my spine, like a premonition, and I hid it under a sigh. "I'll break every heart in sight," I said as bravely as I could. "Some of them twice over! As for missing you . . . I'll . . . do my best." My voice cracked and the look on his face didn't help a bit. "What's not fair, Rob? You said you weren't being fair?"

He took the box from my hands and put it back on the table, and then held me in front of him, his fingers strong where they gripped my shoulders. "This," he said. "Holding you, kissing you. Getting you all warm and tender and then . . . just walking way. The way I have to right now. There's nothing on God's good earth fair about that!"

His kiss was not gentle. It was swift and rough, and when he released me I staggered and then stood there with my eyes tight shut until I heard the door close behind him.

He was right. It wasn't fair. And the pressure of his lips on mine and of his fingers on my shoulders were the salve, not the source, of the pain. I knew then what is meant by "tearing away," and part of me he had reached into and touched was gone, torn away, and the wound that was left, raw and gaping, would not heal until he returned.

I don't know how long I stood there bleeding inwardly, my mind hazed. I know when I moved my feet were like lead. I took the orchid in its box back to my room and slipped the silver ribbon over the vacant finial of the oak chair, opposite the pink one that hung there, that reminder of violent death, and this, crisp and shiny, a symbol of what? Life? Love? Or loneliness? A dead heart and a broken heart?

More to honor the orchid I would wear like a badge on my shoulder than for any other reason, I dressed carefully to go to the Club with Alison and James. The place would be thronging with people, and to me it would be empty. It would be noisy with music and laughter and tooting horns and whistles, and there would be no sound I wanted to hear.

I thought you weren't a baby anymore!

What's being a baby about not wanting to go where you don't want to be?

There's a lot of baby in sulking.

I'm not sulking, I'm just sad. I'm lonely and sad and I don't want to dance.

A lot of people are lonely and sad. They live. So will you.

Don't be bracing. I want to curl my shoulders around my head and cry, and I should do what—grin like an idiot and make small talk to strangers and put on a funny hat?

All that. You have more to be happy about than most.

It's in Chicago, which is the Antipodes, wherever the hell that is. All right, all right, I'll go. I'll smile and toot my little horn and be as bright and amusing as a clown, and no one will know I'm sad and lonely, lonely, lonely . . . But I'm damned if I'll wear a funny hat!

'Atta girl! Rob will be proud of you!

It was reason enough. I dressed with care. I found a long silk scarf that almost exactly matched the orchid and wound it around my waist as a belt between my best silk shirt and the white wool skirt I had brought with me for exactly this occasion. I matched my eye shadow as delicately as I could to the orchid, and pasted a smile on my face. Then I slipped the little heart-shaped stone in my pocket with my lipstick and went to the parlor to twirl for James.

He beamed at me and handed me the beautiful gold bracelet that had been Grandmother's. "I think this should be yours, Joan. Keep it to remember this visit by. In case you're in any danger of forgetting it, that is."

I thanked him and slipped the plain gold band over my hand, and when I looked up at him again he jutted his chin at my orchid.

"Dunstan give you that?"

"Yes."

I suppose he read defiance in my face, but all he said was a kind of humph, and he turned his back on me to stare into the fire. I thought he had nothing more to say, and was leafing through the evening's copy of the *Shearerville Sentinel* when he went on. "The Pettyjohns have gone to New Orleans for the rest of the week, you may be glad to know."

"Oh?"

"Branch was real upset with Myra's behavior. He said to tell you he regrets any inconvenience it may cause you, and that's a quote."

"Right white of him, I must say—and thank you for telling me. Too bad he didn't bring his . . . ah, 'little gal' . . . up to be more responsible!"

James just shrugged and said nothing more until Alison came in, looking like an ice goddess in pale blue satin.

"It's old," she said when I complimented her on her gown. "But I may never be able to wear it again." She ran her hands down her gently rounded abdomen with a laugh. "Does it really look all right? I mean, it's not too voluptuous, is it?"

"Not quite too," I said. "Botticellian, a little, but how could you be more beautiful than that? Us meager women should find a way to look as womanly as you do!"

214

"I'm not quite sure how to take that," she said and quirked an eyebrow at me.

"Don't forget I'm an artist," I said. "I like curves."

"So do I," said James surprisingly, and when he held Alison's coat for her, he kissed her neck—and I let out a cheer for the first public display of affection I had ever seen from him.

I left them there in front of the gas log and went to James's study to answer the telephone. I should say I flew across the hall to answer it. But it wasn't Rob. It was Shirley Perkins, and there was so much tension in her voice I pulled the chair around to the desk and sat down. Something there in her shades-of-pink bedroom was about to break.

I wasn't surprised that it was Shirley's voice. "I am at the end of my rope! I . . . just don't know what to do! I need to know what you think I should do. Do you think I should marry Hayley or not, have the baby or not. What do you think?"

"How can I possibly say? I never met Hayley—and I've never been pregnant. And that's just starters. You walk in your sneakers and I walk in mine. How can I possibly make a sensible statement about what I would do when I don't have the slightest idea?"

"But . . . what do you think you *might* do?"

I finally understood that she was taking a poll, a sample ballot of the opinions of her friends. Well, I have always been her friend. I told her so.

"I know it," she said with a relieved little laugh. "That's why I called. I need to know what you think. What if I tell you I don't want to marry Hayley?"

"Then don't. There's no law that says you have to!"

"But—I can't figure out what will happen then. Everyone will know! What . . . what will people s-say!" The last word came across the wires like the braying of a donkey. I imagined Shirley in her room, taking her telephone poll of her friends to see what *they* would say before she made up her mind which of her few and urgent options she would choose. I told her straight out that what people, whoever they are, say isn't really important. It may not even be what they really think. All she can know for sure is what she herself says—feels—believes and hopes and expects out of her life. And she should decide that for herself. I guess that point hit some sensitive area because there was a long silence.

When she broke it there was a new tone in her voice. "Can you get James to drop you off here on the way to the Club? I think I'll just go to the big bash after all. But I can't just walk in there with Daddy and Mamma. I have to look . . . Will you? You don't have a date, do you?"

"Just James and Alison and a seat reserved for me at the Perkinses' table." And I hope Cat has accomplished her mission or it will be a pretty dismal table, I thought.

"Well, if we could just walk in together I think I might just—Are you almost ready to leave?"

"Yes, but I'm not sure it will do your rep any good to be seen with me! I may be a worse pariah than you are!"

"A what?"

"Outcast. You know—"

"Oh, Myra and her slander." Shirley was silent, and for a moment I thought she was getting ready to back out, afraid that being seen with a reputed junkie might be a greater hazard than she was willing to risk. I underestimated her. "The hell with Myra," she said at last. "If we can't carry this thing off we might as well give up. Let's go."

James was perfectly willing to drop me off, and when Shirley and I walked into the Club together an hour or so later, at least she knew what I would say if she had her baby by herself. "It isn't as though you have to work or have no family to help you. You have a lot to offer a kid."

And Shirley was encouraging about Myra. "Cat did a number on her," she said. "I haven't heard another word about that stuff from anyone—including Cat."

216

We took our places at the Perkinses' table, where James pointedly snubbed Shirley, and Alison talked to her as though she were from outer space. I could have kicked both of them, but I was proud of Shirley for putting on a brave face, holding her small round chin high, and keeping her voice level and her smile intact as she endured the snubs. If she wished Hayley were present to share her ordeal, she never hinted it.

Myra Pettyjohn and her parents were not there, but it wasn't long before I received evidence of the damage she had done me and my family before Cat did her number on her. I realized that Fitch and Ellen were being very protective of me, and even James, rather pale and uncomfortable, jutted his jaw at some white-haired lady who made a point of "humphing" and turning her back on me.

"Who in the world is she, James? I don't know her, do I?"

"Virginia Hilliard. Thinks she's the town's imperial highness—"

"Hilliard? Ellen's family?"

"Just by marriage. She's always been an idiot."

I didn't dare ask him how close a friend Mrs. Hilliard was to Mary Dunstan. I was afraid I wouldn't like his answer. In fact, the mere thought that Rob's mother might have heard Myra's slander—and believed any part of it even for an instant—was almost more than I could bear. I sent a fistful of prayers flying out to Father God and closed my fingers hard around the stone heart in my pocket.

One or two other people pretended not to see me when I smiled a greeting at them. Probably it was only coincidence that several others moved to another table when I walked toward the one where they sat. Another smart-looking matron looked me up and down as though I were a freak in a sideshow, and I have to admit I was getting pretty tired of the pretending to ignore the whole thing some minutes before midnight and was considering going to hide in the ladies' room for a while, when Kenny Haynes walked in.

Looking handsome in his tuxedo and smartly ruffled shirt, his cheeks rosy from the cold and his big brown eyes shining, he stood for a moment on the stage of the ballroom, not quite in the center, and with great dignity ignored the stares and murmurs while he searched the crowd for Shirley.

He found her at our table, and a moment later they excused themselves to dance. I did not see hide nor hair of them again and thought that Shirley had finally found someone who could give her the answers she wanted.

I was more popular than I wanted to be at midnight, but I kept my hands in my pockets and held my face available for the good luck kisses men seem to think they are entitled to at that magic moment, and it was soon over.

Cat was in the ladies' lounge when I went in to repair myself after that. Tall and thin in black satin, she stood behind me while I sat at the dressing table. I waited to hear what she had to say about Myra, but she said nothing about her at all. She reached her hand over my shoulder and with a long crimson fingernail flipped a petal of my orchid.

"Rob's gone, then, isn't he! I told you so. Two dates and he's gone." She put her face down and grinned her three-cornered smile at me. I could see the triumph in her moist red lips and green eyes. She gave my shoulder a short sharp pinch and then patted the place she hurt. "Poor baby!" And she was gone before I could gather my wits enough even to snarl at her.

I was left sitting there, stunned and frozen, while strange women milled around me, gossiping, chattering, and laughing. I scarcely saw or heard . . . I don't know how long it was before one of them touched my arm and asked me if I was finished. I got up and gave her my place at the mirror, and was happy to leave the Club with James and Alison a few minutes later. I was more than willing to take my aching heart back to Woodsedge.

New Year's Day was a dizzy round of making calls and being called upon. I was glad James managed to keep us running on schedule. We never once were at someone's house while they were at ours, and the only confusion was when Alison took me off to the Reeves's and left James to catch up with us at the Hendersons'. We missed him there, and when we got back to Woodsedge I wished I had never left. Perk had called, and I gathered he just told James to say Happy New Year to me for him—kind of in passing. But the call seemed to have done James good. "I'll tell you about it later," he said, but he never did.

I wished, when it was over, that I had kept track of the various odd customs of what will and what will not bring good luck in the New Year. We ate sauerkraut at one house, black-eyed peas at another, and both together at a third. Alison thought her homemade fruitcake would do the trick, and James pooh-poohed the whole thing and stuck to bourbon. I took my share of everything because I had a feeling that I would need all the luck I could get in the coming year. I tossed some heartfelt prayers heavenward, for good measure. There's no telling what will please the fates!

Chapter
Twenty-One

FRIDAY DAWNED IN a turmoil of cold rain and gusty wind. Water seeped through the ceiling in the hall and ran down Alison's lovely creamy wallpaper in a raw brown streak shaped exactly like the map of Florida, while James stood and cursed at it. Wind kept the linoleum on the kitchen floor billowing like a restless sea and blew the windows of the brooder house open, wetting Hector's hay. He was shivering when I went to take him for his morning exercise. I threw ancient corncobs in the barn for him to chase until he was thoroughly warm and bored, and then took him to the kitchen to dry him, which he loved, with Alison's oldest bath towel.

Then I went to town and read to Anne until my voice cracked. They hadn't heard from Rob either and evidently had no idea when to expect him back. I wrapped my fingers around the little stone heart in my pocket and kept my worries to myself.

Shirley was nowhere in sight. I asked Ellen about her, but Ellen only shrugged. She invited me to lunch, and when I appeared at the table she looked at me as though she wondered where I had come from. She never mentioned that I was supposed to be leaving the next day at dawn. She never inquired about my plans at all. She evidently had forgotten.

And I didn't remind her. The last thing I wanted to talk about—or think about—was my departure on Saturday morning. I closed my mind to it and concentrated on entertaining Anne until she was tired enough to sleep. I drove back to Woodsedge in heavy rain and began pulling and hauling things out of the old wardrobe as an excuse not to begin packing Hector's crate. Every time the phone rang I rushed like a teenager to answer it, until I got a scornful look from James. The next time I walked briskly and Alison got there first.

When the phone finally rang for me I was waist-deep in things I had pulled out of the wardrobe, but I ran—stumbled—to the kitchen and skidded to a stop when James announced with fiendish delight that it was Shirley. I gave him a withering look and tried to sound cheerful to the tense girl who called.

"I'm going to Colorado to visit a friend from school. I don't know how long I'll be gone. Maybe six months. But one thing's for sure, Cousin Joan, and that's that Hayley is out of it! Kenny has just gone to Nashville to give him his ring back and tell him I am not going to marry him—no matter what! At least I'm through with that . . . grub!"

"Bravo for you—and lots and lots of luck!" So Shirley has at least identified her problems, I thought. At least she knows what's going on in her life at this particular moment. I wouldn't have traded places with her for anything in the world, but I wanted to know what the Hell was going on in mine!

Just before dark I went walking with Hector, clutching my little stone heart in my mitten whether I was entitled to or not. We slogged through the rain to the copse and waded around it through gluey red mud until it was so heavy on my boots I had to stop and peel it off with a stick. Three times I pried it off before I got back on the farm road to walk through wide lakes of rainwater back to the house, almost too tired to think.

But the phone had not rung. I dried my dog and fed him. I was not quite satisfied that the wind and rain had diminished enough for the fresh hay James had put in for him to stay dry, so I hooked all the windows shut, and then nailed them for good measure before I went back to the house. Still Rob had not called.

After dinner I sat with Alison in the parlor, pretending to watch television. My worry throttled my reason, and my imagination jumped into the saddle and grabbed the reins. I fled to my room so I could pace and wring my hands in peace. My mind started a war.

Cat's voice: "He's gone! Gone! I told you so!"

Rob's voice: "I'll be back, God willing."

Cat: "Two dates is all you'll get. You'll see!"

Rob: "There's nothing on God's good earth fair about this!"

And that was only Friday!

I thought of a thousand things, starting with his believing Myra Pettyjohn's lies and being disgusted with me, to the simple impersonal problem of the airport being closed or phone lines being down. (Ours wasn't, obviously. I would have sworn Alison and her friends were playing their bridge game by phone, they spent so much time calling back and forth!) I imagined Henrietta and Rob quarrelling. Henrietta being a bitch. And her thugs? My mind churned with the pictures. Rob sleeping with a gun under his pillow while she laughed with delight . . . Rob with cold eyes and stony face fighting thugs and rabid bitches with stumbling blocks, fighting his brother's wife for his brother's children. . . .

When I finally was desperate enough to call his house, it was too late. If he were not there I would certainly waken his mother, and if her friend Virginia Hilliard had convinced her . . .

But Myra's slander aside, what right did I have to distrub Mary Dunstan anyway?

War: Phase Two. What claim had I on him, after all?

I had none. He has only told me, *told* me he loves me! He hasn't breathed the word marriage, only bed, and only once. I wear no ring. I have only a little stone heart—and Cat says he has none at all.

Saturday didn't dawn, it sneaked in over cold grey ice on

the ground and under a cold grey sky overhead. Tree limbs, thick with ice, creaked and groaned and broke off with cracks like doom. It didn't take me two minutes to decide that nothing on earth would drag me out on the highway. I didn't need to go. No one expected me. Obviously no one cared a hoot where I was or what I did. I might as well be in Jericho for all anyone cared. But I was not going to leave Woodsedge until I at least knew he was safely home.

I blamed it on the ice, of course, when I went through the kitchen to tend to Hector. James flicked a challenging glance at me. "Weatherman says the sun'll be out by noon. You got your little kiddie car ready to take off when the road's clear?"

"I . . . don't know yet," I said, which was not exactly true, but I slipped out the door before I had to explain what I meant. When I got back they were having breakfast, and I joined them. James asked me again what I planned to do. "I'm not going." I said it flatly, without raising my eyes from the spoon I was polishing with my thumb.

"What?"

"Now, James—"

"I'm not going, not until I see . . . talk to Rob." I hated the way my voice broke when I said it, and I closed my teeth on my lip so I wouldn't risk further words. What more could I say, anyway? It was a cold, hard, absolute fact.

"I told you not to mess with him! I told you—"

I couldn't get out of the room fast enough. Tears were absolutely cascading down my cheeks, and I hated everybody as I slammed through the swinging door and was fairly choking with tears when I got into my room.

That was at breakfast on Saturday!

After I could think again, I called Ellen to tell her I wasn't going until the weather improved. She seemed pleased, but her voice was so flat I wondered whether she really cared. She went on to say the kids were fine, and I don't think anyone noticed that Rob had not called. Anyway, no one said.

At noon I told myself I wouldn't talk to him even if he

223

called me twenty times. Obviously he did not love me at all. Everybody on earth was more important to him than I was! Even Myra Pettyjohn! He could at least have given me a chance to defend myself, if he really loved me.

And it was War: Phase Three.

He could have called if he had wanted to! He would have called . . . unless he were dead! Or unconscious! I imagined him in a mangled heap, left for dead in some Chicago back alley. I saw him crashed and burning in a plane. I saw him driving a rented car over icy black roads, hurrying too fast to get back to those precious children—not to me!—and smashing . . .

He should have called me, and now it's too late! For all he knows I have gone, skidding through the mountains in an ice storm, sliding off the road, my dog hanging on by his toenails, crashing over cliffs, falling into chasms. . . .

He might have called to say good-bye, drive safely, come back soon! Have a nice goddamned trip! But it was too late now! I wouldn't talk to him even if he called all day every day—every hour on the hour! I wouldn't answer the phone at all—ever! Not even if it were Perk! I would be happy—overjoyed not to answer it . . . if only he would call!

Shirley called at midafternoon to see if I had heard anything from Rob! I knew this must be at least as much hell for the children as it was for me, but I was afraid to go near them. In my imagination I saw Anne watching the clock, watching the door, listening for the phone, worrying, worrying without the solace of the physical exertion that kept me from thinking too much. I was afraid I couldn't keep the worry out of my own voice and face, and would tip her over into panicky fear, the kind that can't be consoled with platitudes or pats on the shoulder. I left the children for Ellen to cope with.

I called the airport in Nashville. All flights, said the crisp voice, were on time. Yes, Nashville had been closed for two hours last night. Yes, O'Hare had been closed until this morning. She referred me to someone else who could tell me what flights were coming from there during the day. Only two. One was already en route, possibly over my head right this minute. The other would be in at nine tonight.

Of course it helped. He was on his way, he would be here any minute. He would call the youngsters from Nashville; Shirley would tell him I hadn't left, and then he would call me. Certainly. Of course.

I wasn't tired enough to stop thinking, I wasn't tired enough to collapse, so I took Hector down to the barn and urged him, with great cooing and the false promise of rabbits, to climb the ladder into the loft with me. He didn't like it up there, and neither did I, but it was the last corner of the homestead I hadn't set foot in, and with a kind of perversity I covered every inch of the place. I went cautiously, testing the planks before I put my weight on them and keeping a careful watch for the sudden holes where hay had been dropped down to the horses in the stalls below, but some demon in the pit of my mind told me it wouldn't really matter if I fell through. It might even be a good thing! If I broke my neck I wouldn't have to leave at all!

But I didn't. And neither did Hector. When I had enough of it, I reversed the cooing and the promise of rabbits and ended up carrying my squirming dog down the ladder in my arms. Then I put him back in the pen to roll the cobwebs off in his hay, and went in the house and into my room. I scarcely recognized the haunted face that looked back at me when I brushed my hair. I turned my back on the mirror and pretended to clean and pack and look through the books and photographs and boxes of childish souvenirs that were piled in the bottom of the old wardrobe.

And that was Saturday afternoon.

At five o'clock he hadn't called. At six I called Ellen. She wasn't there. She and Fitch had taken Shirley to Nashville for her plane to Colorado. Christine and Molly were the only ones there.

"The children? Where are Anne and Chip?"

"Oh, he"—Rob!—"picked them up hours ago!"

For an instant I just held my head in my hand. God alone could understand the mixture of relief and anger that held me speechless. Finally I managed just one word. "When?"

"Oh, before Shirley left."

"Did . . . did you tell him I haven't left for New Hampshire?"

"No, I didn't tell him. I don't know if Shirley did."

Of course you didn't, I thought. You didn't even want him to know my name! I let Chrissie chatter on, and from the bursts of confusion I gathered that Rob had arrived just as they had been backing out of the driveway, and I could imagine the hellos and good-byes, the short questions and partial answers that had flown back and forth.

No, that woman (Henrietta) wasn't with him. He (Rob!) hadn't stayed. They (Setsuko and Archie?) had to go off somewhere. He was in a hurry—that point was clear enough. He hadn't taken time to call me from town—If he wanted to talk to me. If he knew I was still here. If Shirley remembered to tell him, he would call me—when he thought of it, when he got around to it. When it was convenient. When he had nothing better to do. Meanwhile, I could wait.

I waited fifteen minutes and then I called him.

The line was busy. Joy! He was calling me. At last! I waited. Then I called again. Still busy. Always busy! I got sympathetic glances from Alison and grumphs from James. I ignored them both and dialed again and again, in vain.

I got more sympathy from Ellen a little after nine when she called to tell me she had forgotten to tell Rob I had not left for New Hampshire. So he doesn't know I have not gone.

I called his house again and this time there was no signal at all. I knew too well what that meant. I would have to go over there . . .

In the dark in the pouring rain to an armed camp, where I wasn't expected and I didn't know the password? Where I didn't know whether I was wanted or missed or even thought about at all? I had no answers. I had no plan. I had not much left even in the way of common sense. I had a tiny shred of pride. It kept me quiet. Kept me from howling.

At ten-thirty Saturday night I called Perk.

I had forgotten the time zones! He answered on the third ring and I apologized for waking him.

"I'll live," said my noble brother, the sleepiness gone from his voice. "What's up?"

That angel! He let me pour it all out, all the fear and frustration in whatever gasps and groans I pleased, helping me along the way with his "Easy, easy Mops. It will be all right." When I finally ran out of breath and could only gasp, he said, "He's back, that's the main thing, isn't it?"

"Yes, oh yes!"

"So you don't need to worry about him, do you?"

"No, I suppose not, but . . ."

"But what?"

"Why hasn't he called me? Why, Perk? I've been right here, not fifty feet from the phone. He can't . . . can't believe that junk of Myra Pettyjohn's, can he?"

"Not a chance. Sandra called me New Year's Day, did I tell you? She told me nobody believes Myra's tales and she's is in big trouble for even whispering such things about you! You can forget about Myra and her slander, Mops."

"Then why hasn't he called me?"

"He doesn't know you're there. He probably thinks you're in Roanoke by now."

"Doesn't he know I couldn't have left without talking to him? Without knowing whether he found Henrietta and that he has the stumbling blocks he needs? Doesn't he know how important all this is to me?" My voice cracked on the pronoun. My heart shrieked silently that Rob should know it is a matter of life and death to me! Perk seemed to hear it in the silence.

"You have to think straight, Mops. He didn't bring Henrietta back with him so he must be terribly frustrated and upset, and the guy can't just go off in a corner and deal with it. He has the kids to cope with, their worries . . . no clear light ahead. It can't be easy."

Little by little I had to accept his consolation. "The guy needs space, Mops, and time. He believes those kids are threatened. He needs to find some answers. Give him a break, Mops. Let him have his space. Talk to him tomorrow. Go over there if you want to. I'm willing to bet he knows damn good and well you won't leave before he talks to you. He got back late. He has the kids on his hands and his mother. . . ."

I had to be satisfied. I would see him tomorrow and then, if he still needed his space more than he needed me, I would give it to him. I would go back to New Hampshire, drive up the long, long road to wherever, by myself.

I've never tried to sleep through a longer night.

Chapter Twenty-Two

I HAD MADE my plans. I was up before dawn, and Hector was well walked and fed by seven. Before eight I started for Shearerville and early church. I had been sending up barrages of tangled prayers and distress signals to Father God for four solid days, and he had seen fit to answer the most important ones and I owed him my thanks; early church exactly suited my requirements. Afterward I would fill my gas tank and go back to Woodsedge, load up Hector's crate, already packed with my clothes and the two ribbons—but not the heart-shaped stone. I would carry that in my pocket one last time. . . .

I would drive through the woods and over the river to the armed camp, only a little out of my direct route to the entrance of the interstate. I would try to get in, try to storm the walls or whatever the barricades were that were designed to keep thugs out and the children safe. If I could get in, could see him, I would simply say good-bye—hand him back his heart and walk away. . . .

But that would be . . . impossible. One tearing-away was enough! More than enough! The wound still pulsed . . . pulsed with pain.

So I wouldn't try to get in. I would leave the little stone heart in his mailbox. Just drop it off, wrapped in a note: "Bring this back when you want me to have it for keeps." Or, "I think you meant this to be a loan, didn't you?" A sheet of blank paper with a few tear stains might be enough.

I didn't know. I only knew that I would not try to see him because . . . I was afraid . . . I might . . . I shouldn't. . . .

So I would simply leave the token, the little talisman, just leave my heart in his mailbox . . . and go!

I chewed my lip to keep the tears that were burning behind my eyes from blurring my vision. I was still fighting them when I turned into the parking lot, nearly filled because I was nearly late, and there, parked close to the parish house wall, was Rob's battered green truck.

Almost numb with emotion and a dozen scrambled thoughts, I pulled in close to it, and then, on impulse, I backed out and came in again so the Volkswagen lay across the bows of the truck and it would be impossible for him to drive away until I got there to move my car. With my fingers gripping the little talisman in my pocket and my heart pounding in my throat, I crossed the street and went into the church.

Rob was easy to spot, kneeling in a pew near the front, with his head on his arms and sunlight through the ruby-and-blue glass windows staining his bright hair. There was a space beside him, and I could have sat there and touched him—but I didn't. I didn't dare. I took a place across the aisle two rows in front of him, beside a comfortable-looking stout lady, where I sat, a little crowded, in the aisle seat, not more than ten feet from him.

Space, Rob, space. If that's what you want, you have it. But you can't raise your head without seeing me, without knowing I am here for you. If you want me!

I fought a running battle to keep my mind on the service. I think I made all the proper responses; I don't know. I went forward to receive communion at the proper time, and I was fairly bursting with prayers and supplications that I could not possibly have put in any coherent words, and I thanked God that coherence wasn't one of His requirements. Never for thirty seconds was Rob and his presence a few feet behind me out of my mind. It seemed to me that vibrating, twanging wires stretched between us, that the air hummed and the floor trembled with them. I held my hands, clutching one another fast to keep from reaching out to him, and I kept my eyes tightly shut. Never once did I hint that I knew he was within twenty miles of me.

When the service was over I walked, head up, eyes down, past his aisle toward the back of the church. I knew he was waiting there. I felt him, sensed him reaching out to me . . . but I didn't look at him. I didn't dare. With the stout woman close behind me I marched on, keeping carefully to the center of the aisle so it looked as though I were content to walk alone.

My instincts were running away with me. They had the bit in their teeth, and if I was going to ride it out I could not afford to let this moment go without the answer I wanted. Do you need me, Rob? Want me? Want me to stay? Or go?

I had to know.

So down the aisle I went, my shoulders squared like a soldier on parade. When I got to the porch I shook hands briefly with the rector, and I still didn't look back to see where Rob was. He might have gone out the choir door for all I knew. He might already have decided that he had more important things to do than have a useless conversation with me. He might dread saying good-bye to me. Manlike, he might go to any lengths to avoid an emotional scene, in public, with a woman whose self-control was hidden under a very thin veneer that was obviously about to crack. Maybe he already regretted getting so deeply involved, maybe he was angry—disgusted by Myra's lies! Maybe Cat was right and I had had my two dates!

Maybe if I hurried I could get to the parking lot before he did, jump in my Volkswagen and speed away before he got there, before I forced myself on his attention again . . . ever . . .

I paced on, stepped down onto the sidewalk and marched steadily across it. I was ready to step off the curb to cross the street when he took my arm, and my heart did a breathtaking backflip at the strength of his fingers that circled my wrist.

"Just . . . merely . . . the longest hour of my life," he said out of the corner of his mouth, and when I looked up at him he was staring straight ahead, marching, even as I was myself. His face told me nothing of his thoughts; his profile looked, if anything, stern and closed, perhaps even angry. I tried to step away from him when we reached the far curb, but his arm behind mine didn't yield an inch and his fingers were not gentle, not even very kind. He marched me like a prisoner straight across the parking lot to where my car was so audaciously parked.

He stopped when we came up to them and surveyed the situation, reading my intentions clearly, of course, and I watched his face for a sign of his reaction, and there it was. The crow's feet around the corner of his eyes were just beginning to crinkle, a muscle at the corner of his mouth just trying to twitch into a smile.

With one quick gesture he moved me around to the passenger side of the truck, to the narrow space between it and the brick wall, and backed me into it so the sun shone on my face, and I knew he could read everything I was thinking. I hoped he could. All I wanted was to get it over with. One way or the other, get it solved. I drew in my breath to say something, I don't know what, but he spoke first.

He dropped his hands to his sides, the steely glint of sternness in his eyes obviously at war with an imp of mischief that lurked around his mouth. I watched, enchanted, my heart thumping, and heard his voice tighten into a kind of roughness. "If you had a grain of sense you'd run like hell!"

With him standing there? Where on earth did he imagine I could, or would, run to? There was no place on earth I would rather be. Running was the last thing I wanted to do, and sense had nothing to do with any of it. I had no sense. I stood in front of him, all my instincts reaching out to him . . . and smiled up at him.

In another instant his arms were around me, gently at first, but I leaned toward him, turned my face up to his. And then I couldn't have pulled away if I wanted to. I couldn't move. I couldn't even get my arms free to put them around him, to hold him as close as he was holding me.

He kissed me over and over again, my mouth, my eyes, my cheeks and chin and neck and mouth until I was breathless under the rising tide of his passion. As I started to drown in it I heard my voice from a thousand miles away. "Mercy, mercy, Rob!" In another moment he held me gently, breathing in gasps even as I was myself, and we stood there, leaning against each other until the world stopped spinning in a crazy spiral and the cold winter morning cooled us back to some kind of sanity.

"I told you to run," he said at last. And when he looked down at me as I stood there, warm in his arms, the smile was in his eyes, the clear and loving smile that was all in the world I had wanted.

"You said if I had any sense."

He cuddled me to him, snugly, with his face in my hair. "I'm glad you didn't, or haven't. Or maybe you have more than enough. I don't know. But I'm glad you didn't. I'm glad it's not too late."

"Oh, yes! But . . . why should I have run?"

He laughed. "I was feeling a little . . . fiercely loving! I was thinking of flinging you into my truck and carrying you off like Lochinvar!"

"Oh, dear!"

"Well, what do you expect? After that last hour . . . ?"

I buried my face in his lapel with a joyous little shudder and clung to him. "Don't hide," he said as he turned my face up to his again. "Did I frighten you?"

"Just . . . delightfully." After he proved he could be gentle as well as fierce, I asked him, "Why is what not too late? I mean, you said—"

"Yes. I'll . . . we'll have to talk. There's a little coffee place around the corner," he said. "Are you up for that?"

We took a table by the window, where the sunlight streamed in, but it was immediately apparent that this was no place for the kind of conversation we wanted to have. Rob left me there, stirring the horrid stuff they served as coffee, and went to the phone behind the counter. I knew he was going to call his family; he would never put his own affairs, be they ever so urgent, ahead of their comfort. Just one of the little bonuses that come with being loved by a man like Rob, I thought, and wondered why I wasn't jealous or angry over his evident neglect of me.

But the warmth of his kisses still tingled on my face. I knew the answer to my question, the most urgent one, at least. I could afford to wait for the rest.

Then he dialed another number and had a brief conversation that seemed to please him. "Will you follow me over to Ellen's house," he asked when he returned. "She will lend us her library, and privacy, for as long as we like, and I do want a bit of privacy with you right now."

The privacy extended to the door being open and not a soul in sight. There wasn't even a car in the garage. I don't know how Ellen did it, I only know it was another of her miracles and I was grateful.

"I thought you had gone," said Rob a few minutes later when we stood together in front of the fire in the library. "I tried to call when I got home but our phone was out. And anyway all I could have said was good-bye. . . . Joan!" He pulled me to him again.

It took me a moment to catch my breath. "I couldn't leave without seeing you," I said.

"I should have known you wouldn't—couldn't, as you say. Not you. God, Joan, have I told you how much I love you? *Can* I tell you?"

"You've dropped a hint or two." His eyes were blazing. I lowered my own from his and put my hands on his shoulders to hold him away from me while I caught my breath. He let me go, and a moment later I sat in the little chair he placed for me in front of the fire. With some idea of lightening the moment, I said, "You've loved me since first we met, I think you said. Didn't we have a bet on it?"

He laughed somewhat ruefully as he leaned against the mantel, looking down at me. "How could I have dreamed I was in love with you all those years? What did I know about love? You weren't even real!" He laughed again as my eyes came back to his in surprise. "I had you fixed in my mind as an ideal, a beautiful little girl with black hair and huge blue eyes and sunburned legs. I kept you as my ideal all through school. There were Christmas letters"—Susan's! She never missed one until this year—"that said you were in the band and on the swimming team, and I imagined you skimming through the water like a slippery little eel, not more than ten years old. And then you sent Ellen some pictures from camp, and you still had the long legs and pigtails and just the beginning of being a woman. I dated every girl I could find who looked the least bit like you."

I settled back in my chair with a kind of interested complaisance and watched him leaning against the mantelpiece, enjoying his memories, putting them into perspective in the dream world where they belonged. It was like hearing a fairy-story in which I just happened to be the central figure.

He went on. "All through school and college there were lots of girls I thought were lovely, but they never rang true. I didn't like their habits, or their families, or what they wanted out of life. All the way along the line there was something wrong. They just didn't measure up to you—the way I imagined you must be."

I understood. I knew imagination was a fickle will-o'-the-wisp. I didn't interrupt him.

"Those Christmas letters kept coming, and every year I knew something more about you and your family, and I liked and sort of recognized them all. You all fit, somehow, into something I know and like. Does this make the least bit of sense?"

"The least bit," I said with a smile. "Go on."

"And every year you were up to something different, busy doing things, changing and growing, and I loved you more. Loved you? I didn't know what love was!" The laugh was short, disbelieving, the look on his face grew more serious as he watched the flames in a reverie for a moment. "Then there was Vietnam," he went on. "And Stanford, and I was too busy to think about girls except as a kind of R. and R.—uh, rest and rehab—"

"I . . . know." I kept my fingers wrapped around the little stone heart in my pocket.

He went on quietly, still reminiscing. "And then there was Andy's mess, and girls weren't fun anymore. I began to want something more. Trust, honor, integrity, and loyalty. Things that don't show on the surface but that make all the difference. I came home on leave before the . . . end of that, that summer before, and went to New York looking for you—and found you wearing that diamond. I won't tell you how I felt. I just came on home and decided I didn't want anything to do with love at all. Girls, yes. Love, no. I thought I was dreaming at Carter's store, and then I knew it was the real you, there in the Co-op . . ."

And it wasn't a fairy-tale anymore. The fantasy was over. His eyes were alight again when he looked at me, alight with warmth that almost pulled me into his arms, but something in his face warned me to wait. I sat still but my heart was pounding.

"You were real, alive, and here, and the sunshine and wind made your cheeks glow, and when you smiled at Anne and looked around to see who she belonged to, I almost walked up to you right then, to tell you this, all this, on the spot, but I thought there was still that diamond, so I couldn't. Until I talked to Ellen while we helped decorate the church and she told me there was no more diamond, and I came alive again."

And suddenly he was on his knees in front of me, his arms around me and his eyes blue flames burning into mine. "I want to court you, Joan. I want to spend big chunks of time with you. I want to take you dancing and to dinner with champagne and candles. I want to give you presents and watch you open them. I want to make you blush and wiggle under a shower of compliments the way you're doing now, and I haven't even started yet!"

My voice was tiny. "Oh stop, Rob. You're overwhelming me!"

He laughed. "That's the general idea! I want to overwhelm you every way I can think of! I want to take you to bed and love you . . . God, how I want to love you! I want to watch you wake up in the morning, watch your eyes look for mine. How do you manage to lift those eyelashes, Joan? Look at me! That! That's the beginning of what I want!"

For a moment, as our eyes met and the world began its crazy tilt, I thought we had arrived at that place, that enchanted place where I longed to be, but I was wrong. Suddenly the veil of sadness crashed down between us again, and he wrenched himself away from me, stood again by the fireplace, his face bleak, deserted.

"But I won't cheat you again. Didn't you learn enough about the pain of it last week? I did. Don't get up. Sit there and let me tell you! I won't cheat you—us—again. You know now what I want, and I can't—I simply can not give it to you. Not now. Not until that . . . filthy mess with Henrietta is cleaned up. I can't even get the kids squared away in school again until I know she's not lurking, waiting to snatch . . . Anne's measles give her a reprieve, but Chip should go back tomorrow. It should be fun and exciting for him, but it isn't. He admitted last night he dreads it because he'll be out in the open, a sitting duck! Good God!"

He gulped down that bitterness, while I watched, wishing I could help, knowing I couldn't. I didn't attempt to speak.

He went on. "I can't let it go on. I have to get it

finished—quickly—for all our sakes. I don't care how messy it is, as long as you and the youngsters and Mother are safe. That's top priority. I have to be sure of that. So please—please go back to New Hampshire, Joan, away from here, out of the mess. And the very minute I get it finished I will go up there, and then—then I can put you first. Hold that as a promise, Joan, as I will."

I had known it was coming, ever since I talked last night with Perk, I had known it. And now that he had said it I knew I would have to go. His eyes were tight on my face, and I kept my eyes on his and hoped they showed only my love and understanding.

He went on. "But fly, Joan, please? I can't live through the thought of your driving all that way alone. Yesterday and this morning, before you sat down there, are all I can handle of that. Fly home to your folks and start collecting your trousseau, or whatever it is girls do, so I can get all this finished and come up there and court you as you deserve to be courted, as I want to. Will you?"

"Yes. I'll go. I'll fly, Rob." I would walk through fire for him if he asked me to. Of course I would go.

He pulled me to my feet then, and the kiss we exchanged spoke more of love than any that had gone before it. While I could still think, I drew myself back from him and said, with my voice as controlled as I could make it, "I guess I better call the airlines—"

"Would you like me to?"

"Oh, yes, please."

"And I'll get you a dog crate."

"I have one. But there's Dad's car—"

"I'll find some soldier at the fort who's going on leave."

"It's like . . . I don't know. For how long, Rob? Can you guess?" I refused to cry, and for once my voice didn't betray me. I turned away from him because I couldn't trust my face.

"I don't know. She's hiding somewhere, the devil only knows where, but she's not in Chicago—not where she said she'd be."

"But she sent you a wire—" I turned to look at him and saw frustration and anger on his face. His voice was brittle with it.

"The telegraph office had no record of it."

"The apartment, that credit thing."

"The manager said he never heard of her, never wrote me that letter. I don't know how or why she managed that bit of deceit. Anyhow, I went to Nadine's, her sister. A real twit! She poked her head through the chain on her door and said she wouldn't answer any questions without her lawyer present. Unbelievable! I finally got her to admit it was she who checked in for Henrietta at the hotel. Henrietta had never been there. Never got off the bus. Nadine hemmed and hawed and finally said she thought Henrietta might have stopped in Champaign to visit a friend, so I rented a car and went down there. Chased around half the night to find the so-called friend, and that was a waste of time. When I finally got back to Chicago I had to run for my plane, and then sat for an hour on the runway. An hour, that is, before they closed down for the storm. And all of it a wild-goose chase. I don't know where the hell she is."

"She's missing then?"

"Or hiding behind a rock somewhere, waiting to pounce—"

I didn't hear him. My mind was caught on the word "missing." "When . . . when did she go, Rob? What day?"

"What? Oh, the twenty-first—Sunday, at three-thirty. I loaded her on the bus myself, in Shearerville."

It wasn't a conscious thought, it was total knowledge. It started, icy cold, near my heart, and waved down my spine and out to my fingertips like some swiftly invading parasite, enervating, stupefying. I could scarcely raise my hands to reach out to him, and my lips were stiff when I spoke. "Blair, Rob . . . did that bus stop at Blair?"

"It always does. That's their depot. God, Joan, what is it? What's the matter? You're pale as a ghost!"

I held on to his hands like a lifeline. My voice was a thread. "Was she wearing a tan jacket?"

"Yes. Fake leather."

"And a pink . . . pink headscarf?"

"Yes. Why?"

"Wait! Can you describe it, anything about it?"

"The color of chewed bubble gum. She said Ramon gave it to her. Hearts or birds on it, in black. Does that help?"

I closed my eyes and leaned my head back on the chair and knew it was over. I recited then, like a litany, the other items of her clothes and features, recited them as I had to Alison and Sheriff Dennis, and Rob affirmed each one until neither he nor I had any doubt that I had seen her, and I ended with the short hard fact, "She's dead." And then went on and got the whole story out, as clearly and as quickly as I could, before I opened my eyes again. He listened to it all in silence, his hands strong on mine, until I got to the end. "They didn't believe me! They thought I had imagined it—or was drunk!"

The tears came then, the relief of them, and the end of the frustration, and he held me in silence, close to his heart, until they, too, were finished.

"Feel better?" he asked me then, as he mopped my face as gently as he had mopped Anne's.

"Good God, yes. Thank you. I . . . I'm all right." And I smiled at him to prove it. "It's over, then, isn't it?"

"Not . . . quite, I'm afraid."

Something in his voice must have warned me, or in his eyes as they bored into mine. Something warned me in time and pushed my face down into his neck. I was hiding there when the hellish thought struck me, a stiletto-sharp, needle-sharp injection of doubt, a hateful demon of doubt and suspicion. My mind raced to fight it before it could numb my senses. I went rigid with the horror of it. How did it dare, *dare* to accuse Rob of . . . murder!

I felt his hands on my face, knew he was going to force me to look at him, and to try to hide would be worse than impossible, it would be unforgivable. My prayer was a cry. Dear God, if ever you did, help me now! For a fleeting instant I resisted the pressure of his fingers, and then, as suddenly as it began, it was over. I knew . . . I could prove a hundred ways . . .

"Say it!" His voice was tight and commanding.

And when I raised my eyes to his, the demon of doubt had gone, gone without a trace—gone as though it had never existed. I met his eyes and knew through the tears in mine he could read my faith and trust and love. "It's gone," I said simply.

He understood. With a little shuddering sigh he pulled me close to him again. "Now it's over," he said. "Thanks be to God, *now* it's over."

Chapter
Twenty-Three

WE SAT TALKING for some time, following lines of thought as they occurred to us, adjusting to the change of course that always follows in the wake of death. Not tragedy, except as the end of life and its potential is always tragedy. "I wish she had consented to get help. Andy begged her . . . and I tried again this fall. But she was hell-bent . . ."

My own principal regret: "If only I had told you when we went to dinner! It would have saved so much pain—for so many people!" When I told him about Myra's attack on my reputation he was surprisingly thoughtful.

"Strange that she knew so much about what happened up there."

"That's what Perk thought, too. Alison says she listens at keyholes."

He continued to look very thoughtful and a moment later looked at his watch. "I may just be able to catch Pete."

"Pete?"

"Pete Strawbridge. I have to talk to him, and the sooner the better."

"Not Dennis?"

"Preferably not Dennis. He is not famous for brains, or an open mind. There's that aspect of things, you know."

"Yes, I suppose so. Can you guess who may have done this thing, Rob?"

"Possibly Ramon. He was here and he was certainly

angry with her about some drug deal she botched for him." His voice was suddenly tinged with impatience. "We can make better guesses when we find her body and know what killed her. Pete may have some ideas. At least I won't have any trouble convincing him you weren't drunk or on drugs."

We parted soon after that, Rob to go talk to Pete Strawbridge and I to go back to Woodsedge. I found James and Alison in the kitchen, and I ran in fairly shouting my news. "I'm sorry I didn't call you, but wait 'til you hear . . . !"

In my wildest imagination I could never have pictured their shocked reaction, the wide eyes and tense pale faces and stiff gestures. Alison reached her hand out to James, and her fingers tighted on his arm, slowly, almost like a claw, and he put his hand over hers in a protective grasp.

Then I realized what I had done. "Oh, God, I'm terribly sorry! I shouldn't have dropped it on you—I didn't think! But you knew her, didn't you? She worked in your office, James?"

Alison, as pale as paper, answered me while James stood immobilized with a dazed expression on his face. "Yes, we knew her. I thought . . . I thought she was going to Chicago." She looked at James with a kind of panic, and her voice was thin with strain . . . or fear. "Wasn't she . . . going, James?"

"What? Oh, yes. I thought she had gone."

His voice was so flat, so vacant, that I couldn't bear to look at him again. I didn't want to see the pallor in his face and wonder how deeply he felt her death. I didn't want to share this thing between Alison and James at all. I looked again at their tightly clasped hands and excused myself. "I'll just go call Perk. I may be able to catch him. . . ."

I couldn't. But because I couldn't contain my excitement and because he had been so helpful, I didn't hesitate to tell Jake the whole story. He listened as patiently as Perk would have, and when I was finished he said, rather flatly, I thought, that he'd have Perk get back to me. "Say in a hour?"

"Longer. It's lovely out, and Rob won't be here until three. Tell Perk I've taken Hector to Fox Cave. We haven't been up there yet, and this is a perfect day for it. The fields are still frozen but there isn't any wind. I can cut across and easily make it home by three."

"Okay. Right. About three, then."

So at high noon I took Hector and started for Fox Cave. Our way took us in a long slanting curve across the midsection of the sleeping-giant field below Corn Crib Woods to the easternmost corner of Woodsedge, to the last acreage Gramps bought "to round off the farm" into a neat rectangle more than two miles long by almost two miles wide. I took the old track that turned off from the wider, better used one that led up to the old corn crib. I looked up the gentle inclination toward the woods and the mound of honeysuckle that was slowly but surely crushing the old landmark into the earth. The old corn crib . . . even Sheriff Dennis had known the place I meant.

I don't know what turn my mind took to arrive at the blue notepad by the telephone and the scribbled hippie face that revealed the words "Blair Hound, 3:30," but for the second time that day I was frozen by a blast of sinister premonition. Stopped short by it, and I stood there gaping while it whipped through me.

In a single word, a single name: James.

It hung in the air around me in a pulsing aura of fear, a stinging icy fear that expanded and contracted as my heart raced and my lungs fought for breath.

James could kill!

I knew it with absolute certainty.

James could kill!

In a kind of desperation I looked back toward the farmstead, hidden now behind the swelling fields I had just crossed, Woodsedge cut off from me, barricaded behind a glassy wall of fear and horror, by the certainty that my cousin, who was there, was a murderer.

"Easy, easy, Mops! You're not thinking straight!"

Oh, God, Perk, what are you thinking? You don't know about the note by the telephone. I never told you about that. You know James, but you don't know about his affair with Henrietta. I never told you about that, either. So you can't put it together. You can't know!

Does Rob? Can he guess? Surely he knows about the affair. But what does he know of James? Of his temper? His violence held on a rein that can break . . .

Blair Hound . . . 3:30! Suddenly in my mind I saw again the face of my cousin, stony, hard with rage when he roared around the corner of the wagon shed in his jeep. Rage . . . but not at me! At what, then? Had he just, only just left that woman—that dead woman, Henrietta Dunstan, up there in the woods, and then after I found her the next day, gone back during the storm on his way back to the farm, and moved her . . .

And left the sack of garbage. . . .

You're guessing.

But it could have happened! Just like that!

You can't do this.

What? What can't I do?

Convict him. He's innocent until proven guilty . . . proven. . . .

The thought hung swaying before me like a lifeline in a tempest-torn sea, a lifeline back to sanity, and I had just wit enough to grab it and hang on. Proven! It has to be proven—beyond a shadow of a doubt!

I was suddenly drenched with shame. Here I stood convicting my cousin of murder—murder!—with nothing but guesses and shadowy circumstantial evidence. There might be perfectly innocent reasons for those words written on that notepad. They may have nothing at all to do with the woman in the pink scarf who Rob put on the Greyhound that always stops in Blair, the woman I found in Corn Crib Woods less than twenty-four hours later.

In my mind I heard Dad's voice, reasonable and cool. You don't have to be the judge or the jury or the lawyer or even a policeman! You don't have to figure it out and understand it. You certainly don't have to guess!

The sunshine on my face began to feel warm again, and I walked on, soberly and slowly at first, and as I went the thoughts of James and murder slipped farther and farther back in my mind. There was one thing I did know and that was that I would certainly not return to Woodsedge a minute before three o'clock, when Rob would be there.

Rob, my other part—the rest of me! Whatever lay around the corner at Woodsedge, around all the corners still to come in my life, I would share with Rob. With my love. . . .

Fox Cave opened on the inside rim of a sinkhole roughly forty feet in diameter, its sides unstable and raw where rocks tumbled down as the ground beneath them sank into the hidden limestone caverns and rivers below the surface. Neither the sinkhole nor the cave could be seen from Blair Road, but local people knew where it was, about three hundred yards in, near the crest of a low hill covered with brush and young trees. We used to take picnics there on hot summer days because the shadows were deep and the constantly dripping water cooled the mosses and ferns that hung over the rocks.

I made all the noise I could as Hector and I approached the place just in case there were hunters wandering around. I shouted "bang-bang" at the top of my lungs when he flushed a covey of quail, and told him to "hunt in there" for the singles, until he paid no more attention to me. One corner of my mind was busily scheming ways to borrow him from the New Hampshire Brandons so he would have the fun of hunting with Rob next fall, as I slipped and slid eight or ten feet down over the frozen vegetation to the place where I knew the opening of the cave to be.

As I went I steadied myself by grabbing saplings that grew along the walls of the pit, young maples and oaks with precarious footholds that hung at angles over the bottom, which was black now with a mysterious depth of water that had drained into it from the hard rains and melting snow of the past week. I skidded over wet moss and lichen on one limestone boulder, and my feet came to an abrupt stop against a soggy blue suitcase. I gave it a kick and was surprised when it spewed a load of bright clothes into the water, where they sank from sight slowly, like jewels into quicksand, and disappeared through the thin crust of floating leaves into the water. The sapling I was holding seemed ready to follow them, so I swung around on it to another and stepped down into the opening of the cave itself.

Everything about the cave had a deceitful look of softness. The ceiling, walls, and floor, and the rounded, smoothly sculptured shelves and knobs and bulges of worn limestone were a rosy beige color, dull and sandy. I walked forward ten or twelve steps to the back, where a last shelf, almost like a couch, was set into a dim alcove. My brothers insisted there was another chamber out of sight behind the couch, but to get to it involved squirming down a narrow tunnel of some kind, twisting around rocks and encountering goodness-only-knew-what lurking things, and I had never tried it. I had looked where they said to look, and never saw anything but blackness.

Today I looked again, looked through the tiny space where they had said so many times, so eagerly, "Can't you see it? Look again!" So today I looked again, and there was more light than I needed. Too much more! A dim reflection of the sky caught the pink scarf in an eerie glow, and glimmered over what was left of a woman's once beautiful face.

Somehow I got out of there. Stumbling, crawling, fighting nausea, I remember hating the beckoning light at the entrance of the cave because I knew it was too far away. I couldn't not breathe that long! I remember the scalding agony of not being able to breathe, as though my throat and lungs were crushed tight together. And then, when at last I was out in the light, the hot pain of pulling air into my lungs, gasping, gaping like a fish, nearly strangled me again. Hanging on to whatever my hands touched of the rocks or ferns, I fought to keep my balance while I struggled to catch my breath.

I don't know how long it was before I could look around, but the first jolt into a kind of aching reality was the sight of my cousin James perched against a boulder across the water from me, his feet braced in a small tree and a shotgun in his hands.

He wasn't looking at me.

I tried to scream to him, but I couldn't make a sound. I tried again and managed a rough croak, but he didn't hear. Then louder, "She's here, James! That body! It's Henrietta, James!"

He seemed to shout something, but what I heard was a booming voice, over my head, slightly to my right—Rob's voice, but distorted, loud and harsh with urgency, a shouted command. "Shoot me, you bastard! Over here!"

There were two shots, but they seemed to me only one, in two parts, and the sound of them knocked against me with shattering force. I reeled from it and fell back against the rocks, and slid down, my hands blocked over my ears that seemed to have burst inward, spattering my brain with sharp spears of noise. I forced my eyes to stay open. I had to see! And through a smoky haze I watched James slide, slowly, gently, forward off his perch, try, half-heartedly it seemed, to hold another branch, give it up, and continue in slow motion into the water below, the young tree slipping with almost delicate precision down on top of him.

Then, like a missile, came Rob, feet first from the rim above me, into the water after James. I screamed his name, although I did not hear a sound except the echoes reverberating in my ears. I flung myself into the tangle of branches after him, into the black chaos, to find some part of him to hold onto, to pull with me out of the insanity . . . or if not . . . if not. . . .

He surfaced before I found a place to stand. I saw his mouth speak and his eyes send a message as he ducked again under the black water. I crashed through the branches toward the spot and was standing knee-deep on something unstable when he reappeared, James' head and shoulders clutched, dripping in his arms. "Stay there," he said in an eerie whisper as I started toward him again. "I'll pass him—"

He said nothing more that I could hear as he struggled to disentangle James from something below the surface. I tightened my hold on the slender tree that had wedged itself across the water and reached out, tried again, and at last caught hold of James's collar and hung on. It was a nightmare, but little by little we got him out of there, out of the water and safe on a narrow, reasonably flat rock, and then we could look at each other.

Blood, thin with water, was streaming down one side of Rob's face, and when I ran a finger over a stinging place on my forehead it came away red. But we were both alive, and for a tiny instant that was the only important thing in the world, but for no more than an instant. We turned back to James, who lay there, deathly pale, motionless. Dead? In a mindless daze I gently pulled a rotted oak leaf off my cousin's face while Rob searched for a sign of life.

"Breathing! His neck—Good God! Here—" I couldn't think, I could only watch while Rob pulled off his own sodden sweater and then his shirt; he wadded them against a red-running place in James's shoulder and tugged the zipper of James's jacket tight again over the mound. Then Rob pulled off his belt. "Hold his head st-straight. Here . . . I'll h-hold, you w-wrap . . . a . . . a k-kind of c-collar—" Rob's teeth were chattering like an Indian rattle by that time, but we got the belt around James's neck the way Rob wanted it. He still wasn't satisfied. "N-n-need a bl-blanket—" He started to get to his feet, to leave—

I felt a soft grey darkness creeping stealthily around me. I tried to shake it away. Rob saw. Rob always saw. "Wait! Here! Put your head down!"

"I'm . . . all right . . . I think . . ."

"C-can't—can't leave you. We n-need help!"

"Reckon so." It was a new voice, and I heard Rob, from outer space, calling to someone on the rim of the sinkhole, somewhere above us. I saw a dim figure and then another emerge from a fog and slide away again into a woolly cloud while I sank peacefully, willingly, into benign and total oblivion.

Somebody put sticks in my bed and propped my feet in a tree. It was waving at me. But it wasn't my bed, it was a hillside, and a blackberry bush was waving at me. I tried to raise my head to look but something was holding it fast.

"Be still." It was Rob's voice but I couldn't see him. I tried again. "Please lie still," said my love, his hand, in a strange dark sleeve, was firm. "Just a minute more. You fainted. You can sit up when the ambulance comes."

There was a rough blanket wrapped around me, much too tight. I couldn't move my arms or legs! I started to try again, to insist! At last he gave up and took me to lie in his arms, my head on his shoulder. "You are worse than a puppy," he said and smiled down at me.

I discovered I could not only hear, I could speak. "I am not a puppy," I said.

"I said, 'worse than,' " my sweet love said and held me close, with his face for a moment next to mine. Then he shifted me so he could search for something in the strange pea jacket he was wearing, while I tried to understand the winking silver badge on its lapel. Then he called to someone down in the sinkhole. "You got that flask in your pocket, Pete?"

A moment later he asked me to swallow raw fire, slowly. And then, since the first choking gasp didn't satisfy him, another. And I was Joan again. Whole, solid, alive, and sane. And I remembered everything.

But I didn't understand any of it.

"What happened, Rob? Where's James?" I tried to raise my head, and I might as well not have bothered. "Is he . . . is he all right?"

"If you'll just lie there, I'll tell you."

"I won't move." I didn't even want to.

After a moment or two of getting comfortable, he began. "James was still unconscious when Pete Strawbridge arrived and you fainted. I . . . well, James wasn't my top priority just then, so Pete sent Tom down to take care of James, and I haven't seen him since. Pete says he's conscious, but not very lucid. We're waiting for the ambulance."

I assimilated that for a moment. "But . . . in the cave—or outside—What happened there, Rob? How did you get up here and why was James up here in the first place and . . .and is it really—?" I couldn't go on. I didn't want to say her name.

"I'll just tell you what I know," said Rob softly, his lips in my hair and his arms strong around me. "It will take a while, I reckon, to piece it all together. Will you just lie still?"

"All right." I snuggled my head down on his shoulder again.

"I was coming back from Blair. I had talked to Pete. We exchanged a lot of information. Did you know Perk kept them working on that body you found? Just nod, don't talk."

I nodded and smiled up at his face, where a streak of blood had been carelessly wiped aside. I wanted to reach up to touch it, but he had my arms inside the blanket again, and in spite of my wiggles, they stayed there. At the pleading look on his face I subsided and waited in silence for him to go on.

"Dennis had shelved the whole thing. But Pete was more suspicious because of Perk's call. He had been digging around at your corn crib place, found the sack of garbage, but figured you would have to be pretty . . . ah, he said . . . I think he didn't mean it to be so . . . you know. Well . . ."

"Don't spare me," I whispered against his neck.

He placed a gentle kiss under my ear, and went on. "Anyway, Pete didn't find anything to say there had been a body up in the thicket. But some guy from Bethesda, Maryland, called him about a missing sister. Did you know anything about that?"

I almost sat up in surprised protest, but Rob prevented me. "I thought you probably didn't," he said. "But he described Henrietta just as you did. Pete got suspicious when he couldn't say what color her hair was. He said she was forever changing it so he didn't know what the current color might be, which sounded reasonable enough, except it left Pete with the idea that there might be something kind of fishy goin' on. So he kept worrying about it, and he talked to the bus driver when he came through again. That was last Friday, or Saturday. Anyway the driver said a woman dressed like that had gotten off at Blair. He thought she must be travel-sick. He handed her her suitcase and went on into the office and didn't see her again."

"It was the pink scarf, Rob."

"What?"

"Nobody could overlook that pink scarf."

"I reckon." He was quiet a minute, remembering it, I suppose, and the woman who wore it. "So when we talked this morning, Pete already had half the story. We spent a while trying to figure where somebody would hide a body on a stormy winter night. Thought of a number of places. Made quite a list, in fact, but Fox Cave wasn't on it."

Suddenly his arms tightened around me in an almost convulsive grip, and his face pressed into my hair. "It was . . . just chance. Good God, Joan! I just happened . . . just happened to see Hector—just a flash of his white up here on the hillside, as I came along from Blair."

I didn't understand then why that was so painful to him. "It's all right, Rob. It's over—it's over." I pulled one of my arms free of the blanket and held his head there against my own and shared the shudder that went through him until, in a moment, he continued, his voice steady again.

"I came up here, thinking we'd have a nice little walk, and there was Pettyjohn, with a rifle pointed—"

"Pettyjohn?"

"Branch Pettyjohn. Didn't you know?" A smile dawned on his face again as he looked down at the bewilderment on mine.

"No! I thought—"

"That I had shot James? My sweet lamb, I would never shoot poor old James. Under any circumstances. Jump him, maybe, if I had to. But I didn't have a gun. Don't carry one as a rule. Well, I didn't have one, anyhow. But Pettyjohn had a rifle. I spotted him through the brush from about twenty yards away, just as you came out of the cave. Heard you calling to James. Pettyjohn raised his gun and then it was . . . just back in the jungle. There wasn't much I could do but yell. Anyhow, he got his shot away. One. He got James in the shoulder, you know. Not so bad, really. Not likely to kill him."

"But . . . I thought the Pettyjohns were in New Orleans!"

"Branch was here. I don't know about the rest of his family."

"So . . . what happened to . . . Branch?"

"Last I saw him he was lyin' in a heap on the ground holdin' his head, and his rifle was a little bent. I don't know where he is now and I don't care . . . a damn."

Neither did I.

The ambulance arrived a few minutes later, and right behind it came Alison in the Lincoln. I didn't even wonder how she had gotten the word so quickly, I just thought how like her it was to be there, bravely marching forward to cope with whatever she faced. She disappeared over the edge of the sinkhole like a mountaineer to go to her husband where he lay on the rocks below.

A small woman in some sort of uniform came up, dabbed

something that stung on my forehead, put a butterfly bandage over the gash, and then did the same thing to Rob's cheek, clucking softly to us as she worked. Then we watched in silence as the stretcher came up out of the pit, Alison beside it.

She stopped for a moment in front of me, where I stood still wrapped in my blanket. "I don't understand, Joan," she said. "I don't know what James was doing up here with a gun. Can you tell me? Why was he here?"

"I don't know. I only know . . . I don't know."

"Rob?" She asked, her eyes flashing with the need to know. But Rob didn't have an answer for her, either. She turned to me again. "Will you take the Lincoln home? I'm going in to town in the ambulance."

"Certainly. Oh, I do hope . . . I pray . . ."

But she was gone.

And then, while the lights of the ambulance were still bobbling over the track to Blair Road, Pete Strawbridge came up to the place where Rob and I stood waiting for him.

"Feelin' better, Joan?"

"Oh, yes. Much better, thanks."

"Ah, you said there's a dead body down there in the cave?"

"Yes. She's . . . it's the same one I saw in the woods, up behind the old corn crib. You know—"

"I know the place. I heard about you findin' that body an' all. Now, Rob . . ."

Another man appeared over the lip of the sinkhole. "She's there all right. In the back . . ."

I listened to them talking in their soft, quick, country voices and tried to understand what they were saying, but I couldn't. Like Chip I tugged on Rob's sleeve when I could bear it no longer.

"Please tell me what's going on! I need to know!"

"All right. We're just going up the hill here so I can

identify . . . Why don't you go sit in the car for awhile? Tom here will drive you back to Woodsedge when we finish."

"Up the hill? She's in the cave! In the back!"

"Right. But we can't get in that way. We'll have to go through the chimney."

"Chimney? What chimney? I didn't . . . I don't . . ."

"Well, there is one, always has been. Joe sure knew about it. Us country boys were forever making it bigger or plugging it up and hiding it again. That's what Pettyjohn was doing when you came along, I reckon. He wanted to go down there, or send Joe."

"Joe?"

"Joe Burden. Pete says he was up here with Pettyjohn and left in a big hurry when they heard you whoopin' and hollerin'. He's waiting in the sheriff's jeep now."

"The sheriff's? Dennis?"

"Dennis is probably at the Nashville airport by now. He's skipped town."

"What!"

"Well, he was in it, too. Now, for a little while . . . Pete's anxious to get this over."

I had no wish to see what they were going to do. I called Hector to me and went down the track to the place where Alison had left the Lincoln. I waited there in the passenger seat and hugged my dog while he busily pulled burrs out from between his toes. I gave up trying to piece the story together and just lolled my head back on the soft cushions and closed my eyes against the rays of the setting sun. I was almost asleep when Hector woofed and then wagged at Rob when he tapped on the window.

He placed a tidy little kiss on my mouth and said, "I'll see you in the morning."

By some miracle I was able to push my protest aside when I remembered that Rob had something more important to do than keep me company. "Shall I come with you, Rob? Can I help?"

He considered for a moment. "Me, yes. Always. But for tonight . . . the quieter we keep things, the better. I hope I'm right. I haven't much experience with this kind of thing. Unless you don't want to be alone? Maybe I'm wrong! Maybe you should—"

I stopped him with my hand on his. There was nothing in the world I would rather do than snuggle under his wing with all the rest of his family. I'd love to. But I didn't say it. They needed all his attention tonight, those two who were orphans now, who weathered the storm and were coming into port, and his mother, tied to her illness, waiting for the news he would bring. . . .

I'd take my turn. I had the rest of my life!

"Much as I'd love to, my love," I said, "I will pass. I'll let Hector be a house dog tonight. His reward! And I'll be there if Alison calls. And I want to call Dad and Perk. Lots of things. I think Dad will come down. Don't worry about me the least bit. I'll be just fine."

Chapter
Twenty-Four

PETE STRAWBRIDGE JOINED Rob and me for coffee at Woodsedge Monday morning. We sat at the long white table, where the sunlight streamed through the chintz curtains, and Hector lay in blissful contentment at our feet. And we began to fit the pieces of the puzzle together. The only big question now was James. His condition was stable. That was all we knew.

A few minutes after he came in, after he had said everything polite the occasion required, Pete Strawbridge put a crumpled note on the table and smoothed it out carefully. "Do you by any chance recognize this, Joan?"

"Why, yes! It's Alison's stationery. Her monogram. I can show you more of it. She keeps it—"

"No, ma'am. That's fine. That's just what I thought it was. Do you want to see if you can make it out?"

"Oh, yes. Let me see." It was smudged and faded, but it was legible and brief. I read it aloud. " 'I know all about your affair with my husband and I have forgiven him for being so foolish.' Signed. 'Alison Brandon.' Well, what do you know about that!"

"That's one way to spike a blackmailer's guns," said Rob while Pete folded the note and put it back in the folder he was carrying.

"Blackmail? Henrietta was blackmailing James?"

Pete shrugged his shoulders and ducked his head, then fixed each of us in turn with a sharp blue eye. "Just between ourselves, then?" We nodded agreement and he went on. "That note . . . ah, we found it in her pocket. Interestin'. She was sure tryin' to blackmail James, but she never got it set up real good. James just told his wife and that was the end of it. But Mr. Pettyjohn, he had to take another way. She had him caught between a rock an' a hard place." There was no smile on Pete's face.

Sometime in the next hour or so I understood a little better.

After her return from Texas, Henrietta had taken full advantage of her position as a receptionist-typist for the Pettyjohn-Brandon office to collect impressive dossiers on the public and private affairs of both men. James, she evidently decided, was a plum ripe for seduction and black-mail, but Branch Pettyjohn was juicier. Using all the talents for intrigue she imagined she had, she insinuated herself into his schemes on one hand and began to steal from him with the other.

"Tom found a wallet of papers floatin' in the leaves at the sinkhole. They're pretty soggy an' it'll take a while to go through them, but looks like she was gettin' ready to squeeze Mr. Pettyjohn with some documents she had, letters, contracts, some certificates—things of that nature." Pete shook his head sadly. "I've been watchin' him settin' up an empire in town for the past six years, but there was never any hard evidence of wrongdoing. Some of the stuff in that wallet will be real interestin' in that regard. Some right funny permits granted, an' agreements." Pete shook his head again while I poured fresh coffee.

In a moment he went on. "Most of them operations was in town. Din't concern us out here in the county. When he reached out here he put Dennis in charge. Dennis an' his pals run a gamblin' hall at Blair, on the edge of the law mostly but . . ." Pete looked through the chintz-curtained window toward the rose garden in thoughtful silence for a moment. "Jus' lately there've been rumors of some kinda sportin' complex with motels an' such." The tone of Pete's voice hardened as he went on. "He was plannin' to change the face of the earth, was Mr. Pettyjohn, but he won't now. Miz Dunstan tripped him up real good." Pete shook his head in the classic gesture of disbelief. "Of course, he's innocent until proven guilty, just like ev'body."

He sighed tiredly. "As for Miz Dunstan, Joe Burden's been helpin' us out. He's pretty keen on savin' his own skin. T'was Joe handed Miz Dunstan that there note when she stepped off that bus in Blair. Whether she had been expectin' the first cash payment from James or not, we'll have to wait for James to tell us, but near as I can figger he never saw Miz Dunstan that day, maybe on purpose, maybe not. I doubt he ever seen that pink scarf. If I know James, if he'd a'seen it he'd a' said. An' Miz Dunstan dressed a lot finer than that as a rule. And you, Joan, you never seen her blonde hair, an' that's why I din't reco'nize your description of her."

And why James didn't recognize it, either, I thought. He might have wondered, even suspected, but he didn't know.

Pete went on to tell us that Joe also delivered the spoken message to Henrietta that Branch Pettyjohn was parked behind the bus depot and would be happy to take her wherever she wanted to go. Joe said he saw her get in Pettyjohn's car and watched them drive away, out the Blair Road toward Corn Crib Woods. Then he brought the Mercedes back to Woodsedge.

Pete didn't know yet how Branch Pettyjohn lured Henrietta up to the woods, or whether he carried her body up there after he killed her. He said there would certainly be an autopsy, but Branch Pettyjohn was well known to have great proficiency in the more lethal aspects of the martial arts. He and Rob exchanged glances I didn't even want to understand.

"Mr. Pettyjohn," said Pete, looking nowhere in particular, "seemed kind of . . . confused when I carried him to the hospital after I seen him limpin' along Blair Road, usin' his rifle like a crutch. Had a real mean lump on his head, now I come to think of it. You know anything about that, Rob?"

"Reckon he hit his head on somethin'?" Rob asked, thoughtfully stirring his coffee.

"Stock of that rifle was a little split."

Rob was silent

"And one of his ribs is broke."

Rob still said nothing, but his eyebrows were sliding up and down vigorously.

"Was you anywhere near them ribs, Rob?"

After a pause, Rob said, "Some, I reckon.

Feet or fists?

"Feet. I needed my hands."

"To swing the rifle?"

"Some," Rob answered with a rather nasty smile on his face.

"Figgers." The deputy sheriff of Brandon County seemed satisfied that he had all the information he needed on that subject. He turned to me. "I don't know what possessed your cousin to be up there at the cave last evenin'. He don't hunt no more I know of. And that old shotgun of his never could hit a barn."

"He had come to meet me. Perk called him after I had left for my walk. I think he just wanted to . . . be there . . . for me." My voice choked a little. James being gallant on my behalf! "Perk thought that was why . . . Ah, Jake, ah, that's Perk's roommate up at Bethesda, said the gun was kind of camouflage."

"Mr. Delano, ain't he? We talked. He had me searchin' around for a sister. Reckon you knew about that."

"Yes. They told me about it last night. He has no sister, Pete, only one brother. He and Perk were just trying to help me."

"Can't say I blame 'em. You had a pretty bad deal on that thing, shuntin' you off like that. That was too bad."

"I reckon Perk knew about that chimney," said Rob

thoughtfully. "Knew it would be a great hiding place. You and I missed that one."

"We sure did, but Perk called me right after he called James and reminded me. I hightailed me up there, just to be handy. Glad you was quicker, Rob."

Silence hung heavy in the Woodsedge kitchen. I had talked it out with Perk the night before, and the idea of first James and then me being shot "like fish in a rain barrel," as Perk put it, no longer churned my stomach, but Rob still hadn't completely passed the anguish of imagining what might have happened if he hadn't been, as Pete put it, quicker. He reached out his hand to me as I reached out mine to him.

Then Rob quirked a grin at me. "Steaks," he said, "nothing but sirloins for Hector as long as he lives!"

I laughed. "You'll kill him with kindness!";

Rob amended it quickly. "Kibble. The very best. May the noble Hector live forever!" The noble Hector raised his head at the sound of his name, and when Rob had petted him sufficiently he went back to sleep. Then Rob explained to Pete why he got to the top of the hill in time.

I had one or two questions of my own. "How much, I mean, how deeply was—is—James involved with Pettyjohn and his schemes?"

"Near as I can figger, James and that office in town was just window dressin', ah, you know, one of the most respected names in the county, that kind of thing, and that there campaign for mayor was more of it. No connection as I know of between James an' the shady doin's in town, nor rackets 'n' vice—other than gamblin'. James has always been right foolish about that."

I wondered briefly whether Pete had any memory of Aunt Caroline, and whether this weakness for games of chance was indeed inherited. I set the question aside for Dad and asked Pete another. "Was it Sheriff Dennis, then, who . . . ah, moved . . . Henrietta that night and left that sack of trash?"

Pete nodded. "But 'twas Joe Burden's idea. He's full of it!" Pete shook his head in wonder at Joe's warped talent, then shrugged and went on. "You surprised them real good when you reported findin' that body. They never figured there would be a girl walking around up there with a dog, y'see, an' the place was posted against hunting. I reckon Pettyjohn thought if the body ever was found up there, it bein' James's land and all and the whole town aware of that affair he was havin' . . ."

Perk had said much the same thing last night, and added that Pettyjohn also had a neat pair of thumbscrews if James got stubborn about trading Woodsedge for that huge debt. Pettyjohn could say almost anything he pleased about James and Henrietta and produce almost any kind of evidence, and if Henrietta's body were ever found at Woodsedge, James, not Branch Pettyjohn, would have a desperate time explaining.

"Pettyjohn overheard you tellin' James about the body you found," Pete continued, while I remembered Pettyjohn also overhearing my conversation with his new receptionist. "He told Dennis to move real fast and they was lucky th' storm give them the time they needed. Him and Joe took th' body away and left the sack of trash in its place. To make you look . . . ah, you know . . ." Pete choked a little, and his voice was rough when he continued. "When we pick Dennis up we'll charge him with accessory after, and destroying evidence, all kinds of things. He's in big trouble." He paused a moment, and when we had nothing to say, he went on. "Him an' Joe just lowered the body down that chimley and shoved stones back over the opening." Pete's lips were compressed with sadness. "Dennis would never of known about that second cave, not bein' a local man, if Joe hadn't a-told him," he said at last. "The boy's right smart to be helpin' us so good with this here investigation."

"And if nobody found the place to open the chimney so there'd be light . . . It might have been years! There's no telling . . ."

"Why *did* Pettyjohn go up there yesterday," I asked, when Rob fell silent.

"I reckon too many people knew about that pink scarf—made him nervous. He was mutterin' last night about it gettin' too much notice. He wasn't satisfied that Joe's hidin' place was all that secure, not if that body you found was to get identified and local people should start scouring the place. I reckon he meant to have Joe go down there and take away that scarf, and then maybe plug up that hole. There was a bag of cement in the back of Joe's jeep, and a bucket. I haven't gotten him to tell me about their intentions yet. Joe says Pettyjohn wanted her to disappear in Chicago, ya' see, not here close to Blair."

"So that's why I got those phony leads to Chicago!"

"Joe phoned that singin' telegram to Andy's kids himself. He laughed when he told me. Thought it was a right good song! And they got the name of that apartment out of a phonebook or somethin', and had some goon—or maybe Henrietta's sister—to mail you that letter. They wanted you to believe she was there, for a time. They din't mind you searchin' up there long as they could go on about their business."

I put my hand over Rob's which was knotted into a fist. We both knew what kind of hell such a scheme would have perpetrated on the Dunstan family. And it almost worked. It might have worked.

If it hadn't been for that pink scarf—and Hector. . . .

I had another question for Pete. "Why didn't I see them, or at least their jeeps, when I got up there? There was nobody around. Even Hector didn't act as though there were."

"I reckon they were all there before you and your dog arrived. If he spotted James he would have known him"—and ignored him, I thought to myself—"I don't know why he didn't bark at Pettyjohn or Joe."

"Noble Hector was down at the bottom of the hill," said Rob. "I didn't see Joan with him, and that's why I figured she was at the cave."

"As for the jeeps," Pete went on, "James's was behind the hill. You wouldn't have seen it, comin' from the direction you did. And Joe left his—it's an old Army surplus still in war paint—in some bushes down beside the track. He ran off from Pettyjohn when he heard you whoopin' an' hollerin', an' was tryin' to get right away when I come up beside him. We was talkin' when we heard them shots, so I just cuffed him to his steering wheel and left him there to think about things."

"So there *were* two shots!"

"James fired all right, but he didn't hit nothin' but air."

Rob put his finger over the little bandage on his face, but he said nothing. I hadn't realized until that instant that he had that gash in his cheek before he went into the pool after James. I put my hand in his again, and he squeezed it tight.

I asked Pete if he knew why James hadn't warned me that Pettyjohn was there or let me know that he was there himself. Why had he been so quiet, hiding there in his tree?

"I been wonderin' that too," said Pete. "I guess he just wanted to see what happened, whether you found anything to speak of, you might say. An' then, whilst you was in the cave, he seen Pettyjohn hidin' there an' figured you was both in real danger. I reckon we'll have to wait for James to tell us."

Pete got up to leave, and while he was tying up his envelope, he stopped and pulled Rob's belt out of it. "Reckon you'll be wantin' this, Rob. It done a right handy job. They said to tell you. Where'd you learn tricks like that?"

"Boy scouts, I reckon. Or maybe Nam. We did a lot of improvising out there."

Pete buttoned his shabby pea jacket with the shiny badge on the breast. "I'll go talk with Branch Pettyjohn. Like to persuade him to make a nice clean confession before he starts scheming up ways not to. Make it a lot easier for everybody. Y'all have a real nice day."

The door closed behind Pete Strawbridge, and Rob and I

were alone together at last, with no ghosts or worries between us. I held my face up to his and whispered very, very softly, "Let the courtship begin!"

His eyes sent me a warm, mischievous message, and an imp was dancing in his smile. "I've changed my mind," he said. "I don't want to court you—"

"Sir!"

"Well, I don't. Not just yet. I want to marry you. Tomorrow."

I admit that surprised me. "So soon! Maybe . . . oh, dear. Rob, wait!"

"Why?"

"But I was looking forward to . . . ah, overwhelming courtship!"

"After we're married. For the rest of your life. I promise. It will be my pleasure! So will you? Please?"

I hadn't much breath, but I made myself heard. "Not tomorrow—Thursday! That's only three days, Rob! Maybe Susan can get here, and the girls. And we should know about James by then."

"I'm being selfish, aren't I?" he said. "It's just I've waited—so long!" After I convinced him he really wasn't selfish, that he was something else entirely, in fact, he told me to hold out my hand.

I put out my right hand, palm up, expecting I don't know what. He put a kiss in the palm and let it go. "The other," he said. I held out my left hand, and he turned it over and examined it thoughtfully for a moment. When he was quite ready he dug in his pocket and found what he wanted, and said, as he slipped a ring over the proper finger, "Mother gave me this to give to you. She's very happy. I'll get you a better one tomorrow."

"Oh, no, you won't! They don't come any better than this!" I turned the small old-fashioned solitaire on my finger. "It isn't the size of the diamond that matters, Rob. It's all those wonderful other things we already have—living things that will grow! I love this ring that your mother sent me! It couldn't be more perfect!" The little diamond winked at me. Can love that is already overwhelming grow any larger, I wondered. Is there a limit to love? Is it endless, like wherever? I expect I'll find out—fairly soon!

The telephone interrupted us a few minutes later. We exchanged sighs. Our peace for the morning was over. "There's the first of 'em," said Rob. "I'll leave you to it." With a warm and slightly rude caress he turned to leave for Nashville. Dad was coming, and Rob was going to meet him at the airport.

The giggle in my voice probably shocked the dear soul who called to inquire about James, and I swallowed it quickly and blew him a kiss as he closed the door. My job for the morning was here, answering the urgent inquiries of all the kith and kin who had heard that there had been an accident at Woodsedge and that James Brandon was in the hospital. I wrote all their names down for Alison, and all their special messages. In any case, their prayers will be greatly appreciated by her, as they were by me—and always will be.

I saved the news of my marriage to tell Ellen first and she couldn't have been more pleased. The lilt came back in her voice as she said she couldn't decide who she was happiest for, me or Rob—"How good it will be for him to have brothers again!"—or her cousin Mary Dunstan, not to mention the children!

"Throw in Terhune and Cobb," I said happily.

"Who?"

"I'm teasing. They're Rob's dogs!"

When I told her the wedding date was Thursday, she thought I was teasing again. Then she laughed. "I keep forgetting how long you have known each other. It really isn't all that sudden, is it? What can I do to help?"

"Everything! Anything you can think of! The church, the rector—Tell everybody! Keep it simple so we can manage, but invite everyone! Tell them all to be as happy as I am!"

She laughed again. "Duck soup! I'll get right on it and get back to you!" I had visions of her rolling up her sleeves. My wedding will be a family affair, an all-hands effort.

Then Bailey Comstock came—and went—and a few minutes later came Alison. One quick look at her face and I knew what her news was, and I jumped to my feet to give her a hug in celebration. "James can wiggle his toes!"

Whoever would have imagined two grown women could cavort around a kitchen because a grown man could wiggle his toes! "One vertebra is broken, and another is cracked, but the nerve damage is minimal. The wound in his shoulder is fairly superficial, and unless he gets pneumonia, he should be fine. He's sedated, of course, but sleeping. He sent me to tell you and to get some clothes. I'm going back. I'll stay at the Hayneses'.

I gave her my own news and she seemed delighted. "Come help me pack and tell me about when Uncle Phil will get here and what else is going on."

One might have thought she had been gone for days! "Rob has gone to Nashville to meet him, and possibly Pip and Jim, too. He took the Lincoln, I hope you don't mind."

"Oh, no! That's fine! It will be wonderful to see Uncle Phil. There are so many questions. . . ." She stood at the window, gazing out at the ruined rose garden. I stood silently and waited for her to go on. "I don't know. What do you owe a man—a murderer!—who tried to kill you?" She shuddered and turned away from the window and began carefully folding clothes. "It all started with his gambling, you know. James had it pretty well under control until that woman got back last fall and . . . teased—*enchanted* him! And Branch just kept lending him more and more—huge amounts, always smiling and willing. 'I know your ship will come in one day,' he kept saying. And James, foolish James, always believed him . . . and went on borrowing. Then in November she began scheming ways for James to pay him back. Ugly ways—stealing things

267

from the safe, and . . . blackmail. It made me sick!" She choked a little over the word and stood with her Christmas negligee dangling limply from her fingers.

Then she sighed and went on. "It made James sick, too, when he knew I knew. That was just before you got here. I have a little money. Not enough, but we could have raised—paid it all back somehow. But then Christmas morning—while you were at church—Branch came by and told James he didn't want money, he wanted Woodsedge. Only Woodsedge." Her voice hardened. "I thought when James stormed out of here he was going . . . to kill him!" She whirled around to hang the negligee back in her closet and snapped the door closed. "But he just went to Blair to watch a college basketball game on the big screen there. He didn't even place a bet on it! That night Branch told him he'd really like to know more about your use of drugs! You know the rest," she said gruffly. "You wouldn't sign that agreement of sale, and James was furious—at himself, Joan! Not at you! So Branch was threatening to take us *all* to court. But now I don't know what will happen. We'll have to talk to Uncle Phil and Fitch—"

"No wonder you both were stretched so tight. I never guessed. . . ."

Alison turned aside with a shrug. "At least we know there won't be a sale—except for just one thing . . ."

I gave her some murmured encouragement.

She turned to me again with a brilliant, if still tearful, smile. "James never told you that when Perk called on New Year's Day he said he wanted to buy into Woodsedge. He wants to fix up one of the cabins or something. He wants to write. They'll have to do a lot of talking about it, of course. They were going to keep it as a surprise for you, but I thought you should know—"

"They never said! Never hinted!"

"I guess finding out about Henrietta sort of pushed everything else out of all our minds."

When Alison left to go back to town, her head was full of

plans for a wedding reception at Woodsedge and how glad her sister, Victoria, would be to arrange it. No trouble at all! I had to laugh at her eagerness. "We have such a lot to celebrate, honey," she said as she left. "James really does like Rob, you know. He will be glad to have him in the family!"

Rob called from Nashville fifteen minutes before I expected them back to say the plane was just in. They would be coming straight along as soon as they picked up their baggage. I told him the latest news of James and then asked, "Who? I mean, are the twins there?"

"You mean Pip and Squeak? They're here!" There was laughter in his voice, and I knew he would have fun on the drive home, getting to know them all, these men in my family, so dear to me. Only one not here. One missing.

I called Perk.

"Delano."

"Jake, it's Joan. Is Perk around?"

"Not at the moment. Shall I have him call you?"

"Please. I have some great news for him—for you both. James can wiggle his toes!" I had to laugh to think how many people would be glad to know this rather intimate thing about my secretive cousin. Served him right! Then I told Jake about my wedding. He said a few rather silly but complimentary things and promised to keep it quiet until I could tell Perk myself.

It was just dusk when I saw the Lincoln turn into the driveway at Woodsedge, Rob driving, Dad beside him, looking wonderfully tanned and healthy. Pip and Jim tumbled out of the backseat, tossed brief greetings to me, and began wrestling with Hector on the grass. And the third . . . another person in back . . . ? I saw the visored cap, the gold braid on shoulder boards. . . .

"Perk!"

He had to keep a grip on the door to receive my hug without being tipped backwards, but he did. I watched him, watched every move as he got two legs—two!—out of the

R25

car, and when Rob handed him crutches he tucked them away where they would be useful with one hand. Not two. The other was made on purpose to deal with the crutch. And there he stood, straight and tall like the Perk of old, and grinned at me when I went to hung him again.

"Easy, easy, Mops! I still rock a little!"

I turned to Dad, who was beaming with pride and pleasure. "He just got on the plane in Washington. I didn't know he was coming until I looked up and saw him standing there laughing at me."

I looked at my love who was lounging comfortably against the fender of the car watching me as I greeted my family. He handed me his handkerchief before I knew there were tears in my eyes.